This is a fiction[...] [...] [...] [event...]
and dates that oc[...] [...]curred [...] similarity [...] :o
real persons, living or dead, is coincidental
and not intended by the author, but some
events were based on real life.

JUNE 21, 2019
CELSO FERNANDEZ

CHAPTER 1

"A time to be born and a time to die; a time to plant   and a time to uproot the plant"   Eclesiastic 3: 3

It was a breezy yet comfortable night in Havana, a salty smell was in the air, men standing in the corners smoking the good old Cuban cigar Partagas or H Upman , a city compared to Paris before the debacle of 1959, our time frame begins on a particular night December 28 1957.

It is around 11:00pm in a street called Galiano a young detective with the homicide squad of the Havana police dept, his name Rafael Chaquet was summoned to his office, immediately he knew the similarities to a case that he is also involve, strangulation, naked body and a hint that the body was of a young prostitute.

Det. Chaquet is an intelligent logical det, born to a Basque family that settle in Cuba at the beginning of the

20's century in the city of Santa Clara located in the central part of Cuba.

Became a rookie officer in 1955 going up the ranks immediately becoming a det at the beginning of 1956, it was on the on the third year of Fulgencio Batista took over the government in a coup de stat.

 his assistant named Gerardo an older detective with a ton of commendation for solving complex homicides noticed a piece of rope that was left next to the body, like other evidence on past homicides.

This is the fourth body found in Havana in the last 18 months, young prostitutes, strangulation, left naked and yes, a piece of rope next to the bodies, is the killer telling us how to solve the crime?

Detective Chaquet live along in an apartment in the section of Marianao, located 10 minutes away from the center of Havana, his wife Zoila Andrade 20 years old, died a year ago of a rare form of cancer, no family so this case took most of his time.

1957 was tumultuous year in Cuba, a year after Castro has landed in the Oriente province with a determination to over-throw the government of Fulgencio Batista an army sergeant that proclaim himself the president of Cuba in 1952 toppling the legitimate president Socarras.

Rafael was going thru some difficult times, his wife death, the reminder that the new government was not legit his determin-ation to solve this case and his future plans, his drinking was consuming him to a point that one night he ended drunk in a bench at the central park in Havana, smelling the Bacardi rum and the vomit that tainted his clothe was repulsive.

His commander reminded him to stop throwing away his life and concentrate on his main priority, solving the case that was assign to him, it was easy said than done he had to many thoughts in his mind, drinking was an escape route to simplify his life, he was wrong.

Eventually he controlled his drinking problem, but not fully, he understood that his career and his personal life were on the line.

He began to get help from a group of fellow police officers that were going thru the same phase in life, a version of AA, there he meet Eduardo Sanguil a veteran police officer that gradually guided him to an improvement in his life, officer Sanguil was going thru the same period in his life divorce, family lost, he lost his older son to a bomb that was placed under his car.

The latest victim was identified as Irma Perales a young prostitute from the adjacent province of Pinar del Rio east of Havana, an autopsy was perform and a final determination was made of neck strangulation also it was noticed that the young woman had several marks in his arm indicating an heroin addict.

Det Chaquet went back to his file and found the same autopsy information concerning the heroin marks, could this be a heroin dealer? or maybe a derange killer associated in some way with a prostitution habit.

From 1956 to 1959 Cuba experience a tumultuous time, bombings in Havana, and attempt by a group of University of Havana students to take control of the presidential palace, led by a courageous leader of the Federacion Estudiantil Universitaria, an anti-Batista group named Jose Antonio Echevarria an a promising young democratic leader that was killed that day. From the Sierra Maestra in the Oriente province east of Cuba Fidel Castro and his guerrilla group advanced west toward Havana fighting a corrupt Batista army, by promising a true democracy after Batista, he rallies the people of Cuba to support his so call revolution.

After enjoying his lunch at his favorite restaurant located next to the 'Plaza de el Vapor' he was summoned back to his office, his assistant det Gerardo receive an anonymous note that morning, the note said the following:

"I will deliver my next beautiful but dirty woman when the next calendar reaches EOM29"

Yours truly Mecias"

"Reaches 29? all months have 29 days, wait except February", Chaquet ask Gerardo.

"When is the next February that contain 29 days?"

Next month! Gerardo shouted.

That was a delicate month in Havana, several bombs, electric post sabotage, it was getting difficult to move around Havana at night, but next month was approaching we needed to gather all the data we have file and see what else we have missed. All the killings are very similar, young women, all from the province of Pinar del Rio, heroin users and no family members in Havana, Pinar del Rio is the most western province in Cuba, mainly agriculturally tobacco growing being the main crop. The 26 of July movement was created by Castro to commemorate the assault on the Moncada barracks on

the 26 of July 1953, that clandestine group which Chaquet Was a member included democratic groups that were oppose to Fulgensio Batista with minimal participation of communist groups, that came later.

Some members of the Havana police dept were also members of this clandestine group but there was a large faction that supported Fulgencio Batista and its regime including Gerardo, Chaquet had to be very careful how he approaches the situation.

The first body was found in the corner of Lamparilla St .and Aguilar St.

The second was found in Compostela St close to Muralla St.

The third was found in Muralla St. and Aguillar St.   The fourth was found between Jesus Maria St. and Merced.

And the fifth was found in the corner of Muralla St. and Inquisidor St.

Chaquet ask det Gerardo.

"Any pattern you see?" no responded Gerardo.

"Well maybe he likes the streets that are within 4 to 5 blocks apart, Muralla St being at the center he or she we don't know, is trying to trace a pattern" Rafael said.

Chaquet Contact within the 26 of July movement advise him that the SIM 'Servicio de Inteligencia Military' the political police of Batista was watching him, be very careful in who to talk to specially Gerardo he sympathizes with this government. He put aside all clandestine activities for the moment, he needed to concentrate on his case, the 29 was approaching.

29 of February 1958, a cool air hit Havana Castro was advancing from the east and the urban guerrilla detonated more bombs in Havana. Chaquet already had selected a group of decent policemen to carry out hopefully the capture of "El Mecias" and no more bodies will be found in Havana, hopefully.

There were 5 teams created they were stationed in different points that det Chaquet have selected, they represented a pattern of a cross, det Chaquet selected this because his theory shows a person who hated women, prostitutes and heroin users, the area of Jesus Maria St was popular with this type of characters.

The teams consist of 4 officers each with one female dresses in provocative clothes to entice the suspect, they were in place around seven pm, enough time since all the homicides occurred between 10pm and 11pm.   Chaquet was in the detail at

Muralla St., det Gerardo was at Aguillar and Lamparilla St. detail, officer Jose Alvarez a sgt with the Havana city police was at the Inquisitor and Muralla St. detail, officer Miguel Diaz was at the Merced St. detail.

At 10:00pm det Gerardo shouted over the radio that another officer was attacking one of the female decoy at Muralla St. and Aguillar St., same place where the third body was found, Chaquet rush to the site where Gerardo was, they apprehended the officer and immediately found out that he was not a police officer he was dressed with the uniform of a police officer killed 2 years ago in strange circumstances, but being Havana anything that happened is of strange circumstances.   The subject turns out to be an ex inmate from the Mazorra mental hospital that was release 2yrs ago, nofamily connection in Havana, ex drug addict and mentally disturbed.

In the mean time when all the details were concentrating at the Muralla St. detail something happened in another Havana St, thru their car radio they heard the police dispatcher that a body was found next to the Malecon across the street from El Paseo del Prado, Chaquet immediately responded to the call and rushed to the scene, " this does not match the information we have gather from the other cases, except the strangulation part". Chaquet thought.

The area was mainly well off, a lot of tourist and a high presence of police, we must wait for the details of this case, autopsy report, description of the victim and so forth.

The following morning, we gather in our office, Det. Gerardo, members of the main detail and Me.   "we need to brainstorm and find out what we have missed" said Chaquet

"This really have caught us by surprise, new area and who knows we might have to proceed with a different route that takes us to a different conclusion"

Chaquet said, everybody agreed.

"Back to the drawing board" Chaquet said.

"Bring those boxes where we keep all the evidence from past cases, we need to reexamine again page by page all the details". Chaquet demanded.

Another 29 was approaching, but not February 29, that was 2 weeks ago "what did he meant by the EOM29"? Chaquet started thinking.

Chaquet was still struggling with his own demon, his drinking even thought he has managed to partially control it he kept a bottle of Bacardi Rum in his desk, if found it will be the end of his career.

The following week March 6 he received the autopsy report about the new case, female, cause of death strangulation, drug markings on his arm, certain

described the victim as a local prostitute even thought this time she was from Havana.

"Not from Pinar del Rio?"

Chaquet said, this is new, also no rope next to the body, at that moment Gerardo appeared, he was holding a note that just arrived at his office, it was from "El Mecias";

"you guys are a bunch of stupid rookies; I am free to keep getting rid of the trash in Havana while all of you keep guessing where I will be next remembering EOM29"

El Mecias

"We have to catch this son of a bitch NOW! "

Chaquet shouted.

What is going with me, Chaquet thought I have being very creative, I know that my drinking is a burden on my personal life but I controlled must of it, Chaquet was going thru a period of his life very precarious his clandestine affiliation with 26 of July Movement was

investigated within the dept, his ineffective way of handling his major case has put him almost to the edge, I need a break I need something to clear my mind and put mi priorities back in order.

Something is going to change in Chaquet life, for the better.

"Hey Rafael, do you have anything to do this weekend?"

Gerardo asked Chaquet.

He answered back, "not why?".

"I have a small gathering at my house and my cousin Eloiza will be there, she is a student at Havana University, also she is very attractive and smart ,maybe she can give you some pointers on how to solve this case, I want you to meet her". Chaquet paused for a moment.

"off course why not".

The weekend arrived, no leads on our case det. Chaquet is very frustrated "what have we missed?"

But today he needed a mental break and the gathering at Gerardo's house will surely be welcomed.

At 7pm Chaquet arrived at Det. Gerardo's house, his home is located in the La Vibora area it is a mix of old and new homes perfect for the growing Cuban middle class, his wife Rosa answer the door, she was in the late 40' a beautiful brunette, she maintained a beautiful figure she was also a Doctor working in the emergency area of the Havana General Hospital.

"Welcome Rafael" she said to Chaquet.

There were around 11 invited guests, friends, acquaintances and members of Batista secret police SIM, they are Gerardo friends.

I better keep my political views in my head, det. Chaquet thought.

When Rafael turned his head, he saw this beautiful young woman, dark hair with a sculpture body.   "Miss Cuba 1957?".

At that moment Gerardo embraced Rafael and said.

"Come and meet my cousin Eloiza".

Rafael was surprise, but a good surprise, it was the same woman he has seen right when he entered the house," Miss Cuba 1957".

They immediately started a conversation, she explained her Medical studies at the University, her vision of Cuba as a nation Chaquet was listening but his mind was somewhere else, he was thinking not only that she is very smart but also how beautiful she is.

They talk about her future career, his present case and many other topics except politics, being Gerardo cousin and Gerardo associated with the Batista government he did not know Eloiza's political view.

It was around 10pm time to live, Rafael excused himself from the people.

"Thank you, Gerardo, for inviting me, I really needed this see you tomorrow at the station, we need to catch this crazy person FAST". Chaquet said.

But before he left, he asks Eloiza if she was willing to have dinner with him sometime, Eloiza said

"Off course, what about next Saturday?"

Rafael responded yes, since she did not have a way to get in touch with her, he gave her his home and station numbers, they parted, you could see that Rafael was beaming with joy, for a change.

New week, new vision about the case a crazy person is roaming the street of Havana we have to solve it, the team involved in the case of "El Mecias" meet that Monday morning with low expectation, new information came in from the medical examiner some blood was found at the scene of the latest victim, they match some with the victim but other drops were not, they found that the unidentified blood contain a percentage of possible venereal disease, may be syphilis.

"this is an information we never received from the previous crimes scene, maybe if he had that before we could have concentrated in a certain group of criminals".

Chaquet said.

There was a limited amount of evidence, a rope, now the blood not to mention the strength of the killer when he strangulates his/her victims.

"People we have the solution in front of us, we just need to look closer, please" Chaquet said.

After the meeting Gerardo ask Rafael what he thought off his cousin, Chaquet like a true gentleman said.

"Beautiful, smart, interesting".

"We are planning to meet on Saturday and have dinner, if that's okay with you Gerardo".

Gerardo responded, "I will not tell her mother she might impose a chaperone for the dinner, for me is fine you are a personal friend of mine and a true gentleman".

The following day a Tuesday our station was bombed, the secret police the SIM apprehended the perpetrators as member of the 26 of July movement, one of them an associated of Chaquet, he might have a problem if he is torture and talk, he belongs to the same conspiracy cell as Chaquet.

In the 1950's the United States and Cuba had a close alliance concerning the apprehension of criminals in either country and a full training agenda that require officers in Cuba going to the US to receive training in the methods of solving and closing a criminal case, well Chaquet was invited, it was going to be in Atlanta, GA in July 1958, maybe he needed that trip, if the person that was captured by the SIM started talking he will be in great danger, if that happens while he is in the United States maybe he can stay there as political refugee, we'll see.

Beside desperate to solve the case he also was excited to meet Eloiza again and figure her more, he was worry about talking about politics you never knew what kind of reaction she might show, but it is okay just to see her was enough to lift my self-esteem, the weekend was fast

approaching Chaquet have not gone out with another female for a while, he needed to brush on the male female etiquette.

On Wednesday afternoon det. Gerardo received an anonymous tip, the serial killer El Mecias was going to strike again the following evening Thursday, how does the tipster know about this, friend, family member, personal enemy what?

Det. Chaquet immediately gather all members of the team for a brief meeting, the area of operation has changed not only the east part of Havana but now the Malecon area, the last victim was found there.

Today is the 28th, tomorrow is the.......29th, the team stop breathing.

Them Chaquet said.

"Yes, people the 29 we must act and gather all our strength and catch this person, we have to!!".

About 2pm the team began to assemble in the designated area, plus another team of roaming officers

will proceed to different areas of Havana, everything is covered, we hope.

Thursday went by nothing happened, maybe the killer was advised about the police details we set up to catch him/her, maybe he decided that he needed to stop for a while and tried to not to leave any more clues, who knows, anyway I was preparing my mind set for the dinner date with Eloiza.

It was tomorrow I need to select a nice restaurant, yes "La Zaragozana" a fancy place, expensive but what the heck my first date in years, it's worth it.

Around 8pm I pick up Eloiza at the steps of the University of Havana, she looked stunning a beautiful blue dress that fit her perfectly it was going to be a perfect night at least I'll try to make it, we arrived at the restaurant around 8:30pm, it was half empty Cubans like Europeans like to eat late, by 9pm it was full the trio was playing beautiful boleros that created a relax atmosphere specially for me.

"So was your week det. Chaquet?" Eloiza said.

"Please call me Rafael"

"Okay Rafael how was your week?"

"it was challenging" Rafael said.

"We are still all involved in a case, well maybe you don't want to hear it". Chaquet said.

"yes, I do" Eloiza said.

"Well is a little complex for a normal serial killer case it involves various women, all of them ladies of the night."

Rafael said.

"You mean prostitutes".

Eloiza said.

"Yes prostitutes, like I said it's complex, Eloiza tell me about yourself, future plans, dating anyone?"

Eloiza started laughing it was a very direct question, but she guests he is a detective he like to prove.

"Not dating, too involved in my studies and other activities related to the University".

"Like what?"

Rafael replied.

"Well we are going thru a period of change politically and morally; we need to define ourselves where we are heading in the coming years ". Eloiza said.

Rafael was intrigue by her answer, is she telling me that a political change is necessary? I need to go beyond and get a definite position from her.

Rafael asked," Eloiza what do you think about the present political climate, you are a student and the attack of university students is brutal".   She responded, "I knew Echevarria he was a friend of mine".

"You know Jose Antonio; he was killed trying to take over the presidential palace" Rafael responded.

"Yes, I know, they killed him in cold blood, it was an assassination".

Eloiza responded very emotionally.

Rafael paused for a moment, thinking can she be trusted don't forget her cousin is a big supporter of Batista, can I ask her is she with Batista or against him, will that spoil the night?

"If you were a friend of Echeverria that means that have certain affinity to a change of government in Cuba, right?"

Eloiza paused for a moment and said.

" Rafael you are a police detective, work for the government am I creating a jeopardy for myself if I answer yes or no?" Immediately Rafael answered, "No Eloiza is just that since I also admired Jose Antonio it was necessary to ask".

Eloiza smiled and said,

"yes Rafael I am not in tune with this government, is that enough?"

Rafael immediately change the conversation.

"Eloiza let's talk about our self".

Eloiza started talking about his medical education how she plans after getting her doctor degree to help the needed people of Havana, how by doing that she can accomplish her goal of helping the new generation of Cuban society, Rafael was quiet admiring the beautiful woman sitting in front of her, how she moves her lips when she spoke, the softness of her voice.

Them, Eloiza stop talking and asked Rafael what are yours goals for the future?

Rafael answered, "the same as yours, I want to confess something to you I also want a political change in Cuba".

They place the dinner order and after a while the band was playing, they decided to dance, they felt an unexpected mutual attachment, it is the first time Rafael

felt this way since his wife pass away his heart was melting while embracing this beautiful woman.

After a couple of dances, they went back to the table, Rafael asked Eloiza.

"Are you enjoying this night?"

"Yes, it is the most beautiful night of my life".

At that moment Rafael kissed her hand, a positive smile appeared on Eloiza's lips.

It was past 11pm, Rafael drove Eloiza to her apartment closed to the University of Havana, both step up to the door of her apartment and Eloiza raised her face toward Rafael and closed the night with a spontaneous passionate kiss, while walking to his car Rafael ponder, is this relationship will be the answer to my mental solitude.

The following morning the team meet at the station programming the next step into solving this case, it was

beginning to overwhelm the Havana homicide squad it was already two months since the serial killer struck.

"We need to figure out what "AOM29means"

Rafael said.

after the meeting Gerardo asked Rafael how was the date with her cousin Eloiza, Rafael smiled, it was a perfect encounter between two persons of the same frame of mind, Gerardo could not figure out what Rafael meant, so he ask again was it good?, Rafael answered it was perfect.

Det. Rafael sat at his desk in the station, is was around 7pm, his phone rang, he answered, it was Eloiza at the other end, Rafael answered and said Eloiza you don't know how happy makes me hear your voice, Eliza immediately answered me to .

"The reason I am calling is to see if we can meet tonight and have dinner, there is a nice Chinese restaurant around the corner from my apartment can you make it?"

Rafael answered yes off course.

"I have been thinking of you all day" Rafael said.

"how about 9pm?" Eloiza asked Rafael.

"9pm it is" Rafael said.

PEKING is a restaurant that cater mainly to University students and certain groups of writers and poet, not expensive but great Chinese food, Rafael arrived there 20min late there was series of bombings closed to the University put there by a student clandestine organization, Eloiza was there, she looked happy was Rafael could see that she was anxious she embrace Rafael gave him a kiss and started crying, Rafael immediately thought that it was related to her clandestine student activity.

"Eloiza was going on?" Rafael said.

Eloiza was sobbing,

"Rafael my roommate Gladys, was detained by the SIM tonight, they are saying that she planted the bombs that were detonated tonight, I am afraid that if they torture, her she can implicate me, I don't have to many options, either I can go to the mountains and join the rebel forces or stay here and keep working with my clandestine cell, Rafael I don't want to leave Havana, I am beginning to fall in love with you, if I go there is a chance I will never see you again".

Rafael was shocked but at the same time happy now I can tell her of my involvement in the 26 of July Movement.

Them Rafael said to Eloiza.

"Don't worry I have to confess something to you, I am a leader of a cell in the 26 of July Movement that is involved in the military and police forces, I will not abandon you I also love you passionately".   At that time the shared a long and lasting kiss.

Rafael proposed to Eloiza a safe place at his apartment while he can determine what the outcome with her friend will be, she accepted after finishing their dinner they drove to Rafael's apartment, Rafael assured her that he was a gentleman, she replied, I know I trust you, the University of Havana was closed that night by Batista security forces.

Even thou that Eloiza was in his mind Chaquet needed to solved serial killer case that taking his time and personal life over, while sitting at his desk he opened one of the drawers, a bottle of Bacardi Rum appeared, he looked at it even thou he needed a drink he closed the drawer and started thinking about Eloiza, she has cleared my mind, I think I can handle this drinking problem now.

Gerardo began to ask around about her cousin Eloiza, with no answer he turned to Rafael and ask him.

"Rafael have you seeing or her from my cousin, her mom is anxious to know".

"Oh yes she told me that since the University was closed, she was going to take a trip to Matanzas province with a group of students, don't worry".

But Gerardo was worry, the rebels are advancing fast toward Havana and Eloiza might be cut in the middle of the fight.

Rafael immediately phone Eloiza at his apartment and instructed her to call Gerardo.

"Eloiza please call your cousin and tell him you are in Matanzas with a group of students not to worry".

Eloiza after finishing the conversation with Rafael called her cousin Gerardo and explain where she was, Gerardo was now more relax.

After a couple of weeks the University was opened, Eloiza planning to go back, but her attachment to Rafael was very strong , she wanted to stay but Rafael decided that it was better for her to go back to her apartment, her roommate was freed and no connection to Eloiza was stablished, Eloiza was almost ready to move back but a passionate desire engulf her mind, she turned to Rafael and said, Rafael I love you have being a true gentlemen but my desire for you is unstoppable, Rafael approach her and embracing her and a passioned kiss they ended up making love, it was her first experience, they promised true love and never to be separated, for Rafael it was the beginning of a true love, his first love his wife pass away 2 years ago his life have being taken over by his work and yes alcohol, now he found a true calling in Eloiza, he loved her immensely and did not want to loose her, the same with her.

Now that Eloiza situation was stable he needed to get back to his main case, like always a meeting of the team went thru all available evidence;

The rope, yellow was manufacture in the US, precisely in Illinois, sold anywhere in Cuba.

The blood, O Positive with a trace of Syphilis.

Human hair dark, Male, Caucasian.

No eyewitness, all victim's female, prostitutes. AOM29? what does it means? we think that 29 means a day, AOM? A another? O on? Month?, wait, wait, Another Odd Month on the 29, it that makes sense?

May is now, odd month on the 29.

Chaquet Said "let's go ahead and target the 29th of May, we can get lucky and catch this SOB!"

Eloiza and Rafael spoke almost every night, wishing to be together again, they have set up another meeting at Rafael's, apartment he was very edgy, but they made love passionately and promised never to leave each other's side.

The following day the 29th of May around 8pm the teams were in place, Chaquet took the Galiano St .detail, the night was breeze not to hot clear night.

It was around 10:45pm Chaquet saw a captain in the Cuban Army approach a street prostitute at the corner of Galiano and San Rafael after a couple of minutes he saw the captain grabbing the prostitute and later put a rope around her neck, this is it!, he called all detail to his street .

"WE GOT HIM; WE GOT THE SOB!"

It took a couple of officers plus Chaquet to handcuff him, he was very strong.

His name Hilario Diaz a captain in Batista Army, he confessed to the crimes and said.

"I   wanted   to   clean   the   street   of   Havana". The reason was that a prostitute has transmitted syphilis to his system, it was pure vengeance.

So, at 10:45pm we caught "El Mecias "on the 29th case closed.

After searching Capt. Hilario house they found several pieces of personal belonging from his victims, also at his house they found pictures of his daughter, she died of an overdose of heroin, she also have become a prostitute to support her heroin habit, it was a terrible situation all over.****

CHAPTER 2

"Yesterday is not ours to recover, but tomorrow is ours to win or lose"

Anonymous

July 1958, Chaquet will be spending 2 weeks in the United States taking a course in "modern criminal detection tactics", the week was quite considering the fact that the rebels were closer to Havana, the Havana police dept. was busy not only solving crimes but also lending a hand to the SIM, in apprehending rebel factions inside the capital, not many professional officers participated most of them were anti Batista.

Eloiza and Rafael were making plans to wed when he got back from the US, they were much in love, she still was participating in anti-Batista activities inside the University but the relation with Rafael was very firm, they both were hoping that the coming year will bring a real change for a Democratic Cuba.

Det. Chaquet flew from Havana to New Orleans on Delta Airlines, from there he flew to Atlanta Georgia, arriving in the middle of the day an officer with Georgia bureau of Investigation was waiting for him, an officer named ralph Scotts he was a LT. at the GBI, they drove to Decatur Georgia where the Headquarters of the GBI is located.

There were agents from all over Georgia, the only foreigner was Chaquet, he spoke some English, enough to understand the agents and the course.

There he meet Agent Charles Lynnard of Marietta, GA, pleasant fellow spoke some Spanish so they hit it off immediately, the week end before leaving back to Cuba Lynnard invited Chaquet over for dinner at his house, his wife Rachelle was a beautiful Georgia Peach, 2 teenagers, Dolly 15, Eileen 16, and the big boy 4 years old Karl(active was his middle name).

During dinner we spoke about the course, the political situation in Cuba, as a matter of fact President Eisenhower had suspended all shipments of arms to the

Batista regime back in May, my personal life I mentioned that Eloiza my fiancée and me were going to wed before the end of the year, not knowing that our destiny as Cuban citizens will change.

It was an intense course, also my mind was shared, thinking about Eloiza, the political situation in Cuba and the future that I will experience when I arrive back, his return will not be as he has expected.

The day of his departure, Lynnard took Chaquet to the airport telling him that anything you need please do not hesitate to ask, their friendship was cemented that day.

He flew the same way he came, Atlanta to New Orleans and back to Havana.

At the Havana airport he was meet by Det. Gerardo, Rafael immediately asked for Eloiza, she was supposed to be at the airport to greet him.

Gerardo looked at Rafael and said. Eloiza had a problem", Rafael moods immediately changed and asked, what

happened, Gerardo directed him to the next set of benches at the airport and gave him all the details.

"Eloiza was setting up an explosive devise about 2 blocks from the University when without any warning the devise exploded killing her immediately".

Sobbing Gerardo said to Rafael.

At that moment Rafael could not contain his emotion and started crying, the woman he truly loved was gone, she was the one that lift him out of his alcohol dependence, they were going to be marry soon, why did it happened to me, he shouted!

After the body of Eloiza was recovered from the Central Morgue, her family and Rafael made arrangements for the funeral, during the wake the coffin was closed due to the damage the bomb have done to her body, Rafael could not contain his crying, their rest the woman he was going to marry live next to her and have a family.

Batista must go! the young are dying.

After the funeral mass at a local Catholic church Eloiza was laid to rest at the family plot at the Colon cemetery, what would happen now to Rafael, will he go back and started drinking again?, Eloiza family was suffering a young woman with a future ahead of her have left, the priest at the funeral mass said, she is going to a better place, but Rafael and her family wanted her here.

These was a big to blow to Rafael, his life was turning for the better, not anymore without his Eloiza. ***

CHAPTER 3

"The light of the Moon will be like that of the Sun, and the light of the Sun will be seven times greater"

Is. 30: 26

It was past midnight 1958 that Fulgencio Batista president of Cuba left the country, next stop Dominican Republic, Che Guevara took Santa Clara and on January 1, 1959 Fidel declared that Cuba was "liberated".

It was pandemonium in Havana as members of the 26 of July Movement started looking for criminals within the the Batista regime, that day there were several murders caused by personal revenge, Chaquet assumed the administration of the Havana Police dept on a temporary basis until the Revolutionary council named a new director.

It was not until January 6 that Chaquet was promoted to director of the Havana police force under its new name (Policia Nacional Revolucionaria), its main commander

was Efijenio Ameijeiras a ruthless commander that fought with Castro on the mountains of Sierra Maestra.

Due to Chaquet participation in the 26 of July Movement at the beginning of Castro taking power he was treated with respect.

A new beginning for Rafael now Director Rafael Chaquet, but without his dear Eloiza his personal demon will be out again, his new bottle of rum took a part of his desk, his friends at the station always reminded him to clean himself up, he smelled like a pig, his barhopping after hours in Havana began to take its toll, one night on a bar in Old Havana Federico an old friend from his clandestine days approach Chaquet saying

"Oye chico estas borracho" (man you are drunk), Chaquet immediately turn around recognizing his friend and said.

"No solo es un trago" (not, only one drink) But Chaquet was having trouble walking, Federico hold him and said.

"Rafael get your life in order you need some help". Chaquet keep saying, is only a drink and immediately collapsed.

The following day Chaquet woke up in his apartment with a terrible headache, it was not the first time he could remember any conversation he had the night before, he surely needed help.   The first 6 months of 1959 were very traumatic, personal revenge, political posturing and the creation of a so call government of unity, off course the communist advance within that government was notable.

Director Chaquet was involved in a couple of cases , it was mainly political revenge and husbands killing their wife's lover, in July 1959 there was an interesting case involving a 15 yr. old girl, she was found raped, and her throat slashed from left to right, the girl was from a middle class family, no hint of any criminal activity and her father was a prominent supporter of the Castro regime. Immediately Director Chaquet was called by the commander of the National Police to get involve in the case, det. Gerardo was not available, he was   apprehended the first week of January 1959 on suspicion of torture to a member of the 26 of July Movement, Chaquet testify on his defense, after the hearing with no evidence against him they let him go and a week later he took a flight to Miami, FL.

Political persecution was in full force, your neighbor, any family member, or any stranger who wanted to do harm on a certain individual can testify on the so-called Peoples Courts and your life as a human being was destroyed.

July is a hot month in Havana men walking wearing their Guayaberas, women dressed nicely but the breeze from the Ocean kept the day livable, Director Chaquet made his way to El Cotorro, a suburb of Havana where the girl family live, they were Mr. and Mrs DeLeon their daughter Rosa DeLeon was the girl that was found dead in Havana the prior week, they were middle age with a high degree of intelligence after interviewing the mother he began to interview her Dad, he was 56 yrs. old wore spectacle and had noticeable scar on his right face, and accident or a fight.

He began telling Chaquet of his role in the Revolution a Lawyer he helped young rebels that were caught by the Batista secret police win in court, for that he was rewarded after the Revolution with a judge post in the main court in Havana, he proceeded to tell me that he meet a young rebel captain Ray Sosa, he was around 25yrs of age tall and a ladies man, Mr. DeLeon began to invite the young Captain to his house for dinner that's when he notice his 15 yrs. old daughter began to get infatuate with Captain Sosa, he was the son of one of Fidel Castro aide so this require a very delicate approach.

The following day Chaquet and his new assistant Det. Raul Sains visited Captain Sosa at his headquarter in La Cabana, a Spanish built fortress that was used as a political jail and headquarter of the G2 the feared political police of the Castro government. Director Chaquet introduced himself and his assistant, he began by telling Captain Sosa the reason he was there, Captain Sosa knew about the murder of the dead girl, according to him he read it on the Havana newspaper, he preceded to say, "what can I do to help?"

"Well Captain Sosa it's seem that the murdered girl had a crush on you and will have done anything to make you notice her".

Rafael said.

Captain Sosa responded.

"I had a respect for her, every time I went to have dinner at the DeLeon house, I knew she had an infatuation with me, but I tried to stay away from her as much as possible".

Director Chaquet and det. Sains left Capt. Sosa's office with more questions than answers, he said he never took her out of the house for a walk or to the movies, that contradict an statement made by the girl's father in which he described how Capt. Sosa took her for a walk in Havana and later to the movies, of course my wife was the chaperone, now there was an instance when Capt. Sosa took the girl for a tour of La Cabana his headquarters, and introduce her to his father comandante Sosa, she went alone with him, odd right.

After dropping det. Sains at the station Det. Chaquet made it to his apartment, there he drowns himself in sorrows, his job was getting to him, Eloiza his beautiful Eloiza, he immediately went after the bottle of rum next to his bed, it was almost 6pm.

At 2am he woke up, sweaty and a daunting and yes smelling like a pig because of his headache he could not sleep any more took a shower and made to the station, he arrived at 2:45am, there was a message in his desk it was from Alex another officer at the station, the note read; "meet me at the corner of Galiano and San Rafael I might have some information for you concerning the girl killing, but please keep it to yourself not even your assistant can know, let's make it around 6am".

It is almost 4 hours from now, I can prepare for the meeting and leave before det. Sains shows up.   He did not have a close relationship with officer Alex, but according to some other officers that knew him they all said he was very professional in his work.

The corner of Galiano and San Rafael was not busy at 6am, it was mainly shops and restaurants, some will open at 6am to serve breakfast others will open at 9am, Director Chaquet did not know officer Sosa that well, but could recognize him, he was standing next to the door of a coffee shop, he indicated to Director Chaquet that he will meet him inside, Alex was from the interior of Cuba, due to the fact that the police force was being clean of Batista sympathizers they were short of officers so they decided to bring officers from other parts of Cuba.

They sat in a corner table; Alex began talking.

"Director it is a pleasure to meet a hero of the Revolution, your leadership in the urban clandestine movement was superb".

Chaquet immediately cut him and said.

"Cut the crap and tell me what you know".

Alex was surprise, he started talking.

"There is a rumor among the G2 operatives that either Capt. Sosa or his father Comandante Sosa might be implicated in the girls murder".

Okay Director Chaquet ask Alex.

"Do you have any evidence that can connect either one of them to this crime?". Alex responded.

"No just the rumors, you might want to look into both of them and them where about the day of the crime".

They had a latte and some biscuits, the smell of Cuban Coffee was overwhelming, Alex started to ask Director. Chaquet about the way the revolution was going, about the talk that the government was moving to the left, about certain members of the government that are communists, Director Chaquet was surprise, he sounded like the Batista secret police trying to find your political position, but why me I support the Revolution was a member of the movement, why is he asking all those questions?, Director Chaquet thought. He responded to Alex. "Thank you, Alex, for the information, I will surely look into the rumors you just mentioned, concerning the Revolution, we will wait and see where it will take us".

In about 2 years Director Chaquet will find out, for the worse.

Director Chaquet arrived at the station around 10:30 am, det. Sains was already there, he was looking into the evidences they already had, an autopsy report confirm that she was raped, them det. Sains mentioned to Director. Chaquet that an officer from G2 was requesting the same evidence, Director. Chaquet thought, the rumors that officer Alex mentioned, they might be true?

That afternoon he was trying to get an appointment with Comandante Sosa, he had to be very delicate how he handles this situation, Comandante Sosa is very influential a close aide to Fidel Castro and the chairman of the newly created Integrated Revolutionary organizations (Organizaciones Revolucionarias Integradas).

Chaquet was given 25 minutes to ask Sosa any questions, Director. Chaquet and Det. Sains drove to the Miramar section of Havana, an affluent neighborhood full of empty houses that used to belong to associates of Batista, those houses were assign to a close circle of Fidel Castro friends and their families.

A post manned by army soldiers was setup at the entrance of the neighborhood, they showed their badges them the soldier proceeded to call Comandante Sosa to confirm their meeting, an okay was given they drove to the house, it was the house of the past president of the Cuban Supreme Court a member of Batista circle.

By the door there was another member of the army, they directed us to leave our revolvers outside, very odd since we are there as officers of the law, Comandante Sosa was seating in a sofa facing the patio, talking with someone, after he finished the conversation he was very polite and directed us to a small office next to the living room, them he began to speak.

"Welcome to our home, or may I say the people's home, this house was given to me by the commander in chief Fidel Castro a true hero of the Revolution".

Director Chaquet almost feel sleep by listening to the same revolutionary rhetoric, Sosa resumed his speech.

"Director Chaquet you are also a true hero of the Revolution".

Chaquet change his conversation and started to direct his dialogue with Sosa toward the main reason he was there, he had to be very careful how he conducted the questions.

Director Chaquet began by saying. "Comandante Sosa the reason we are here is to get as much information about the case involving Paula DeLeon that was found murderer in Havana 3 weeks ago, we understand that you and your so you know De-Leon family".

"Mr. DeLeon is a judge in one of our Revolutionary courts, a fervent supporter of our revolution, I have been to his house several times with my son, it is terrible

what has happened to that poor girl, she was intelligent and beautiful, anything that I can do please let me know".

Sosa concluded. Chaquet push forward with his questions, "Comandante Sosa at any time you or your son were along with Paula, either for a walk or going to the movies?".

Sosa began to be annoyed, "what kind of question is that? are you assuming that either my son or I are suspect in this case?"

Director Chaquet immediately said.

" No Comandante I just need to clarify certain information, all persons associated with DeLeon family needs to be asked".

Suddenly Sosa said, "Director Chaquet your time is up, have a nice day".

Chaquet and his assistant left the house it was a palace but according to the rhetoric of the revolution it was not supposed to be that way, all members of the government will have to sacrifice with the rest of the Cuban people, Director Chaquet was beginning to understand, there is a Cuban saying that goes like this 'quitate tu pa ponerme yo' (get out of the way so I can step in).

The following morning Mr. DeLeon was waiting for Director Chaquet at the station, they sat in Director Chaquet closed the door and Mr. DeLeon started to talk.

"Director I found something in my daughter's room, it is a diary, on page 16 there is a description of a man that kissed her and promise her true love, she kept writing that even thou he was older than her he was very sweet and gave her a true loving experience".

Director Chaquet was baffle, an older man who knew her, Director Chaquet asked DeLeon.

" Were there any more persons that associated with your daughter?"

"well beside the Sosa father and son there was also our neighbor Miguel, he is a little strange, low IQ and a problem trying to communicate with people, also across the street Joaquin a 21-year-old welder, he works at the port of Havana, you see my daughter did not go out that much and associated with a limited amount of friends".

Director Chaquet asked.

"did she have any boyfriend or male friends at her school?"

DeLeon answer "well there is Luis Alvarez he was Paula's boyfriend for a while, she broke with him and he was very distress about the situation".

Director Chaquet asked again. "could you provide me with the name and addresses of this people?", DeLeon said off course.

The list of suspects kept growing now there is 5 suspects added, who knows it might grow even more.

Director Chaquet supervise a department of 98 detectives in the metropolitan district of Havana that covers several neighborhoods, Old Havana, Atares   section and other areas of Havana, it was a large area for the amount of detectives available to him, no female detectives, if he needed a female he will have to request the aid of a female police officer, by the way there were not that many either, like he told Alex, "we will and see where the Revolution will take us".

They already have interview the Sosa's, father and son now they needed to interview the rest of names that Mr.DeLeon has provided, they started with Joaquin the welder at the port of Havana, we arrived at the offices of the Cuban Shipping Lines talk to the supervisor and asked for Joaquin, after 10 minutes Joaquin arrived he was short maybe 5'5", weight approx. 130 lbs. and a quiet appearance.

After introducing our self we began to tell him the reason for our interview with him, asked him about his acquaintance with Paula and when was the last time he saw her, with a very low voice he began to describe his knowledge of Paula, he saw her several times outside of her house, sometime said hello, sometime she   responded, she was very beautiful but never to close, one time he saw his boyfriend looked like a jerk push her, could not hear the conversation but he was very mad, like I said a jerk, after 30 min. interview Director Chaquet and his assistant left, they determined that Joaquin was not his man but they will keep an eye on him.

Her ex-boyfriend was next, Luis Alvarez is 17 years old attend a Havana high school located about 30 min. from our station an area called Marianao, like always after asking the principal for permission to talk to Luis he showed about 10 min. later, 5'8" muscular figure maybe 156 lbs. he was an athlete at the school, we began by asking about when was the last time he saw Paula, he began to be aggravated.

"That girl, you know she broke with me threw me out of the house and told me she found a better man and they were going to live together someplace outside of Cuba".

" Was that the last time you saw her?" Luis responded "yes, I was very mad and wanted to find a way to get   back to her telling her how much I love her, but she did not want to talk to me".

"When did all of this happened?"

Director Chaquet asked.

"It happened about 6 weeks ago", again Director Chaquet asked him if he knew the name of the man she was going to go away? "Luis answer no, but it must be somebody with a lot of resources to leave Cuba".

They left Miguel the neighbor for last.

Director Chaquet still attend the AA meetings, even thou they have been cut from 4 a week to 2 a week, according to the revolutionary government they represent an idea from the past, they have set a goal to eliminate all negative part of the society by 1961, that includes prostitute, drunks, homeless and so on, good luck with that, Director Chaquet was beginning to question in his mind the future goals of the revolution, this is not what we have fought for, it was the beginning of the loss of personal liberties, between these and the case of Paula DeLeon his mind was running wild, he needed Eloiza now more than ever.

After interviewing Paula's neighbor Miguel, the following week Director Chaquet concluded that he was not a suspect anymore, the week of the crime he was with his family someplace else outside of Havana.

It was now 6 months since the homicide of Paula DeLeon happened, Director Chaquet and his assistant Det. Raul Sains went thru the evidence every day, there have to be something here that we have miss Director Chaquet said, we need to concentrate on the man that appeared in Paula's diary, the man that kissed her and promised her the world, that man has power and of the persons we have interview the ones that support those qualities are the Sosa's father and son, we have to keep digging.

The following day an informant with the Havana Police called Director Chaquet, he had some information about the Sosa family, they decided to meet the following day. Just before the meeting with Director Chaquet the

informant was found dead in a street in the old Havana district.

Chaquet was not surprise, having information about a famous revolutionary family like the Sosa's can put you in danger, Chaquet was beginning to see the case evolved around a group of members of the Revolutionary council, Comandante Sosa and Captain Sosa his son.

January 1960, after 6 months no clear solution to the Paula De-Leon case, there were other cases, the case of Paula was taking most of the time with Director Chaquet, it was like his inner demons was calmed by this case, he could not forget Eloiza the wonderful time they spend together their future plans all in the past, he needed to start planning for his future personal life but first his drinking needed to be controlled.

1960 began with the realignment of the Policia Nacional Revolucionaria (Revolutionary National Police), 3 different branches were created it was under the command of the Ministry of the Interior, Security, Technical Operations

The last Internal Order was veiled in mystery, Director Chaquet was assigned to Technical Operations which included homicides, he was immediately named commander of that division in Havana and it's several jurisdictions a big promotion, how long will it last?, to his surprise he was given a new apartment next to the Havana Bay, it used to belong to a businessman that left for the US a year before, a big surprise for the new commander Chaquet.

The old 26 of July Movement members got together at least once a month for lunch or dinner, Commander Chaquet started to noticed that every time he attended a meeting more members were missing, he asked several of his old friends and nobody knew were they were the organizer of those meetings called their homes and try to get more information into their whereabouts to no avail, something was brewing and Commander Chaquet needed to find out. Even thou Commander Chaquet had added responsibilities he stayed in the Paula de Leon he had no idea that it was going to explode in front of him.

A couple of weeks after his promotion a police captain called Commander Chaquet with some information about a prostitute that was beaten and left on the sideway in the small town of Bejucal, she was alive in the hospital but said to the captain she had information about DeLeon case, Bejucal is about 1:30 hours from Havana, he called det. Sains to accompany him to interview this woman, they arrived at Bejucal around 1pm the woman was very bruised and spoke with some difficulty, the captain that called Commander Chaquet was there too, they began the questioning by asking her name, "my name is Sara Lopez, she said, my age, 24yrs,"

Det. Sains took over, he asked her.

"who did this to you Sara?" with great difficulty she described the man who first enticed her for sex and when they finished, she demanded the payment and

instead he beat her up, det. Sains followed with more questions.

"can you describe him". She said, he is a client of mine he is in the government, always bragging about how he can have any girl, when I say girl I mean minors, usually around 16yrs old and convince them to have sex with him, he was telling me about a girl he tried to have sex with him but she was very difficult and had to pressure her, she kept on stopping him so he did not have any choice but to raped her and dispose of her later, and you know he describe all of this smiling, what an ass".

Commander Chaquet asked Sara" what do you mean by dispose of her?". "I don't' know he said disposed of her maybe left her a bus station or something, I don't know".

the most important question.

"Sara since he was your client, I assumed he engaged having sex with you before do you know his name".

"No, he always used Carlos as his identity".

"Could you give us any more information on this Carlos guy?", det Sains asked Sara.

"he is a little overweight maybe 5'10" very vulgar in his way and yes lousy client".

det. Sains asked her. "them why do you keep on seeing him if he is such a lousy guy?"

Well Sara said" he provided me with certain needs I have".

like what det. Sains asked, Sara said "I am a drug addict he provides me with cocaine that's why I keep seeing him"

Commander Chaquet asked the captain if he can moved her to a safer place until we can have a more clear picture of the whole situation, the captain agreed and ask Commander Chaquet if he could talk to him alone, Commander Chaquet and the captain went to an empty room in the hospital. The captain started the conversation.

"Commander Chaquet my name is Roger Ruiz and I am a good friend of Alex, you know him, right?"

Commander Chaquet was caught off guard.

"yes, I meet him, why do you ask?".

Captain Ruiz continue, "well the reason I called you is that there is possibility that the beating of Sara might be related to the homicide of Paula DeLeon, also Alex, me and a group of fellow officers have a sense that maybe, and let me repeat maybe Comandante Sosa or his son might be implicated, please Commander Chaquet don't take this the wrong way but there is a lot of corruption with the new elite in the government, we want to save the revolution". Captain Ruiz concluded.

Commander Chaquet listened and began asking to himself, have the new order replace the old one with the same methods and kept the system of corruption?

After captain Ruiz finish his conversation commander Chaquet said.

"well Comandante Sosa and his son are a couple of persons that are in my list of suspects that does not means that they are involved but only that some aspect of their testimony has certain flaws".

Commander Chaquet was trying to keep this investigation as tight as possible , it involves a high ranking member of the government he didn't want to rock the boat until all the facts were available, det.Sains asked what did the captain say, Commander Chaquet did not want to share the information with the det., yet he did not know if det. Sains was too close to the elite of the government.

The following day det. Sains arrived at the station very early Chaquet was already there, immediately they began to reassess all the information available;

There is no physical evidence of the crime.

The suspects; Paula ex-boyfriend: Luis Alvarez, was mad that she left him for somebody else, no alibi the day of the crime.

Neighbor/next door: Miguel, alibi he was out of town with his parents.

Neighbor/across street: alibi, he was working a shift at the port of Havana the day of the crime.

Captain Sosa: G2 Captain (secret police), no alibi, according to him he was alone in a park with a woman friend.

Comandante Sosa: high government official, close to Fidel Castro, no information into his whereabout that day.

Paula's diary: information about a man that kissed her and made sexual innuendos, a man that had a lot of influence in our society.

There were other homicide cases in Havana that year but commander Chaquet was mentally and emotionally involved with the Paula Deleon case, if it shows that a member of our government is in any way connected to this case it will be a blow to the ideals that made him participate in the fight against Fulgencio Batista.

Commander Chaquet still had a personal problem, now more that ever his drinking increased to a point that the police in Havana found him sleeping in a bench at the Havana Central Park, it was around 2am, he was taken to his apartment and commander Chaquet stayed in bed for 2 days, he was close to the bottom of the barrel.

After several months into the investigation into the Paula DeLeon case there was a complete frustration within the dept., Commander Chaquet was forced to get involved in other cases that were not as delicate as this one, something was brewing, Comandante Efigenio Amejeiras the head of the Cuban National Police called Chaquet and instructed him to desist in his participation into the Paula Deleon, no reason was given just get out of the case, that was a shocker, now Comandante Amejeiras and Comandante Sosa are close friends both fought in the mountains with Fidel Castro and both are considered in Cuba as heroes of the revolution is this a signal that either any of the Sosa's are involved, Chaquet wondered. I advised det. Sains of the order, and them called officer   Alex and captain

Ruiz about the developments, they were not surprised, a week later captain Ruiz call Chaquet and told me that a couple of officers from the G2 interview him concerning Sara Lopez the prostitute that was beaten in the town of Bejucal, also the same week det. Sains was also summoned to the main office of the G2 and asked to handout the file on Paula's homicide, off course he refused until he spoke to commander Chaquet, he advised det. Sains to go ahead and forward the file to them, this situation is over the head of commander Chaquet, whatever happens we will never know.

That week Chaquet meet with various ex members of the 26 of July movement they were dissatisfied with the way the Revolution was moving, corruption, leftist influence and political persecution that look very similar to what Batista did, something had to be done, but what? Chaquet asked, Federico his old friend was present he mentioned to Chaquet about several sectors within the revolutionary council that were beginning to plot an overthrow of the leftist faction within the government, Chaquet interrupted Federico and said.

"Federico don't you think is better to approach the main leaders of the revolution and present our points of disagreement instead of getting into a fight against them?". Federico said.

"Rafael, you are so naïve they don't give a shit, they stole the revolution from us they are not going to let it get out of their grip". Chaquet was worried, my close friends are planning an insurrection they already have one in the Escambray mountains, am I missing something?

1960 is turning to be a challenging year for the Cuban people, for Chaquet next year will be even more challenging, the meeting with his friends was on a Tuesday, on Thursday around 6:00pm his assistant Sains contacted Chaquet.

"Commander Sains said a couple of G2 agents just came by the station and took all the remaining file about DeLeon case they told me to get out of the office and be   quiet,

I tried to get in touch with you, I also called the head of the National Police to no avail, I am worry this is getting very complicated ".

Don't worry I will take care it in the morning Chaquet responded to Sains, but Chaquet was worry to he immediately hit the bottle it was the only scape he could find all the work he did to get rid of Batista was for nothing a new elite was there and more repressive than the last. ****

CHAPTER 4

"If you don't have a plan for life, you'll never have order"

Jose Maria Escriva

FELIZ ANO NUEVO, "happy new year, for commander Chaquet was not going to be, 1961 is here there is still fighting in the mountains of Escambray by anti-Fidel forces most of the fighters were members of the rebel army that fought against Batista they turn against Castro because of the affiliation with the communist faction inside the revolution, in April of 1961 Bay of Pigs had occurred, after supporting the invasion the Kennedy administration without any prior notice dropped the support, with no definite solutions in sight the people were beginning to questions the true direction of the Cuban Revolution.

Like every morning commander Chaquet arrived at his office very early, he was mainly involved in administrative duties, his detective work was limited,   one thing he noticed was that some of his comrade in arms in the fight against Batista were beginning to disappear, some were forced to move to low level jobs others were detained and accused of plotting against the state, things were changing in Cuba, for the worse.

In the middle of all this change was his inner demon, his drinking was a scape from the realities of the time, the AA meetings was reduced even more, his contacts within the government were being diminish, somethings were not going right for him, he found out that his friend Federico was detained 2 days ago and charged with counterrevolutionary activities.

In the middle of the night one day in the summer of 1961 the G2 broke into Chaquet apartment and detained him, accused of counterrevolutionary activities he was taken to the G2 head-quarter at the Cabana Fortress, the same place Captain Sosa was assign, this fortress was built by the Spaniards in the 18th century, the third largest in the America in it used by the government as a prison complex.

Initially he was interview by a Lt. Hernandez a G2 official, he was a young fellow out of the University of Central Cuba, a true idealist, with communist leanings he started talking about the future of the revolution how Cuba will surpass the US in total freedom and in the production of goods," with the guidance of our leader comrade Fidel Castro we will achieve our goals" he said.

Then commander Chaquet asked.

"Okay but why am I here? are you accusing me of any crime? or this is a tactic by the government to convince the people that the revolution is right no matter what".

Them LT. Hernandez again said to commander Chaquet.

"There is proof that you have engage in activities contrary to our leaders and our revolution".

Chaquet asked "which leaders?"

The LT. said. "Well members of the army command, the same comrades that gave their lives for the revolution". Chaquet was shock but not surprise, Comandante Sosa he immediately thought, yes, we were too close to the investigation of Paula De-Leon homicide.

After spending a couple of hours in the interview room Hernandez proceeded to read me the accusation that will be presented to the people's court the following day, Chaquet later found out there were several others involved in this so call plot, the government elite was determined to close Paula's DeLeon case.

Chaquet was placed in a small cell, next to it he could hear the suffering of his fellow inmates, they were not legally accused of any crime but to the government they were already guilty.

The G2 was already using the Soviet method of interrogation, Chaquet thought that since he was not involved in any conspiracy he will be freed soon, wishful thinking, around 7pm a bulky sergeant from G2 appeared in Chaquet cell, he began by saying.

"Comrade my name is Jose Gonzales, but you can call me cheo".

He smelled like he had smoke a package of Partagas a Cuban brand of cigarettes.

"Now we are going to find out everything about you either you sign this confession, or we are going to make your life miserable".

With a big smile he opened a small briefcase, another interrogator was in Chaquet cell, this one tight Chaquet to his bed and made a remark.

"Cuidado con cheo el no cree ni en su madre". (be careful with cheo he doesn't gives a shit not even to his mother).

At that time cheo took a syringe from the briefcase and a small bottle of some liquid, smiling he turn to Chaquet and said." In a little while you will be singing like a bird."

Chaquet knew what he was going to do, inject him with the famous true serum.

Chaquet began to twist, moan, and began talking about everything except any involvement with a conspiracy, cheo and the other interrogator administer more of that true serum, but no result were obtain, Chaquet was unconscious to much of that serum, a doctor was called he began calling the 2 interrogators you 2 are stupid, you can kill him them what, no answers to the high command, quick give him an anti-serum doses so the rest of the interrogation team can have an answer, estupidos you almost kill him.

After a couple of days Chaquet was back to normal, he had a headache it was like the ones he had when he drank to much, well at least I was happier Chaquet thought, that afternoon lt. Hernandez came to his cell, Chaquet made a comment.

"Hernandez, I going to vomit, you smell as bad as cheo, is this a requirement among the G2 interrogators to smell like shit".

Immediately Hernandez gave Chaquet a big punch in his face.

"Shup up your miserable scum you are the one that is in big trouble, let's say in deep shit".

Hernandez said, he showed a sign confession from one of the accused policemen that were taken with Chaquet.

"That is all a lied". Chaquet said.

"You probably torture him or terrorize his family you piece of shit, all of you are a bunch of sons of a bitch, you hear me SONS OF A BITCHES!!!".

Hernandez got real mad and began hitting Chaquet several times, he had no food for the last 2 days only limited water so he was very weak and immediately fainted and collapsed, Hernandez was furious his higher up needed Chaquet to start talking now he laid in his bed unconscious and unresponsive, Hernandez left Chaquet cell but was immediately reprimanded by his superiors, what Chaquet did not know is that in the next room listening to all the conversation was Capt. Sosa, he was mad he needed Chaquet to start talking about any involvement with the so call conspiracy, it was not going to happen. Chaquet woke up the following morning still hurting from the hitting and the chemicals that was administered by the interrogation team, tight to his bed, his head was spinning but at least he was alive for how long he did not know.

It was 3 weeks after being detained that Chaquet appeared in court, it was August 21, 1961 sitting next to him was det. Alex, Capt. Roger Ruiz of the town of Bejucal and 12 more members Cuban National Police all accused of counterrevolutionary activities, they were assigned a defense lawyer but he didn't show any sympathy for the group he was more in tune with the prosecution.

The group was accused of being agents of the US working for the CIA ' under the Cuban communist system anybody who is not in tune with the government is a foreign government agent', the trial lasted for 3 weeks they had police officers testify against the group with wild and false information, nothing was true but it did not matter they knew what was going to happen, family members of the accused were not permitted to attend the court hearings, it was all a farce.

On September 10, 1961 the group was sentence to 15 years hard labor at the Isle of Pines prison located of the western coast of Cuba later the name was changed to Isle of the Youth and the prison was closed", all the remaining inmates were send to various prisons inside of Cuba.

Rafael Chaquet political inmate #4657 was entering a new phase of his live, he could not had imagined that after fighting to topple the Batista dictatorship his own principle of freedom and liberty were being tossed in the garbage by the same group of people he fought with.

Rafael was transported to the Isle of Pines prison with a group of 40 prisoners some ex members of the 26 of July movement and other democratic organizations, Rafael was assign to gallery 2 cell 44, several inmates were also placed to the same cell, all political prisoners, he was among friends.

On December 2, 1961 Fidel Castro declared himself a Marxist Leninist and the revolution that was fought by many democratic groups were taken over by the communist factions within national movement, nobody at the prison was surprised they knew that Castro was not a true Democrat he only used sectors of the Cuban society to put his plan in motion.

Rafael stayed in the Isle of Pines prison until 1967 when it was closed due to several riots and hunger strikes by political inmates, he was transferred to La Cabana fortress the same fortress where the Captain Sosa was assigned, Rafael will soon receive a visit from Sosa.

About a week after his arrival Sosa meet with Rafael, they spoke about different topics but when they jump to the Paula DeLeon case captain Sosa immediately said to Rafael.

"I was not involved in this crime, I liked her a lot but not to the point of raping or killing her, you and your group of detectives were put into this situation just because of that case, and that's my last word on it".   Rafael immediately thought It all make sense now if it not   Captain Sosa who else have the power to persecute and put us in this situation if it's not a real higher up?

By that time a large group of rebel commanders that fought with Fidel Castro were eliminated, William Morgan an American, Sori Marin, Hubert Matos, Cubelas, Quevedo and many more that belonged to the Democratic front, between 1959 and 1968 the communist takeover of the Cuban Revolution was in full force, by 1965 the Escambray fighters were almost all liquidated, it's leaders Porfirio Ramirez, Evelio Duque, Joaquin Membrive, Ramon del Sol Sori, Tomas San Gil, Francisco Lopez Blazquez Chaplain of the group, and many others were eliminated due to their anticommunist believes.

By the end of the 60's Cuban was solid under the Soviet dominance, military, internal security and the economy were in line with the Soviet system, Rafael and all political prisoners began to fill the pressure, they were order to change their political prisoners clothe to the   regular common prisoner's cloth, the majority refused it was an intense period of Rafael interment.

Between 1965 and 1968 the government decided that prostitutes, homosexuals, homeless, religious involved persons and any other "social affliction" will be dealt by sending them to special camps called UMAP, (military units for to help in production of goods), in other words concentration works camps.

Cuba was changing for the worst, during his time at the prison he began with the help of an University English professor that was also a political prisoner to learn basic English, it was not easy they were awaken almost every night at around midnight and naked began to run inside the prison for 1 hour, the prison guard were always laughing, they were trying to break the morale of the prisoners since the majority were there for political reasons.

Rafael was assessing his life, from a star homicide detective in Havana to a political prisoner, nothing to be ashamed most of the fellow inmates were professionals within the Cuban society but their dedication to stablish a true Democracy have clashed with the dictatorial regime of Fidel Castro, in 1959 more than 95% of the Cuban population supported the regime but by 1961 more Cubans realize that a communist system was not to the benefit of the people.

Rafael began to reanalyze where he went wrong in reference to the Paula DeLeon case, all the limited evidence recorded, all witnesses were interview, but something was missing the sudden close of the case, the investigating team accused of counterrevolutionary activities it came from high in the elite group of Fidel Castro collaborators, my conclusion Comamdante Sosa by now head of the Ministry of Interior with the G2, National Police and several other counterintelligence agencies under his command was involved.

It was the beginning of the 1970's that Rafael and a group of inmates began to hear rumors, the government was implementing a program "for the cleaning of corruption"in the different agencies within regime, including the Ministry of Interior that means Comandante Sosa, in 1972 Sosa was eliminated from the government, he was caught with a minor doing drugs he was sent to a Cuban rehabilitation camp where he died 3 years later, his son Capt. Sosa was sent to prison and accused of "sexual deviation" Rafael thought Fidel was very benevolent with his friends he didn't kill them, in Cuba the only persons that can be corrupted and get away with it is the Castro family.

Chaquet was at peace with himself counting the days he will leave that hell hole; he will be surprised soon. ****

CHAPTER 5

"Uno sabe donde nace, pero no donde va a morir"

One knows where he is born, but never where he will die
Juan Antonio Corretjer

Rafael Chaquet was released in 1975 a year earlier thru the intersection of an American Congressman, the first stop was Miami, FL there he contacted several friends from prison that were released early, he also contacted Gerardo his old assistant, they immediately meet and began talking about past cases and the future that Rafael will face, he also found out about Capt. Sosa he was shot in prison trying to escape with another prisoner.

With close to 1 million Cubans in Miami it became a true Cuban city, business flourished opened by entrepreneurs that left Cuba in the 60's, restaurants catered to Cuban food and it was a unique experience of freedom, Rafael started to work in one of those restaurant where Cuban lawyers, judges and professional people worked that's what Rafael called an 'Intellectual kitchen'.

After several months in Miami Rafael decided to contact his friend in Georgia Charles Lynnard, immediately Charles recognize him and offered Rafael to go up to Georgia and settle there, after Rafael gave it some thought he decided to take the offer, heck working in a factory or a restaurant in Georgia will be a new challenge for him. Arriving in Atlanta on February 1976 was no fun, it was cold, he spoke limited English, but he could manage, the Southern accent was a different matter, the Lynnard family welcomed him with open arms and will help him to accomplish his future.

Rafael Chaquet was no longer a detective, his new life began to unravel, at night his thought took him back to Cuba, his favorite restaurant where Eloiza and him used to spend precious moments, their walk thru Paseo del Prado, a wide and beautiful avenue filled with trees and flowers that smelled like a French perfume in each side   restaurants, clubs and commercial establishments ending at the famous Malecon.

His parents came from the city of Irun in the Basque region, they died when he was very young, taken in by his aunt an old lady that had a thick Basque accent, she died in 1958 in the city of Santa Clara, Rafael life in Cuba was always challenging, his wife dying of cancer, his alcohol problem but none of that impeded his creative detective personality he needed to proof to himself that he can succeed after all of that and his past politically prison time.

Det. Charles Lynnard's kids always asked Rafael about his life in Cuba, and his achievements as a detective, and many more topics about his homeland.

In one of those conversation Rafael said to the kids.

"Did you guys know that during the American Civil War the assistant to Confederate General Beauregard was a Cuban, His name was Ambrosio Jose Gonzalez, he was a coronel and oversaw artillery in GA, SC and FL for   the Confederacy, he also participated in the battle of Honey Hill".

Also, Rafael said. "Also, the National Capitol building in Havana was built with marble from Georgia".

The kids were amazed.

'Yes, my future', he was already 42 years old with no special skills except solving crimes, he could take a job at a restaurant, hotel or even a factory, eventually he will have to figure it out, there were a few Cuban families closed by in Atlanta area that he had meet, maybe they could direct him in the right path.

He kept quoting in his mind his favorite poem from Cuba's national hero and poet Jose Marti;

"I have come to the strange ball

Where tails and gaiters abound

And the best hunters the year round

The new year wait to install.

A violet duchess careens

In the arms of a red coat:

A painted viscount of note

Keeps time on a tambourine.

And the red waistcoats whirl by,

And the flaming tulles are flowing,

As dead leaves the wind is blowing

In front of a blind man's eye".

Jose Marti

"My future plans, oh my future plans".

Charles wants to talk to me in the morning.

"Is it about my future plans?".

"Rafael, I want you to meet John Carlisle, he is the head of the Georgia Bureau of Investigation (GBI) Lynnard said, he wants to make you a proposition".

John Carlisle began to explain the cold case to Rafael.

"We have a cold case dating back to 1961 of a white female, Hispanic that was choked to death, we only have several clues, it happened in the city of Decatur which is in De Kalb county, I have assign det. Kurt Janus of the GBI to this case, he is fluent in Spanish and according to Lynnard you have the necessary background to assist him, we can not offer to much in compensation but at least it can give you a start on your new life".

"Can we count on you?"

Rafael was overjoyed, here is an opportunity for his future to work.

"Director Carlisle I will be blessed and proud to join your team, compensation is a minimal requirement, I will be doing it as a gift to the state and nation that open their arms to me at the most negative period of my life".

"Thank you, Rafael welcome aboard, I will instruct Officer Kurt to brief you on the case". At that time Rafael, Charles and John open a bottle of Makers Mark.

The aromatic smell of the Kentucky Bourbon overwhelmed the room.

John said." Gracias Rafael" (thank you Rafael).

At the same time Rafael said, "Gracias a ustedes dos por darme esta gran oportunidad" (thanks to both of you for giving me this great opportunity).

The next morning Officer Kurt was on the phone with Rafael and gave him all the pertinent information about the case, it was a complex case full of characters and places, from Georgia to Alabama and South Carolina, since the body was partially decompose the exact date, motive and method cannot be completely stablish.

Rafael gather in a notepad the following information;

RACE White

NAME Alisa Roques

AGE From 24 to 26 yrs. old.

ETNICITY Hispanic/Puerto Rican

MOTIVE N/A

METHOD Rape/Strangulation

CHARACTERS Many

ESTIMATED YEAR OF THE CRIME 1961.

STATUS Married or Single N/A

INITIAL DETECTIVES ON THE CASE Peter Smiths and Robert Muncy.

Indeed, it was a complex case, it has been cold since 1961 when the body was found, certain details have perished or file the wrong way.

Rafael knew that technology have changed all the parameters of a crime investigation but applying the basic criteria to this case he can incorporate sufficient experience and move forward, officer Kurt is planning meeting Rafael that afternoon around 5pm by that time they will probably have a bite to eat and later strategize on how to face this complex crime, In the next 2 weeks.

Rafael and Kurt met almost every day; Rafael incorporated certain tactics reminding Kurt "that Sherlock Holmes did it, why not us".

Kurt reminded Rafael that they might have to travel to Alabama next week to interview the sister of the victim, he interview her 6 months ago but by taking Rafael this time he can experience her demeanor and stablish if it is feasible to proceed with this witness, even thou she was born here she spoke fluent Spanish, a plus for Rafael.

Rafael took that weekend and visited a Cuban family leaving in Atlanta, he meet the husband back in 1971 in prison, an ex Naval officer named Carlos Urquiza they enjoyed a nice Cuban meal prepared by Carlo's wife Leonor a beautiful woman, she was an architect in Cuba now working in a dept. store in Atlanta, he was caught in one of those so call conspiracy plots that the Castro regime fabricated to get rid of democratic elements within the revolution they talk about their time in prison Rafael asked Carlos.

"Carlos do you remember Capt. Sosa".

Carlos responded." Yes, off course that son of a bitch hit me a couple of times, I think he is in prison".

Well Rafael said he was in prison and was shot trying to escape with another prisoner.

The following week June 16 1976 a Wednesday Rafael and Kurt drove to Dothan Alabama, a small town Southwest of Alabama close to the border with Florida to interview the sister of Alicia, her name is Raquel Daryls, age 62 married to an alfalfa farmer with approx. 150 acres plot, they have being married for over 35 years, they met initially in Georgia but later moved to Alabama after Mr. Daryls father died and left him the alfalfa farm.

Rafael and Kurt arrived around noon, Raquel and her husband were not too happy, Raquel thought that she has answer all the questions posed by det. Kurt when the first interview was done 6 months ago but officer Kurt wanted Rafael to get his impression of both Mr. and Mrs. Daryls, Rafael mainly tried to concentrate on the particular reaction to a particular question.

" What was the demeanor of your sister just before she was kill", or to Mr. Daryls" how was your relation to Alicia", all those important points to determine a trend in the family relationship prior to the crime.

Kurt and Rafael were there for almost 3 hours, on the way back to Georgia they stopped at a near country restaurant, even thou

Rafael have being experiencing the best Southern food, eating out in Alabama was a new experience for him.

Grits for lunch? Collard Green? Now meatloaf was like a Cuban dish called "Pulpeta", the smell of onions, garlic transported him to his beautiful Havana, the food it is good. While waiting for their lunch they began to go back and forth with the information they gathered at the interview of Mr. and Mrs. Daryls.

"what do you think?" Kurt asked Rafael.

Rafael responded. "Mrs. Daryl seems genuine in her responses, now Mr. Daryl showed certain body language that makes it questionable, now that does not make him a suspect".

Kurt had the same impression, Rafael asked Mr. Daryls a couple of question that made Kurt suspicious, I guest is the modality and by asking those questions we might get a cleared picture of the crime, Rafael said.

They made it to Georgia later that afternoon, Kurt dropped Rafael at Charles house, the kids were there with some of their friends after a Braves game, they asked Rafael if he wanted to see a Braves game, off course, Rafael said.

"Did you know that baseball is the national game of Cuba, everybody plays starting very young, I played my self with the local school team".

After enjoying a great southern dinner Rafael retired to his room and began to set up a file with the information Kurt and he have gathered on their trip to Alabama,

Rafael broke it by section, each section contained the name question and responses from a particular witness also the body language, he needed to adapt himself to certain legal restrictions that exist in the US compare to Cuba, I know that Kurt will provide that information , it was almost 12 midnight he was ready to go to sleep.

The following morning Rafael was pickup by Kurt and both

went directly to main headquarter of the GBI in Decatur ,GA, Rafael was given a tour of the facility and he was introduce to several members of the Bureau, he was impress with the technological advances that have being made in the forensic field, fingerprint evaluation and data analysis, he asked Kurt.

"When was the last time evidence from our case being summited for evaluation?" Kurt responded.

"It was about 10 years ago, why?"

"Well, 10 years ago none of this improvement was available, maybe if we analyze the evidence again, we can determine new data on the case".

"Great I will resubmit the evidence again to our forensic dept". Kurt said.

It was almost noon time and Kurt asked Rafael.

" Are you hungry?" Rafael immediately said yes, Kurt took Rafael to a BBQ place in Decatur, the best pork ribs you can eat Kurt said, while they were having lunch Rafael asked Kurt about a young Hispanic woman, he meet at the GBI headquarter.

"Oh, you mean Yolanda Valdez, she surely is beautiful also Hispanic, I think she is from Puerto Rico, would you like to meet her?", off course Rafael said.

After lunch they went back to GBI and as promised Kurt introduced Rafael to Yolanda.

"Yolanda, I want you to meet Rafael Chaquet he is from Cuba and is helping us with a cold case".

"Happy to meet Rafael".

"It is my pleasure Yolanda". Rafael said she surely is beautiful I wonder if she has a boyfriend or married

Rafael thought, Yolanda explained to Rafael her duties as a forensic scientist and how they analyze evidence even if they are old.

"Yolanda if we provide you with new evidence that we have gather for our file will you be able to analyze it?"

Rafael asked. "Off course anytime" Yolanda said.

Kurt and Rafael them went to Kurt desk in the floor above where Yolanda office is located, Rafael asked Kurt.

" Hey Kurt, do Yolanda have a boyfriend or is she married?" Kurt answer back.

"Well Rafael I can see that Yolanda have captivated you, no she is single and dedicated to her work, maybe you can ask her for a dinner date?"

Rafael was resurrecting his romantic spirit, what the heck I am only 42 years old Rafael thought.

On their way out they stopped at Yolanda office.

"Yolanda, I have some evidence we need to analyze, will

you be willing to meet with me anytime this week so we can discuss it?" Rafael asked Yolanda.

"Sure anytime" Yolanda said.

"Lunch or Dinner?" Rafael Asked.

"Lunch is almost impossible how about dinner let's say Friday?"

"Fine I will have to find a car so I can pick you up", Rafael said.

"Well don't worry, where are you staying?"

"In Marietta, at the Lynnard, s house I think is to far for you to drive".

"No, I live in Sandy Spring, which is only 15 minutes from Marietta, how about I pick you up around 8pm".

"yes, that's fine see you them".

Rafael was overwhelmed with happiness, it will be the first date with a woman since Eloiza, this is a different culture and a different approach toward women Rafael thought.

It was a Wednesday and Rafael needed to buy a nice set of clothes, he only had the same he brought from Miami, he was limited on his finances but he had enough money to buy the clothe and pay for the dinner with Yolanda as long is not too expensive.

That week Kurt and Rafael made plans to visit the following week another person of interest in South Carolina, it was Master Sgt. Robert Dunlap a retired army soldier that lives in Gaffney SC very close to the NC border he was a boyfriend of Alicia Roque in the 60's when he use to live in Decatur, Kurt already got in touch with his wife, they will meet the following week, while Kurt was going thru the evidence filed in a carton box he found an interesting note, it was from an anonymous person to Alicia dated July 1960, in that note the person express his or her desire to be close to her, to caress and develop a thru relationship Kurt needed analyze the hand writing or any other information he might take out of that note, how come nobody made any comment on this note? Kurt thought.

It was Friday, Rafael was a little nervous it has been more than 10 years since he had any interaction with a female, plainly put he was rusty even thought Rafael was not to religious he prayed for a positive encounter, he knew Yolanda was beautiful she looked a lot like Eloiza, smart creative and very strong, what a combination can I handle that? Rafael thought.

At 7:50pm Yolanda was at the door of the Lynnard's in Marietta, when Rafael opened the door, he almost fainted, Yolanda was wearing a red dress that showed her beautiful figure athletic but very feminine again his thought came back, can I handle this? The best thing was that Yolanda spoke fluent Spanish that made easier for Rafael he could express his emotion easily and with firmness, he hoped, he mentioned to Yolanda that he did not know any restaurant in the area so she will have to make the choice.

"Do you like Italian?" Yolanda asked.

"Yes, I can eat anything that sounds great".

Before they left Mr. and Mrs. Lynnard said hi to Yolanda, Mr. Lynnard knows her they work at the same building they made a comment to her.

"Yolanda take good care to our Cuban Sherlock Holmes he had gone thru some rough time in his life".

"I will Charles", Yolanda said.

They arrived at the restaurant about 8:20pm, it was a nice cozy place not too expensive and the food was great they ordered lasagna and some red wine, they began exchanging impression of the Alicia Roque case but Rafael's mind was toward Yolanda looking at her face, her personality reminded him so much of Eloiza, now a more personal conversation began.

"Rafael how long have you being in the US".

"Not more than a year" Rafael kept saying it's nice to find somebody I can talk to; I mean in Spanish".

"yes, I know Rafael me too the majority of my time is spend talking in English" Yolanda said.

"Well Yolanda tell me about yourself".

" I was born in Humacao Puerto Rico but came to the US when I was 2years old, you see my father was in the army and we moved between bases for a while until finally my father retired from the Army with his last assignment at Fort Benning Georgia, so our family stayed in Georgia where I attended High School and graduated from the University of Georgia, there is my life".

Yolanda finished but them Rafael wanted to find out more, so he asked her about her personal life any boyfriend, Yolanda laughed.

"Not now I am single dedicated to my job don't have time for a personal life".

"That's not good you need some distraction" Rafael said.

Now it was Yolanda's turn now.

"Rafael tell me about your life".

Rafael started to tell Yolanda about his work in Cuba, his political prison time and finally his arrival in Miami and Georgia.

"That's amazing Rafael you had a busy life, now is my turn to ask do you have a girlfriend now?"

Rafael immediately answered." No, I don't have a girlfriend now but who knows maybe I can find a wonderful woman in Georgia".

Off course he already had somebody in mind, she was sitting across the table from him.

Around 10:30pm Yolanda drove Rafael to the Lynnard's home.

"This have turn out to be one of the most wonderful time in my life" Rafael said.

"Me too Yolanda express the same emotion can we meet again, yes, maybe sometime next week".

Rafael reminded Yolanda about his next trip with Kurt to SC. "I will talk to you when I return from my trip."

And with that Yolanda kiss Rafael on his cheek. "Rafael it has being a wonderful night" ***

CHAPTER 6

"Others go to bed with their mistresses, I with my ideas"

Jose Marti

It took Kurt and Rafael 3 hours from Marietta to Gaffney SC, they arrived at Sgt. Robert Dunlap home a modest ranch house not well kept in an old neighborhood they were greeted by his wife Joann.   "I am officer Kurt from the GBI and this Rafael Chaquet we spoke with you concerning an interview with Sgt. Dunlap relationship with Alicia Roque in the 1960's we needed to tight some loose ends in the murder of Alicia Roque back in 1961".

"Well good luck with that".

"Come in please" Joann responded; she was referring to the fact that her husband was developing Alzheimer.

Sitting in an old recliner was Sgt. Dunlap he retired from the army about 5 years ago with a disability he got while serving in Vietnam, the humidity smell of the house was overwhelming, Joann offer Kurt and Rafael some coffee they accepted Sgt. Dunlap seem aloof, looked confused and it looks that his disability kept him for walking to much, Kurt started the interview.

"Sgt. Dunlap first thank you for your service".

Dunlap interrupted Kurt.

"Well, you are but a few people that have said that, I, was treated like a criminal when I arrived from Vietnam sorry officer Kurt please proceed".

"Well Sgt. Dunlap did you knew Alicia Roque?".

"Yes, Dunlap answered, she was beautiful young woman it was my senior year of HS in Decatur Ga when she disappeared, all the boys were in love with her, she was a little crazy if you know what I mean".

Them Rafael jump in.

"Dunlap when you say crazy did, she hang around with a determined person or just hang around with the group?".

"You know I am sorry Chaquet, you sound like a Louisiana Cajun my last post before Ft Benning was in Fort Polk LA, it was in the middle of the Cajun country".

"No, I am not from Louisiana now Dunlap do you remember any person that hangout with Alicia, any boyfriend?"

"Yes, there was this guy Jim something, I do not remember his last name he was sort of her companion at school it is interesting after Alicia disappeared Jim left Georgia".

Rafael turned to Kurt and asked.

Do we have any information on this guy Jim?"

"No Kurt responded".

That is odd Rafael said.

"Didn't all the person of interest were interview?"

"Yes, but I did not see a Jim in our file".

At about 1 hour they finish the interview with Dunlap them they headed back to Georgia.

Back at Kurt office in Decatur they began analyzing the information they gathered from their visit to Sgt. Dunlap it was almost 7pm and Kurt wanted to get home, his older son was playing football at his HS he didn't want to miss it so they left, since Rafael did not have a car Kurt had to take Rafael home when they were leaving they pass by Yolanda's office, she was still there involved in another investigation Rafael stopped and said to her. "Yolanda seeing you in person is better than giving you a call, you see I made it back and the first person I see is you, good omen?"

"She laughed, yes, it is a good omen."

them she asked Rafael how he was getting home.

"Well Kurt is taking me, but he is in rush to see his son play football".

"well in that case do you mind if take you?" Yolanda said.

"No, I don't mind I will be very happy if you do".

Rafael responded, Kurt immediately said in that case I will make the game on time.

On the way to drive back Rafael they pass a Chinese restaurant, Rafael asked Yolanda if she was hungry.

"yes, let's stop here I heard the food is great."

Rafael got out of the car went to Yolanda's door and opened for her, immediately he kissed her.

'Yolanda, you revived my inner soul, I am beginning to fall in love with you".

I feel the same way". Them, she moves forward and gave Rafael another passionate kiss.

They stayed in the parking lot for about 5 minutes caressing and describing their true love for each other.

The Chinese restaurant was not to elegant but the smell of their food was inviting, Yolanda asked Rafael if he ever had Mongolian Beef, no but he will eat anything recommended by Yolanda, they both ordered and also asked for some drinks, the night was bright not so hot and most important they were together, will this be the "future plans" that Rafael was always thinking, hope so he thought, Yolanda drove Rafael to Lynnard's house in Marietta, when they arrived again, they embrace, kissed and planned for the next date, they were truly in love for Rafael all those years in Cuba were beginning to disappear, from his mind his alcohol problem was all but gone and his new friends in Georgia have treated him like a human again.

Rafael was already making plans to get his own place, GBI already promise him a car, if he passed the driving test and he was already making enough to sustain his personal needs, life was beginning to look positive again.

Charles Lynnard was already a captain at the GBI, he was promoted 2 weeks ago, the only drawback was that he needed to drive to his new office in Decatur the headquarter of the GBI every day.

The following morning after breakfast with his family, Charles drove Rafael to his office, Rafael's office was located in a small corner of the 2nd floor it used to be a supply closet but it was big enough to put a desk and a phone line and off course he was close to Yolanda, immediately after arriving at GBI Rafael went directly to Kurt office they began to talk about all the information they have gathered, at one-point Rafael asked Kurt if any of the detectives assigned to the original case were available.

"They both retired several years ago, we know that Robert Muncy pass away last year, the whereabout of Peter Smiths in unknown, the last time we heard and that was about 5 years ago he was living next to Lake Hartwell on the SC side."

"Can we check his widow out, he might have some information about this Jim guy"

'Yes, we can start to see what address she is using to get his retirement and SS checks".

While they were at Kurt office Yolanda showed up with some coffee and donuts, Yolanda asked Kurt about his son game last night.

"it was great they won 28 to 7, Alex Corbin son played too, they beat a great team, I was proud my son, he is a linebacker and stopped their running back several times, he is a wall".

Rafael could not get his eyes off Yolanda even thou she was wearing her regular uniform she looked terrific her beautiful smile and her athletic figure was showing.

Kurt immediately saw the fusion between them and suggested a get together for both at his house, "I make the best barbeque in Georgia" he proudly said, Yolanda and Rafael walked out of Kurt's office before getting into Yolanda's office she said.

"Do you want me to cook you some dinner tonight"

"Yolanda remember I don't have a car yet, how I am going to get to your place?"

"Rafael we can leave here this afternoon together and later after dinner if I can remember where Charles lives drop you off" she laughed.

"That's great I don't remember where Charles lives either we might get lost in Marietta, I don't want that".

Kurt was already working on the new address for Peter Smiths, he was running into some problems, it seems   they were mailing his checks to a foreign address in Costa Rica, why Kurt thought something smell rotten he immediately meet with Rafael and asked why?

"Rafael something is wrong, I know they do have a large American retired community in Costa Rica, but his health was not 100% and according to his last annual check up he needed medical assistant fast" "is there any way we can talk to him, or maybe go there and interview him, we need to know about this Jim fellow there is something about him I don't like he might have some important information about the case."

"I'll get on it", Kurt rush to his boss office he needed his approval to interview somebody on a foreign country.

It was already 6pm and Yolanda was ready to leave, she went by Rafael's office and signaled that the day was over.

"Hoped you liked my cooking" Yolanda said with a huge smile on his face.

"Yolanda I will love your cooking, just thinking about how those beautiful hands prepared the food, it will be heaven".

"Like a good Hispanic your words are full of romance"

They departed, Yolanda's place was about 30 min. away, the traffic was light considering it was rush hour.

Yolanda's place was modern spacious and in a nice complex, family, seniors and single people mingle around it was a true community, she went directly to the kitchen open a bottle of red wine and after giving Rafael his glass they toasted for a lasting relationship, they were truly in love.

"Rafael, I have never met such a sweet loving man and by toasting this wine with you I pledge my lasting love toward you".

Rafael could not contain himself, he grabbed her by her waist and kissed her passionate, caressing her and pledging true love, dinner was put to hold, they entered her bedroom and made love, it lasted almost all night they could not stop.

It was almost 10pm before Yolanda walk to her kitchen, she whispered something into Rafael ear, he smiled and said, "me too", Rafael was still in bed admiring Yolanda's curves as she walked away.

Yolanda had her dinner prepared, she only needed to put it in the stove and in 25 min. the dinner was ready, Rafael made it from the bedroom emotionally charged he sat and finally drank his wine, it was spaghetti and meat balls. "Rafael, I don't think I will take you home".

"Yes, we might get lost going to Marietta, I can sleep in the sofa".

He knew that was not going to happen Yolanda's bed was more comfortable, they sat to eat beside the personal conversation Yolanda asked Rafael how, was the case going. "Well we have interview 4 persons, none seem capable or able to kill Alicia Roque who by the way was Puerto Rican descent, we need to interview one of the original, detectives involved in the case, no luck, an exciting evening, it was not planned this way. ***

CHAPTER 7

"Our greatest glory is not in never falling, but in rising every time we fall."

Confucius

Rafael was ready to make a personal move, he was looking at an apartment in Roswell, GA it is almost in the middle between Decatur and Marietta not to big but spacious enough, nice complex almost new it was built about a year ago, he informed Charles and his wife while they were having dinner that night they express that he did not had to move so fast, Rafael felt like they are like family.

"Charles, Susan, Kids I want to thank all of you for opening your house to me a complete estranger with no future plans when I arrived and now thanks to all of you I can say with firmness that my future plans are solid, not only workwise but also for meeting a wonderful woman Yolanda".

"Rafael, we consider you another member of our family, this is also your home and you will always be welcomed here."

That week Rafael passed the driving test, He and Yolanda celebrated it by having dinner at a nice restaurant in the Buckhead area of Atlanta.

"Yolanda, I need to tell you something"

"Good news or bad news".

"No good news and better news, first the GBI has assign a car to me, not a new car but it runs good, and I and getting my own apartment in Roswell"

"Wait, why are you getting an apartment in Roswell when you can move in with me, you don't love me anymore?"

"First I do love with all my heart, second you never mention the move with you was an option to me"

"Now I do, do you agree?" Yolanda said.

"Yes, I do". Rafael responded.

And even thou a table was between them they exchange a beautiful kiss.

Everything was set, next week Rafael will move in with Yolanda, the Lynnards were happy and all Yolanda friends were also happy, she has found the right man to share for rest of her life, Yolanda was 7 years younger than Rafael but looking at them seems age was not a factor both look athletic, no known illness, smart and very creative in another word made for each other.

Wednesday of that week Kurt called Rafael and told him to come to his office he had information concerning Peter Smiths. "What information you have"?

"Rafael not so good, it seems Peter does not live in Costa Rica at least as Peter Smiths, his checks disappear when they arrive at a post office in San Jose, according to the authorities the PO# belongs to a person name Ernie Callan no deposit transactions or cashing the checks either, is truly a mystery". "Does the government of Costa Rica have any information on Callan?"

"Ernie Callan does not exist, no Costa Rica entry visa, no departure from the country, no Social Security record, no driving license record, nothing it looks like he has been fabricated by whom we don't know"

"We have to keep looking for Peter, but at the same time we might go to the HS in Decatur where Alicia and Jim attended, we might look to any yearbook or personal record of this Jim fellow".

"That sounds good Rafael, I will set an interview with the principal of the school for tomorrow morning"

"Great, we might also visit the house where the other detective used to live, Robert Muncy and ask his widow for any document he left in the house, is that okay?"

"Sounds good, I will get Robert Muncy address".

The following morning Kurt and Rafael arrived at Decatur High School, the principal a Mr. Jacobs direct us to his office.

"Mr. Jacobs I am Kurt and this Rafael we represent the GBI, we are investigating the murder of one of Decatur High student, Alicia Roque it occurred in 1961"

"I arrived here in 1969, but we can look into our records to find the personal data of Alicia, it will take me at least a week since all the records from 1961 are in the main DeKalb county building"

Rafael jump in and asked Mr. Jacob.

"We are also looking for another student name Jim, no last name available but maybe if we could get all the files of students named Jim that were seniors in 1961, we surely will be very grateful"

"The only thing I can say, I will try to find them"

"Thank you, Mr. Jacobs, that's all we ask, we will contact you sometime next week".

Kurt and Rafael headed back to their office to find out if any other information concerning Robert or Callan was received, there was also a note on the desk of Kurt from   the widow of Robert Muncy she said that Robert left a box full of files in the attic, you are welcome to take it, immediately they called Mrs. Muncy and set up a meeting for the following day so they can look at the files and determined if any additional information is there in relation to the case.

Around 6pm Rafael stopped by Yolanda's office, she was still involved trying to define evidences from another case, he went back to his office and waited for her to finish her job, while sitting at his desk and going true Alicia's file his eyes move toward a missing person report from 1961 that it was filed by det. Peter Smiths concerning Alicia disappearance, in that report that was called in by Alicia's sister described the time and place where Alicia was seen for the last time.

It's curious that the last time according to this report where she was seeing or the date do not concur with crime report that officer Smiths made, in his report he put Alicia in South Atlanta not Decatur also the person that found the body was never interview and no written information of that person was filed, also the day is one week before the missing report was filed.

Kurt was still in his office so Rafael called him and asked him to come over.

"Kurt, I found the missing person report for Alicia, there are some information that do not match, here look at it I have marked the areas of discrepancies".

Kurt looked at it and immediately saw the discrepancies, something is wrong here, he thought.

"Rafael, I don't know why this report was not checked before for any discrepancy, I am without words".

At that time Yolanda arrived at Rafael office asking if he was ready to go but found both confused and the mood was not to positive.

"Is everything okay"

"Well we have a missing person report that do not match the crime scene report made by det. Smiths".

"Well, she was reported missing in Decatur, but her body was found in South Atlanta, what is wrong with that?"

"Nothing is wrong with that but look closer and you will see that the day and location of the missing report have being altered to match the crime, report that's what is wrong".

"You are right Rafael, who did the altered report?"

"None other than det. Peter Smiths, the missing detective".

"We have to find Peter, he must be in his 70's by now, we have to find him", Kurt said.

"Kurt, at what time we are meeting with Mrs. Muncy tomorrow?"

"Around 11am, she lives about 2hrs away from here so let's try to leave around 8am give or take".

"Will do". Them as Yolanda and Rafael left, he asked her if is possible to stay overnight so she can drop him that early at the GBI headquarters.

"Yes Rafael, instead of waiting for next week to move in with me why not do it now, I don't mind".

"I know that is my desired, but I don't want to impose on you a change in our plans".

"Remember Rafael that a good relationship is reach by understanding trustfulness".

"Them what I will do tomorrow after the meeting with Mrs. Muncy is to go directly to the Lynnard's and pick up the rest of my things, and take it to your apartment is that okay?"

"Yes, Rafael I will be waiting for you".

From the GBI headquarters in Decatur to Rome GA where Mrs.

Muncy lives you take I-285 W where it will take you to I-75 N toward Rome, on the way there Kurt and Rafael stopped by at a Cracker Barrel restaurant and had a good Southern breakfast, 2 eggs bacon and off course grits, by now Rafael was a fan of grits it reminded him of maiz blanco(white corn) that his mother use to make.

While they were sitting having breakfast Kurt reminded Rafael about next weekend, he will have a barbecue at his house the Lynnard's will be there plus some other friends from the GBI, off course Yolanda will be there with you.

"Kurt, Yolanda and I will be there I understand that your barbecue is the best in Georgia"

"Well, not the best in Georgia but very close".

Both laughed.

They arrived around 11:45am, 45min late but Mrs.Muncy understood, traffic is miserable specially from the Atlanta area. They began by thanking her for her prompt response and facilitating all the files that det. Muncy left at his house, it was a big box with maybe copies of 100 files from past cases that he participated thru his long years at the GBI.

Mrs. Muncy offered them coffee, they gladly accepted, them Rafael asked her about his husband, did he   mentioned any case that he investigated and left a mark on him or any rumors within the GBI?

"There was a couple of cases that kept him wondering if he could have done more, but the case of a girl missing and later found dead in Atlanta tops it all, sometime he will wakeup in the middle of the night shouting and screaming "we screw it all", he also spoke of his ex-partner Peter how he was always complaining about how he needed more money to survive, he had a wife that lived beyond their means"

Rafael and Kurt looked at each other with amazement, are we

going to find a copy of Alicia Roque file in that box and if we do will any important information be there?

Rafael and Kurt thanked Mrs. Muncy for her assistance and reminded her anything you need please let us know.

"Kurt, if you don't mind will take me to the Lynnard's so I can pick up the rest of my stuff and later drop me at Yolanda apartment".

"Yes, I can see that you and Yolanda have hit it off really good, Yolanda is a wonderful woman dedicated and smart ".

"I know Kurt, I am very lucky, by the way tomorrow we can go over that box, we might be surprised".

"If we find something it will make my day, not my year".

Rafael was beginning to understand all the slang used in the US, he liked it, Rafael was happy, move in with Yolanda, the opportunity the GBI have given him to put forward his knowledge in solving crime, "my future plans", yes with the help of real friends here in the US my future is taking shape.

Rafael arrived with Yolanda at the GBI headquarters around 7am, after enjoying some coffee both sat down and waited for Kurt, he showed up around 8am, confessing that he had a terrible night could not been able to sleep that well.

"Just thinking about our case, every time we received different information the case changes, it is weird".

"Kurt, don't worry we'll figure it out, drink some coffee and them we can go into the box full of files that Mrs. Muncy gave us"

Rafael sat at Kurt office and began looking into the box of files, they dated into the 1950's det. Muncy was very meticulous he kept every information of any case from the opening to the close, he even added newspaper clips that gave information on the trail and conviction of the perpetrator. Right in the middle of the files was Alicia Roque, but there was a problem it was empty.

"Shit, why is it empty it suppose to contain something"

Kurt said.

"Did anybody else knew about these files, maybe det. Smiths?" Rafael asked.

"We have to call Mrs. Muncy and ask her if anybody went into the box and pick up the case information"

"I will get on it". Kurt immediately called Mrs. Muncy and asked her if anybody else knew about those files.   When she answered the phone Kurt asked her, she responded.

"Well I know that sometimes Peter sat with my husband and looked into the files, they always said to remember the good old times".

There it is, Peter took the information inside the files, for what reason I don't know he Thought, he immediately thought he passed the information to Rafael and they both agreed, we have to find Peter he can have some answer to this case, but where was Peter.

Rafael and Kurt spend the next two days going thru the files, Kurt recognized a couple of cases when he was in HS.

About 11am on Saturday Rafael and Yolanda headed to Kurt's house a beautiful ranch house in Sandy Spring, the lynnard's were already there plus John Carlisle the GBI director and about 4 more couples, Rafael was introduced and immediately grabbed a beer, good old Schlitz beer.

Director Carlisle approach Rafael, he was very happy to see Rafael and Yolanda together.

"Rafael, you have chosen right I hope that you and Yolanda enjoy and be happy together".

"Thank you, Director I know she is an exceptionally woman and the more I am next to her the more I fall in love"

"Good, by the way Rafael we will have a car ready for you on

Monday not new, but it can run, also I heard from Kurt that you guys have encounter some roadblocks on the Alicia Roque case, don't despair everything will be fine"

"Thank you, Director we will solve this case, I can assure you that"

At that moment Yolanda showed up after saying hi to Director Carlisle she directed Rafael to where Kurt was doing his barbeque, it sure smell great, hamburgers, hot dogs and a variety of vegetables.

"Are you ready to eat the most wonderful food in all of Georgia Rafael".

"Bring it on Kurt, my stomach is empty, I am all yours".

Rafael and Yolanda had a busy weekend Kurt's barbeque on Saturday, on Sunday they headed up to Helen , a beautiful town in Northern Georgia Rafael was amaze at the beautiful scenery it reminded him so much the landscape in Cuba, communism can take the material possessions but not the natural beauty. They headed back to Sandy Springs and spend the rest of the day talking and planning the future, where it will take them.

By 8am on Monday Rafael was at the office already, 15min later Kurt showed up.

"Kurt, I have gained 10 pounds from your barbeque on Saturday, it was good".

" I am glad you like it, our family specially the kids enjoyed your company your personal story was very impressive, by the way in about an hour I am going to call principal Jacobs".

When Kurt called Mr. Jacobs, he mentions to Kurt that he found some information on Alicia and 5 files with first name Jim were also found.   "Mr. Jacobs, when can we go and pick them up? Anytime, det Kurt, just let me know the day so I can put it aside for you"

"How about right now, we are only 20 min away from your

school"

"I will be waiting for you", Mr. Jacobs said.

When Kurt arrived Mr. Jacobs immediately gave him 6 manila envelopes containing the information about Alicia Roque and 5 Jim's, all during their HS years.

Kurt was static, can we find the real Jim here he thought.

When he arrived at his office Rafael was waiting, he already drank 3 cups of coffee, he was nervous anticipating a good result from those files.

"Rafael, here they are, Alicia and 5 young men first name Jim, can we start?" Yes, Rafael responded.

First they started to look into Alicia's file, nothing spectacular, 2.4 gpa, average grades, enrolled in a beautician course sponsored by DeKalb County several detentions, due to a rebellious personality also and this is interesting, taking to the hospital for unknown reasons a couple of weeks before they found her dead.

"What hospital?" Rafael asked.

"Emory University Hospital", why Kurt asked.

'we need to know what kind of procedure they perform for Alicia that day"

"I'll get on it" Kurt said.

"Kurt, let's look into the rest of the files that contains information about the 5 Jim's."

The first is Jim Kelly, graduated from HS in 1961, attended UGA and became a Veterinarian, African American, lives and practice in Atlanta.

The second Jim is Jim Roberts, graduated from HS in 1961, joined the Army and was killed in Vietnam in 1964.

The next is Jim Silas, drop out of HS in 1960, whereabouts unknown.

It followed by Jim Slinkis, graduated in 1961, attended UNC and graduated as Doctor, lives in Raleigh, NC.

And last Jim Donners, Honor Roll Society, attended Harvard and joined Sigma Alpha Epsilon presently a well to do lawyer in Atlanta.

"Well, Rafael we need to move fast, we can start with Jim Kelly, he is close by in Atlanta, I'll find his present address".

Doctor Kelly's vet hospital was in Smyrna a city north of Atlanta, Rafael and Kurt arrived around 10am it was full, dogs, cats and other animals that I can't describe, his assistant took them to Dr. Kelly, s office.

"Dr. Kelly my name is Kurt, and this is Rafael we represent the GBI, we are looking into a homicide that happened in 1961, the victim was Alicia Roque, do you remember her?"

"Yes, I know she was Hispanic, and beautiful".

"Anything else, Dr. Kelly?" Rafael asked.

"Well there was this guy Ernie or Arnie, something like that, he was not accepted by the majority of the students because he was a little bit weird, she always hang around with him and another guy named Jim, I don't remember his last name."

"Dr. Kelly, you have given us some important nformation, we appreciate your help" Kurt said. As they were leaving Dr. Kelly's office, Kurt asked Rafael.

"What do you think Rafael?"

"I think we have a dandy in our hands."

"We might need to go back to Mr. Jacobs and ask for any information on an Ernie or Arnold and they interview Jim Donners the Atlanta lawyer."

"I will call the office of Jim Donner and set up an interview".

Kurt said.

"What I am wondering is why initial assign det. didn't follow any information we just uncover" Rafael ask.

"Rafael, I was wondering the same thing."

The following morning Kurt received thru a warrant the file containing the procedure done to Alicia Roque 3 weeks before her killing at the Emory Hospital.

Kurt called Rafael and relay the information.

"Rafael, Alicia was treated for a miscarriage she had during a fall at school".

"That's is interesting, that means she had intercourse 3 weeks prior to her murder, no determination was made at that time who was her sexual partner, this is interesting"

It was the middle of next week when Jim Donner, the lawyer gave Rafael and Kurt an appointment for an interview, they arrived at 10am and immediately Mr. Donner's secretary guided them to his office.

"Mr. Donner first thank you for giving us some of your precious moments, Rafael and I are reopening the Alicia Roque homicide case that was perpetrated back in 1961."

"Detective Kurt, right? I am a bit busy, so I'll give you about 20 min. to answer your questions, why are they reopening the case now, wasn't that case closed many years ago?"

"Well sir you should know that a homicide case is never closed, until the perpetrator or perpetrators are caught"

Rafael entered the conversation.

"Mr. Donner we are looking into several avenues on this case, according to information we have received you were one of Alicia's friend, we need to confirm that information"

"det. Rafael I detect an accent, Spanish right?"

"yes, actually Cuban".

"Mr. Donner can you confirm your relationship with Alicia around 1961?"

"I'll tell what, first your 20min are up and secondly I will not answer any more questions until you really tell me the reason you guys are here"

"Sir no specific reason, just gathering more information about the case." Rafael said.

"Well anyway I don't have any more information for you guys, have a nice day" Donner replied.

Rafael and Kurt left Mr. Donner's office confused and at the same time wanting to gather more information about Donner.

The moment they reached the parking lot, Rafael shouted in Spanish. "que come mierda!!".

Kurt looked confused.

Sorry Kurt, it means what an ass hole in Spanish."

Kurt concurred.

"You know Kurt it reminded me about my last case before going to prison in Cuba, we were very close in finding the perpetrator, but our main suspect was in the inner circle of Castro, nobody could touch him, he also gave us 20 min. to interview him."

Rafael, our last person is Jim Slikins the doctor that lives in Raleigh, I will call him and makes an appointment to see him next week".

Rafael and Yolanda have made dinner plans in Carlos Urquiza's home, they arrived around 8pm Leonor his wife had prepared a typical Cuban feast the moment she opened the door the smell of Garlic, black beans and fried plantains was delightful.

"Hola Rafael, and this must be Yolanda a true beautiful woman" Carlos said.

Leonor approach the couple hugging them and thanking them for coming over for dinner.

When they sat at the table Yolanda explained that Cuban and Puerto Rican are almost similar. "We don't call them frijoles we call them habichuelas, the seasoning is the same, there might be some variations both taste good". ****

CHAPTER 8

"The future depends on what we do in the present"

Mahatma Gandhi

Rafael and Yolanda left around 11pm, after 30min driving they arrived at their apartment had a night cap and went to bed.

The following morning like always they arrived at the GBI headquarters around 7am, Kurt was already there.

'Rafael, I have some news"

"Yes Kurt".

"Mr. Donner was shot over the weekend, he is in ICU, the case is being handled by the Atlanta Homicide squad, a good friend of mine det. Jerry Sanders is handling the investigation he will keep us posted for any development"

"What was the reason, robbery, family dispute was it in his house or someplace else, those are the initial answer we need to know" Rafael said.

"We should know by 6pm, Jerry is coming over with more information". Det. Sanders arrived around 5:45 pm at the GBI headquarters with more detail information.

"Jerry this is Rafael Chaquet he is helping us in the cold case of Alicia Roque that happened in 1961"

"Nice meeting you Rafael".

They shook hands and Rafael began asking questions.

"Jerry, what else can you tell us about the shooting, attempted robbery, domestic dispute or any other information?"

"Well, it was at his house around 10pm he received 3 shoots, 2 to the stomach and 1 to the head nothing was taken from the house, he gets along with his wife and kids, the only thing we can think is a disgruntle client, Donner was a criminal lawyer and handled some famous cases in Georgia".

"How is he doing now", asked Rafael.

"He is still in ICU in bad shape".

"Thank you, Jerry, please keep us posted, we interviewed him this past week, he was very apprehensive". Kurt said.

Two days later Donner pass away, Rafael and Kurt decided to obtain a search warrant for Donner's home, they ran into some roadblocks, it seems his wife thru her influence on the local legal circle have blocked the search warrant, no reason given.

"Don't worry Rafael we will find a good judge to give us the search warrant". Kurt said.

The Director of the GBI with his connections found a friendly judge to issue the warrant, so Rafael, Kurt and 2 more GBI agents drove to Donner's home, a beautiful home off West Paces Road about a block from the Governor's mansion, they rang the bell Mrs. Donner opened, she was surprised stopped them by the door while she called her lawyer, he gave her the okay to let them in. "Mrs. Donner this warrant gives us the right to search your home, we ask that you find a place to stay while we do our work, in advance thank you for your cooperation. "Kurt said.

Mrs. Donner reluctantly selected a sofa in the main living room to sit while the GBI searched her home, Rafael and Kurt went different directions, Kurt an office in the main area of the house, Rafael went upstairs to their rooms, the 2 other agents went thru the living room and the rest of the downstairs.

There were several file from past clients of Donner at his office, one file caught the eye of Kurt a Mr. Jim Silas convicted in 1965 of armed assault on a group of young people from Georgia Tech, sentenced to 5 years, but according to the file he only served 1.5 years, the presiding judge Henry Callan, the judge pass away in 1973, Callan, Kurt thought the person in Costa Rica a guy by the name of Callan.

At the same time Rafael looking thru a dresser in one of the upstairs rooms found some bank statements under the name of E. Callan from San Jose, Costa Rica.

Rafael, Kurt and the 2 other agents took about 5 boxes of documents from the Donner house dating back to the early 60's, they will look into all of them very carefully, they have a lot of work to do.

In the meantime, Kurt made arrangement to meet with Dr. Jim Slinkis in Raleigh, NC. The following week.

"Rafael next Monday we'll meet Dr. Slinkis"

"Great we'll be ready."

Rafael and Kurt spend the rest of the week and part of Saturday looking at the files they removed from the Donner's, a couple of them seem interesting enough for more investigation.

"This Callan fellow seems to be very closed to Donner, handling his case but also his bank account, something smells like mierda, I mean shit" Rafael said.

"Well Rafael, we might be into something here like you said client is one thing but also his bank account, it is rare".

Monday came Rafael and Kurt left their office around 5am, it will take them about 6 hours to arrive at Raleigh the appointment is for 3pm so they will be fine, they stopped at a Cracker Barrel on I-85 for breakfast Rafael was fascinated with the place.

"Two eggs, bacon and off course grits, the perfect morning" Rafael said. Kurt had the same.

They arrived at Raleigh around 1pm, they sat in a park closed to Dr. Slinkis office, there they prepared the questions to be asked, also determined his personal emotion concerning the case.

Arriving at 3pm they were directed to the Slinkis office, Dr. Slinkis is a successful Pediatrician in the Raleigh area. Dr. Slinkis came into the office.

"Dr. Slinkis, Rafael and I are special agents with the GBI, first thank you for giving us some of your precious time"

"Anything to help the law enforcement community" he graciously said.

"Doctor we have opened the case of Alicia Roque killed in Decatur around 1961, do you remember Alicia?"

"Yes, we were friends, she was very active with all the boys at school, beautiful full of life, but why after so many years you are opening the case?"

"Dr. homicide cases never close, this is what we call a cold case". Them Rafael entered the conversation.

"Dr., did you know a Mr. Donner, he was a lawyer in Atlanta area, also a member of your HS class".

"Yes, we were good friends he used to be my sister boyfriend, even after she was found dead, we kept in touch, he also was a constant companion of Alicia and Jim, I have not seeing Donner in 10 years, is he okay?".

"Well Mr. Donner was murdered last week in Atlanta; nobody has been caught yet". Kurt said.

Dr. Slinkis was shocked, but not surprise Donner was involved in those strip clubs, well I guess it can happen to anyone.

"What was Jim last name?" Rafael asked.

"Now let me see, yes Jim Silas a real troublemaker".

"Going back to Alicia, do you remember when she disappeared, were you in Decatur at that time?"

Rafael asked.

"I think it was during the summer break, I was at the beach in Florida with my parents when that happened".

"Dr. you mentioned about your sister, she was found where?".

"Somebody murdered her, they found her body 4 weeks later in Mableton, GA. I thought you guys knew, it was also in 1961, as I remember maybe a couple of weeks apart".

"Dr. what was your sister name?" Rafael asked.

"Rosanne Slinkis, they never caught the person who did it, maybe you guys can get involved in her case to".

"Dr. I promise we will".

Rafael immediately started to think, maybe a serial killer, now there two women murderers almost at the same time, from the same place with the same group of friends, a coincidence maybe we'll find out.

After 2 hours of interviewing Dr. Slinkis Rafael and Kurt left but not before asking the Dr. if he remember anything else concerning Alicia or his sister please give them a call.

"What do you think?" Kurt asked Rafael.

"The Dr. seems fine no immediate link with Alicia's case, but I am beginning to wonder that maybe the killing of the Dr.'s sister might be tight to Alicia's case, Kurt we have to reopen Roseanne case immediately". Kurt concurred.

Rafael and Kurt arrived very late at their office, they decided to meet early the following morning and put all the information they have gathered together and investigate Roseanne Slinkis case, it was going to be a very busy week.

The following morning both Rafael and Kurt were at their office by 6am, Yolanda also was there in case they needed any help, it was going hectic. First Kurt went to the storage room where all the cases are filed and got the box containing Roseanne Slinkis evidences, it was dated June 1961, she was raped and strangled very similar to Alicia's case, on the notes that the detectives made there was a couple of interviews, one to Jim Silas another to Robert Donner, also to several others in the HS she attended. The case description went as follow:

NAME. Roseanne Slinkis

AGE. 18 years old.

METHOD OF MURDER. Rape and Strangulation.

BODY WAS FOUND. Mableton, GA.

AGENTS ASSIGNED TO THE CASE. Peter Smiths/Robert Muncy.

What! Smiths and Muncy, Kurt was amazes wait until Rafael sees this.

"Rafael, I got Roseanne file, look who at the agents that were assigned to this case". Kurt said to Rafael.

"Well, you know what Kurt, it does not surprise me at all, specially Peter Smiths the missing person".

"Do we know if Peter Smiths is alive, if he is, he must be close to 90 years all by now". Rafael asked Kurt.

"We have to solve the mystery, is Peter in Costa Rica, is he back in the states, did he ever leave, where is his wife Joann? All mysteries, Kurt we have to solved them".

"I know, let's concentrate to find any link between Alicia and Roseanne murders, we might find the answer to Peter Smiths mystery"

Rafael responded.

They went into the box that was given to them by Mrs. Muncy, there they found a file on the Roseanne Slinkis case, looking at the time frame it was realized that the date and time did not match, the body was found according to the official files in June 1961, but the file   that Muncy had showed August 1961, the time didn't match either, official files 6pm Muncy file 9pm either the agents did not have a watch or did not know how to read a calendar or they did this to cover something or somebody, like the file of Alicia the only thing that was there was the information page, no notes on interview, cause of death or any other pertinent information.

"Kurt I think this 2 cases are related, same HS, same year proximity of the bodies I think they were killed in Decatur but dump in different areas of Georgia to confuse the investigation, I also think that Donner had something to do with this".

Kurt responded. "It looks that way, did Muncy changed the data or was it Peter, remember what Mrs. Muncy said that Peter's wife was living beyond her means and Peter was always looking to make more money".

That same day Kurt called Dr. Slinkis and asked him if any agents from the GBI interview him or any person at school in 1961.

"Well I remember that an agent, I don't remember his name did interview me and several students".

"Let me refresh your mind, was this agent name Peter Smiths?"

"You know what agent Kurt, I think it was Peter Smiths, wait yes, I am certain it was him".

"Thank you Dr. Slinkis, we'll be in touch".

Them Kurt turn to Rafael and said.

"Guest what Rafael, Peter Smiths interviewed Slinkis and several students when the body of Roseanne was found, where is that information?"

"Kurt, between Donner, Peter and this guy Ernie Silas we might find the answer to both cases, the trick is finding them, we know that Donner pass away, what about Peter and Silas".

"Don't forget Callan". Kurt said.

"Yes, Callan whoever he is". Rafael responded.

Rafael and Kurt left their office around 7pm, Yolanda was already at their apartment waiting for Rafael she had prepared a Cuban dish, a chicken fricassee and fried plantains, off course a bottle of red wine was also included, the moment Rafael entered the apartment the aroma of the food made him hungrier, Yolanda was happy.

They sat at the table and Yolanda asked Rafael "How was your day?'

"Well Yolanda it was an interesting day, I think there is a connection between this 2 cases, Alicia Roque and Roseanne Slinkis, same HS, same year, same set of friends both of them were raped and strangled, both 18 years old". "Do you need my help?" Yolanda asked.

"We probably will, your expertise in new areas of investigation can solve a couple of questions Kurt and I have".

"by the way how is the chicken?". Yolanda asked.

"It tasted like you sassy and yummy". ***

CHAPTER 9

"It doesn't matter how slow you go, as long as you don't stop"

Confucius

Rafael and Yolanda were getting ready for a quick trip to Aiken, SC where Yolanda's mother lives, a very active 72 years old widow, Yolanda father pass away 2 years ago he was 78 a retired Army Sergeant Major who served in 3 wars, Yolanda was very proud of him a true American hero.

The trip takes almost 3 hours from Sandy Spring to Aiken SC via I-20, they arrived around noon time Cecilia Yolanda's mother was anxious waiting.

After introducing Cecilia made a comment.

"So, this the man of your dreams right Yolanda".

"Yes, mother and Spanish speaking too, what more can I ask". Yolanda responded. "Cecilia, I love your daughter with all my heart and since we are all together here, I will like to propose to your daughter, Yolanda will you marry me?"

Yolanda was caught off guard, but her answer was a resounding YES! they both embraced and kissed, Cecilia joined the celebration, what a surprise the only thing missing was the date of the wedding.

Rafael, Yolanda and Cecilia had a delightful lunch with a wonderful toast to their future, Cecilia reminded them she wanted to see grandkids before she died, off course Yolanda is only 35 years old and Rafael 42 they do have a lot of years in front of them.

On their way back from Aiken Yolanda could not stop kissing Rafael.

"I love you Rafael, I thanked God every day that I meet you".

"I love you too Yolanda, I want to spend the rest of my life with you".

They spend a quiet weekend talking and planning their future together, for Rafael the case of Alicia Roque and Roseanne Slinkis was also on his mind, let's hope that this coming week will bring some answers.

Monday was like any other weekday, Rafael and Yolanda arrived at their office around 8am, Kurt arrived right after them, he immediately went to his office and a note was on his desk, WHAT! Kurt immediately shouted.

"Rafael come quick I have news about Peter" Kurt said.

Rafael entered Kurt office and saw the pale face of Kurt.

"Kurt are you okay, you look like you have seeing a ghost what it is?"

"Rafael, we have found Peter Smiths, he was killed 2 years ago, his body was found in Tennessee, he was shot execution style two shoots thru the head."

"who found the body?"

"It was found by a farmer back in 1974, nobody claimed him, so he was declared a John Doe, but since we started looking for him all over the US, the Tennessee Bureau of Investigation link John Doe fingerprints with Peter and they matched."

"Peter dead, Donner dead, Alicia and Roseanne killed, Kurt do you think there is a link somewhere?"

"Is beginning to look that way." Kurt said.

"have the APD found anymore evidence about the killing of Donner?" Rafael asked.

"I will call my friend and find out." Kurt responded.

In the meantime Rafael set a chart at his office with possible connections with relatives of the victims, Mrs. Donner and Mrs. Muncy were eliminated from the list of possible persons of interest, Joanne Peter's wife have not being located, according to information Rafael obtained from the GBI she was last seeing in Macon, GA at a friends house about 6 months ago, her friend Mary Lundqist was very close to Peter and his wife, she is a widow, her husband left her a sizeable sum of money which she expends like there was no tomorrow.

Kurt rushed into Rafael office and said

" Rafael my friend at the APD said that they found some fingerprints at Donner's house, it is being analyzed now, let's hope that a link can be found".

"great, we need to set up an interview with Mary Lundqist a friend of Peter' wife Joanne, I have created a chart of possible connections with the cases of Donner, Alicia and Roseanne, can you get in touch with her and set it up?"

"Yes, do you have the phone number?"

"Here, is in Macon, GA".

When Kurt left Rafael's office, he continues with the possible links set up at his chart, looking at persons already known and adding other names provided by different sources inside the

Bureau. on Peter's side we

have a bookie, a pastor and a lover all with close links to him.

Let's begin with Bookie Gerald Mark, he is in his fifties, spending time in prison now, living in Atlanta with his brother, his booking activity gone he is a janitor at an Atlanta public school. Mark was also a bookie for Donner before he went to prison.

Next, Pastor Henry Wall Baptist, now retired last known address Kennesaw, GA, was very closed to peter's wife Joanne to an extend that probably they were having an affair.

"Rafael, they have not been able to match two fingerprints from the Donner's house, they will keep looking, they have a theory, maybe it belongs to some longtime hoodlum from the Atlanta area, maybe connected to the old Dixie Mafia".

Kurt said.

"Dixie Mafia?" Rafael asked.

"Yes, an organization that has being active since the early sixties comprised of hoodlums from the southern US, involved in Prostitution, drug trafficking, killing and any other illegal activity you can think of, our bureau is very involved in the apprehension of this criminals".

"But why the Dixie Mafia, have Donner tried any case involving them, and if yes when?"

Rafael asked Kurt.

"That's the next thing I was going to tell you, it looks like Donner was defending several members of the Dixie Mafia between 1974 and 1976, some of them were set free but some did not, one individual, Ruzzo was defended and won his case thanks to Donner, so the motive for revenge is out".

"Interesting, do we know where Ruzzo is now?"

"According to the APD his last address was in Birmingham, AL, they are checking on that". Kurt said.   "Kurt look at this chart, it describes the names and association of several friends and member of Peter's and   Donner family that can be linked to the Alicia' and Roseanne cases." Rafael said.

In the chart that Rafael did some names were connected to both Peter and Donner, like Gerald Mark the bookie, Joanne, and Mary all of them had in a way close personal encounter with both. Kurt already called Mary; the meeting will take place next Tuesday in Macon.

By 1pm Rafael stopped by Yolanda's office and invited her to lunch with him, she immediately said yes, "how about Chinese"," yes let' do it" Rafael said.

At lunch not only did they talked about their wedding plans but also about the case of Alicia and Roseanne, it is consuming him, he ask Yolanda for her understanding and support.

"Rafael, I will always support you and remember my department is always ready to help you in any way you choose".

Rafael was listening, but his eyes could not move away from Yolanda's lips, he felt like grabbing and kissing her passionately.

After lunch Rafael went to his office, he was desperate for an answer, anything that could tied some knots to any of the cases in front of him, what about Callan the unknown person in Costa Rica, who was him?

Does Ruzzo have any relevance with the cases or only Donner, after an hour in his office Kurt showed up with Ruzzo's address.

"Rafael, we found Ruzzo's address".

"Where?"

"Kilby correctional facility in Montgomery, AL, he was apprehended a week ago on a parole violation".

"Can we interview him?" Rafael asked Kurt.

"I am working on that". Kurt said.

"Maybe the knot to tie all the loose ends might be close". Rafael responded.

Weekend has arrived, Yolanda took Rafael to stone mountain he commented that some stone mountain marble was used in the Havana Capitol Building and the University of Havana, she made a comment "marble from Georgia to Cuba, Rafael from Cuba to Georgia, I like that part" she said and both laughed. The weekend was gone so Rafael prepare for a busy week, interview in Macon and maybe another in Alabama with Ruzzo, still waiting for an okay on that.

Monday Rafael and Kurt were getting ready for the interview with Mary Lundqist the following day, will her interview bring any clarity to her association with the Peter and his wife Joanne? we'll see.

Mary lives in a fairly large house located in a 5 acre lot, she looks very athletic that makes her younger than the 56 years she have, she shares her home with her "fiancée" named Leo aged 25, a muscular fellow that looks like is more interested in her money than her, immediately after we arrived he went to the basement of the house where his true love lives, his gym.

"Mrs.Lundqist, thank you for giving us the time to ask you some questions, my name is Kurt and this Rafael we represent the GBI, please if you don't feel comfortable with any question you don't have to answer it, like I mentioned in our phone conversation we are here to ask you about Peter and Joanne Smiths, is that okay with you?"

"Yes, they were good friends of mine, specially Peter".

"when you said specially Peter, what did you meant by that". Rafael asked.

"Well we were friends since HS, I loved him, he loves me, if you know what I mean, later we found each other again in a HS reunion we went out, to be more blunt we had an extra marital affair for almost 15 years, he was married so did I, like I said we loved each other, what else you want to know".

Rafael was quiet for a moment, then he composed himself. "What about Joanne?"

"She was okay, never found out about our relationship until a year before Peter pass away, I guess she never cared she was too greedy always complaining about Peter lack of financial stability, Peter gamble a lot I guessed that he thought he could get out of his financial problems by gambling, by the way she also had an affair with Donner, this conversation is so interesting".

"How long did that affair lasted?" Rafael asked.

"Not to long, Donner's wife found out and threat Donner with a costly divorce if he didn't finish the affair."

"Do you know a man by the name of Gerald Mark?" Rafael asked.

"Yes, he was Peter bookie always owed him money, peter always came to me, looking to helping him out, as you know my husband was wealthy so I could ".

Kurt entered the conversation.

"Mrs. Lundquist" started by saying them Mary interrupted.

"Please call me Mary, Mrs. Lundquist sounds to old".

"Okay Mary, you knew Jim Donner, anybody else closed to him?"

Mary stayed silent for a moment them she answered.

"Yes, I did specially his cousin Willie Donner, charming fellow, real southern I think he was involved with some outlaw group from Alabama, we had a brief fling, not to romantic".

Well now we are getting somewhere, Rafael thought.

"I don't know if you are aware that Mr. Donner was assassinated in Atlanta last month". Kurt said.

"Yes, I know what a shame, any lead on who killed him?"

"We might". Kurt responded.

"Mary by any chance do you know where Willie or Joanne are right now?" Rafael asked.

"The last I heard he was in prison somewhere in Midwest, that was 2 years ago, about Joanne the last I heard was 6 months ago she came by to ask me for some   money she needed some surgery after that don't know, anything else?"

"Have you heard the name Ruzzo by any chance?" Kurt asked.

"I think Willie mentioned his name sometime in relation to his car".

"Mary, sorry one more thing" Rafael asked.

"Mary, do you know a man by the name Jim Silas?"

She tried to remember, took 3 min, and said.

"You mean Silas, that guy was weird, one time he just went into the girl's bathroom and put down his pants to show his parts, not to impressive, but yes very wired by the way an acquaintance of Donner".

"Anything else Mary?" Rafael asked.

"No, also you guys might want to check a couple of Donner's family members they are powerful individuals in Atlanta".

In a flirtatious way Mary also said to Rafael.

"By the way, you have a beautiful accent".

"Thank you for your comment Mary". Rafael giggle.

"You guys have a lot of information you can actually do one of those sex novels". Mary laughed.

Rafael and Kurt left Mary's house with a lot of information, they were amused by the easygoing personality of Mary, what a character. On the way back to GBI headquarters they began to plan for the next interview, Mr. Ruzzo in Alabama.

The following day Yolanda woke up with a terrible cold, Rafael after given her some medicine left for his office, it was pouring rain arriving around 8am he stopped by Kurt's office, he arrived by 7am.

"Rafael, remember what Mary said about the conversation that Willie Donner and Ruzzo had about his car?"

"Yes, anything Important?" Rafael responded.

"It seems that they had a chop shop operation in Decatur and Birmingham back in 1973, they were caught and prosecuted, they spend 3 years in prison, they got out this year, that is the reason Ruzzo is back in prison he broke his parole."

"Kurt can you enlighten me with the definition of a chop shop".

"Sorry Rafael, a chop shop operation is when they steal a car them break it down so they can sell the parts of the car in the black market".

"You know Kurt, if these people put their mind to work on something legal, they will be very successful, they are very creative". Rafael commented.

"Maybe when we interview Ruzzo we can find out the whereabout of Willie, by the way Rafael the interview is for Friday in Montgomery, AL, we should be leaving here early Friday morning, by the way we are not going to mention his fingerprints at Donner's home".

"Great Kurt, we have a day to prepare". Rafael said.

When Rafael got home that day Yolanda was feeling a little better, no fever but a lot of coughing, Rafael made Yolanda some chicken soup and added a lot of lemon juice, "Vitamin C", Rafael said.

Yolanda had the soup and went back to sleep, it was almost 10pm and the phone at Yolanda and Rafael apartment rang. It was Kurt.

"Rafael sorry to bother you at this time, but I just got a call from Mary in Macon, she was beaten badly and her boyfriend also beaten is in ICU, even thou they were wearing mask she thinks it is Willie and 2 of his friends, I have advise the Macon police dept. to put an officer on guard at the hospital".

"Do you think this might had something to do with the interview we had with Mary?" Rafael asked.

"Rafael, I think so, but I don't understand how the heck Willie found out we were there".

"We might look into the possibility that maybe somebody inside the GBI might be a friend or connected to Willie in some way, it is getting interesting, I'll see you early in the morning at the office so we can plan the next step". Rafael said.

"I will see you then". Kurt responded.

Rafael and Kurt arrived early the morning, they began by putting all the pieces of the information they have together and tying them to different individuals, Willie and Ruzzo, Jim Donner and Alicia and Joanne, the bookie and Donner, Willie and his cousin Jim Donner, Jim Silas and Callan who the heck are these guys?, Peter Smiths and his wife, we'll get it done, Rafael thought.

"Kurt, when we go and interview Ruzzo we need to act like we know somebody inside the GBI is connected to him or Willie, we can check his reaction and determine if it is true".

"That's a great idea, I will also tell the Director about our hunch and get his approval for an investigation inside the GBI". Kurt said.

"Now, going back to Ruzzo, we know about association with Willie, what about Jim, did he know him?". Rafael said.

"We will know tomorrow Rafael". Kurt said.

All day they prepared for the interview with Ruzzo, at the same time Kurt spoke with Mary about an update concerning her and her boyfriend.

"He is doing much better, still in ICU but the doctor might move him today to a regular room, as for me my face looks like a car run thru it but beside that I am fine, any word on the people who did this?"

"The Macon police dept. is handling the case; I have advised them to put a guard in your boyfriend room".

"Yes, they are doing that, thank you".

Mary responded.

The following morning Rafael and Kurt left for William E. Donaldson Correctional Facility a maximum-security prison in Bessemer AL, about 3 hours away from Decatur,

they arrived around 11am, they were directed to a reception area where they will meet Ruzzo, he showed up handcuffed and sat in front of Kurt and Rafael, a guard was standing behind him, with a smirk smile he showed insolence and a combative personality.

"Mr. Ruzzo my name is Kurt and he is Rafael, we represent the GBI and we want you to answer some questions, off course you have the right not to respond".

Ruzzo stretch back and answered.

"Okay what's your first question?"

"First, do you know where Willie Donner is?" Kurt asked.

"No, but if you find him tell him that I want to beat the shit out of him".

"Why Ruzzo, didn't you guys have some kind of an association together?" Rafael asked.

"Yes, that was a couple of years ago, but you see he still owe me money from our past association, he is a scum back".

Rafael immediately confronted Ruzzo about an inside connection with the GBI.

"Ruzzo we have some information connecting you and Willie with personnel inside the GBI, if we conclude that you are involved, well I guest you might die in prison because at least you are looking for 50 years inside this walls, you can tell us know and we might give the authorities a good personal referral on your behalf, like they say in Georgia the ball is in your court".

Ruzzo paused for a couple of minutes, asked for a cigarette and began talking.

"ha, ha, they finally found out about Peter, well that's the guy Peter Smiths".

"Ruzzo, you have to do better than that, Peter pass away several years ago, we are talking about the one that took his place". Rafael responded.

"There was another fellow, younger he was a close friend of that Jerk Willie, I don't know his name".

"50 years is a long time behind these walls, think Ruzzo" Rafael asked.

"Man, I don't' know, do you think I am stupid you are right 50 years is a long time, you give me time and will find out".

"Okay Ruzzo, we'll give you a week, now I am going to give you several names tell me about them, if you know them or were, they your partner or anything that you might think". Rafael asked.

"Okay", Ruzzo said.

"Jim Silas"

"Weird guy, a true killer".

"Alicia Roque".

"You know what, Willie mentioned her name some time ago, it

was a conversation relating to his family something about his uncle". Ruzzo said.

Immediately Rafael thought about the remark that Mary said, "check the Donner family they are weird".

"Ruzzo, can you explain about Donner's uncle".

This time Kurt asked.

"His uncle a big shot judge in Atlanta, he is a senator now being married 3 times with younger women, he is loaded, like to gamble a lot, weird man, weird".

"His name". Kurt asked again.

"Judge or Senator Charles Springdale".

"We have two more names for you Ruzzo, Roseanne Slinkis and a fellow his last name is Callan".

"Roseanne yes, she used to dance in a strip club with Alicia, concerning Callan don't know, give me a week and I will find out who guy is inside the GBI".

"Okay Ruzzo, we'll be back in touch with you". Kurt aid.

By that they both departed the meeting, when they reach their car, they began to put together all the information that was given by Ruzzo. "Rafael, you were right somebody is inside the GBI feeding information to a group of hoodlums, we have to find out who he is before more damage is done, I will relay the information to our director as soon as we get in our office".

"Yes, in order for Willie and his accomplice to beat Mary and her boyfriend a day after our meeting somebody supply that information from within the GBI". Rafael said.

Immediately upon arriving in Decatur Rafael left, arriving at his apartment he found Yolanda feeling great and cooking a pasta dish.

"Rafael, hope you like it".

"Anything coming out of your hands I like". Rafael responded.

"A glass of wine and a kiss, the perfect combination" Rafael grab Yolanda by the waist and gave her a never-ending kiss.

"Rafael the food is getting cold". Yolanda said.

"Yolanda, I love you so much".

"Rafael, I love you too". They embrace again and finish with a kiss.

While they were sitting eating Yolanda's pasta, she mentioned to him that they might need to take a couple of days off, "maybe go to Savannah for a couple of days" Yolanda said.

"Yes, that will be great I need a couple of days off so I can figure out where we are in relation to our cases, yes let's do it". Rafael was enthusiastic about the trip.

"How was the meeting with that guy in prison today?"

"You know Yolanda, there might be somebody at the GBI supplying information to a group of hoodlums, we need to find out as soon as possible".

"Any idea who might be?" Yolanda asked.

"No, but this guy Ruzzo might give us some information next week".

After dinner they went back to their bedroom and engaged in a never-ending love affair.

Yolanda and Rafael finally went sleep around 11pm.***

CHAPTER 10

"The truth is rarely pure and never simple"

Oscar Wilde

The weekend came and Rafael and Yolanda were on their way to Savannah, beautiful day, sunny not cold for the middle of September, they are staying at the Planters Inn in the Historic district of Savannah built in the 1800's the hotel is a jewel in the city.

They spend 2 wonderful days together, but you could feel that Rafael was anxious to get back and immerse himself in the cases of Alicia and Roseanne.

Rafael and Yolanda arrived at their apartment late Sunday evening, they were tired, so they grabbed a bite to eat and off they went to sleep.

The following morning Rafael left before Yolanda, around 6am he arrived at his office, he needed to go back to his chart and incorporate the information they receive from Ruzzo, some links have been stablished but we needed more, Kurt arrived around 8am, he asked Rafael how the trip was.

"Kurt it was great, anytime I spend time with Yolanda is heaven, but my mind was also occupied with our cases".

"By the way I have advise our Director of mold inside the GBI, he told to go ahead but be very cautious this can explode in our face". Kurt said.

"Great Kurt, we will proceed very carefully, not to give an impression of a corrupted Department".

Rafael commented.

"Any word from Ruzzo?"

"Not yet Rafael, let's give him until the end of the week".

Rafael needed more information about Jim Silas, a person named Callan and now Judge or Senator Springdale, needed to link them to something, will begin with Springdale, he asked Kurt to find out about Senator Charles Springdale.

Immediately Kurt came back with information about Springdale.

"Rafael, Senator Charles Springdale, being a Senator since 1972, was a judge before at the Atlanta Superior Court a yellow dog Democrat and a true Southern, there you have it".

"Kurt enlighten me, what is a yellow dog Democrat?" Rafael asked.

"It is a political term applied to voters in the South who voted solely for candidates who represented the Democratic party, it

has been used since the 19th century these voters would vote for a yellow dog rather than a Republican".

"well, that means he is truly a Georgian". Rafael said.

"I guest you can say that". Kurt responded.

"Them the other 2 names that are pending are Jim Silas and Callan, first name unknown."

Rafael commented.

By the middle of the week they have not heard anything from Ruzzo so they decided to call the prison warden, and were advised that Ruzzo was transferred to another prison due to the fact that he have received death threats the day after he meet with Rafael and Kurt.

"Can we see him, speak to him or what do you suggest?" Kurt asked the warden.

"I can not give you that information now, he was transferred 2 days ago, and we need 1 week of processing before we can give you guys any information concerning an interview". The warden said.

"Thank you for your help, let's hope he doesn't get killed before". Kurt angrily said.

"Does it take a week to process a prisoner?"

Rafael asked Kurt.

"Rafael every state has its own rules and regulations, except if you are federal prisoner, the whole federal system abides by one set of rules and regulation".

"okay, them we have to wait for a week before we can talk to Ruzzo again, and like you said if he doesn't get killed before". Rafael answered.

Them Rafael asked Kurt.

"Kurt do think we can get and interview with Senator Springdale this week?"

"I'll try to get one, no promises Senators are very special they think they own the world, but I'll try".

"Great, we need to know what kind of relationship he had with his nephew Jim Donner". Rafael said.

"I'll make the call today". Kurt responded.

Kurt finally received a call from the warden at the facility where Ruzzo was incarcerated, they agreed that Ruzzo will see them the following week, he needed more time to get the promised information, in the meantime Kurt received a phone call from the office of Senator Springdale, sorry but the Senator cannot see anybody now he is in the middle of a floor debate and need all the time in the world, Kurt was not surprised.

Rafael called Mary at Macon to check on her boyfriend, when she answered the phone her voice sounded a little shaky, Rafael asked her.

"Is there anything wrong, you sound nervous".

"My boyfriend is doing better, but last night there were several phone calls made to my house, when I pick up the phone the person at the other end hanged up, I think that they are trying to scare me". Mary responded.

"I will tell Kurt to call the Macon police dept. and report those calls, you have our number, please don't hesitate for one minute to give us a call". Rafael said.

"I will". Mary said.

Where the heck is Jim Silas? Rafael thought, he can be the missing link to both cases, but we need to find him first, Rafael started to investigate several notes made in conjunction with all the interviews he and Kurt conducted.

Going one by one Rafael eliminated a group of persons he considered not important to the investigation, he started with the Daryls, Raquel Alicia's sister and her husband, even thou he sounded nervous but after looking into several leads he was not in the vicinity of Alicia's or Joanne murders, of all the Jim's in the list only Jim Donner was active, even thou he was killed his name might be connected in some way with the pending cases.

Ruzzo, Willie Donner, Jim Silas and off course the mysterious Callan, we can also add Senator Springdale, we might get a clearer picture about him when we get an interview, Kurt is trying hard.

Late that day Kurt received a phone call from the Alabama warden where Ruzzo is being held, he confirmed that Ruzzo will be able to see us by Friday, Ruzzo insisted that they bring a carton of cigarettes to the interview, Kurt will comply.

"Rafael, Ruzzo will be ready for an interview on Friday we have to bring a cartoon of cigarettes to the interview, in prison that's like gold". Kurt said.

"Everywhere are the same, common criminals in Cuba always demanded a carton of cigarettes before an interview, in contrast Political prisoners never demanded that". Rafael responded.

Friday was here, Rafael and Kurt left Decatur very early, they were going to Holman Correctional Facility located in Escambia AL in the Southern part of Alabama close to the Florida border where Ruzzo is being held, about 4 hours away they estimated time of arrival around 12 noon.

Rafael and Kurt were directed immediately toward a meeting room where Ruzzo was already waiting for them, they began by shaking hands, seated and began the interview.

"Well Ruzzo any news?" Rafael asked.

"Rafi, here is the deal, I need to get out of this hole, to many enemies they want to kill me, you assure me that that is possible and will give you his name in a silver platter, deal?".

"Ruzzo, first my name is not Rafi is Rafael, got that, Rafael, now concerning the deal my partner Kurt will give you a more precise answer, got that Ruzzo". Rafael answered with a sarcastic look.

"Rafael, please don't get mad I was just trying to be friendly, ha, ha".

Them Kurt entered the conversation.

"Ruzzo, regarding the deal I cannot give you an answer now so you have to trust us, you give us the name and we'll recommend that you get a good deal, now give us the name of this guy inside the GBI".

Ruzzo opened the cigarette carton took out a pack, open it and took a cigarette out asked for a light and began to smoke, after several puffs he started talking.

"Are you guys ready, his name is Alex Corbin I don't know his department, but he has been helping us for a while, there you have it".

Them he kept on smoking waiting for an answer.

Kurt was petrified, he knew Alex Corbin, his son plays football with his son, Alex have been to Kurt house several times, as a matter of fact he was at the BBQ when Rafael was there.

"Kurt are you okay?"

Rafael asked, he knew immediately something was wrong.

"Rafael, I know this guy, he had been with the bureau for several years, he works in the Special Cases Section, 2 floors above us, I have to call the Director right away and give him the news".

Rafael was not surprise, for Willie or any one in their organization to do the things they have being doing an inside informant was needed.

Kurt was in the phone with the Director, informing him of the news.

"The Director says, this information stays with us, he plans to isolate Alex refer the case to internal affair so they can verified all the facts and detain him, we also need to move Ruzzo to a safer place", he is working on that, Kurt said.

Kurt looked somber, a colleague, a friend is now his main enemy he had put the lives of all the GBI agents in jeopardy.

"So, this guy took the place of Peter Smiths, and provided inside information to a group of hoodlums, that organization also needs judges and politicians". Rafael commented.

They waited until Ruzzo was put under protective custody, the warden assured them he will be guarder 24 hrs. a day, they were satisfied.

They left the correctional facility around 3pm, arriving in Decatur late, Kurt was still astonished by the revelation of agent Alex Corbin who thru all this year have served the GBI honorably, that's what they thought.

Arriving in Decatur around 9pm, Rafael and Kurt departed to their respective homes, Yolanda was waiting for Rafael, she immediately thought something was wrong, the expression on the face of Rafael was a giver.

"How was its Rafael, you don't look to good".

"We have uncovered the mold within the GBI, Alex Corbin he took the functions of Peter Smiths and disseminated privilege information to Ruzzo and his organization, we have to keep it quiet for a while, his case is being handled by Internal Affair, it was devastating to Kurt". Rafael responded.

Yolanda could not speak, she also knew Alex, very impressive agent, married with 3 kids.

"My God, this will be very traumatic for the Bureau, he is well liked even thou his wife is a little bit eccentric". Yolanda was in shock.

Being a good detective, Rafael asked Yolanda.

"What do you mean eccentric?".

"Well, Cynthia, that's her name, she liked fancy clothes, went on trips with her girlfriends and no, Alex did not go, they actually lived in a big house, I think she was living above her means". Yolanda responded.

"I am pretty certain that the GBI will investigate all avenues, including Cynthia".

Yolanda and Rafael have eaten already so they sat in the sofa located in the living room, after having a glass of wine Rafael fell sleep, he went thru a hard day, it is not easy to find out that a fellow law enforcement officer is involved in illegal activities. *****

CHAPTER 11

"Success is how high you bounce after you hit bottom"

General George S. Patton

Fall was almost over, leaves were changing, for Rafael it was a beautiful experience, Cuba being in the Caribbean leaves stay green and temperatures are very mild compare to Georgia, but according to the local weatherman winter will bring low temperatures, and maybe some snow.

GBI Internal Affairs was already setting up a trap for agent Corbin, they needed to get Ruzzo to cooperate, for that Kurt was also involved.

"Warden, we need to use Ruzzo in an important sting, I can not give you more information about the case but when we finally get it done, we will give you a full report".

Kurt said to the warden.

"No problem I will instruct the personnel to move Ruzzo to the main reception area so can use him for this sting".

The warden responded.

"Great, I will be there tomorrow with Rafael and set it up, please don't mention any detail to Ruzzo, we will do that ourselves, and again thank you for your cooperation". Kurt said.

The following day Rafael and Kurt arrived at the prison where Ruzzo was held, immediately they were directed to the main interview area, Ruzzo was already there, Kurt started by instructed Ruzzo how we were going to conduct the trap.

"Ruzzo, if we are successful on this you can count that I will do everything possible to get you out of this hole".

Kurt said.

"Okay let's get it going". Ruzzo said.

"Here is what we will do, you are going to call Alex Corbin at his office and say that you got out of prison and need some money, and if he does not do anything to get it he will start talking to the authorities about their relationship, and by the way I need about $5,000.00, okay Ruzzo can you do that?"

"A piece of cake". Ruzzo said.

At GBI everything was set to tape and follow Alex to the delivery of the money, Ruzzo will give the instruction to Alex to where he needed to drop the money, it was at his Grandmother house in Doraville, GA close to the Atlanta airport.

"Ready Ruzzo?" Kurt said.

Both Rafael and Kurt were also listening to the conversation.

The phone rang at Alex Corbin office he picks it up and began to talk.

"This is agent Corbin can I help you". "Alex my friend, this is Ruzzo, how are you doing?" Alex was quiet for a couple of minutes and began by saying.

"Ruzzo why the hell are calling me at this number, this is my office, what do you want?"

"Alex my brother, I just got out of prison, man I am broke need some money, and if you fail me, I will be going to your superiors and talk about our relationship, is that clear?"

Alex was quiet, could not talk, here is this scum bag doing this to me, do I have any choice? Alex thought.

"Okay Ruzzo how much are we talking about?"

"Not much Alex, let's say $5000.00".

"That's a lot of money, Ruzzo".

"Well Alex, you can ask your wife for the money, every time I screwed her, I gave her $150.00, and we did it several times, she was good".

"You son of a bitch, I will get you the money but stay away from my wife and me or I will kill you".

"Okay Alex, don't be to defensive, you knew about our fling now you are mad, now I need the money to be   delivered to my Grandmother house by tomorrow, she lives in Doraville, GA at 1202 Lumpkin rd., I will be waiting don't disappoint me Alex, it can cost you big".

Ruzzo hang up the phone and said.

"How did I do guys?"

"Ruzzo you an ass hole, but you did fine, is Cynthia also involved?" Kurt asked.

"Let me tell you about Cynthia, she used to hang around with Willie, them Willie got tired of her so he pass her to me, she is con artist always needing money to live a life she could not afford, if you can get her she will give you a lot of information about our group, now what's next?"

Kurt immediately call his office and asked the Internal Affair people if they got all the information on tape.

"Yes, we did Kurt, bring Ruzzo to Georgia, everything is set with the Alabama authorities, so he can finish and get the bribe money, tell Rafael that you guys did an excellent job".

"Will do" Kurt responded.

"Now Ruzzo, we will take you to Georgia so you can get the money, after Alex hand you the money and the procedure is done, we will take you back to Alabama, because you have co-operated with us a special parole hearing will be held for you next week, if everything goes right you should be out of prison soon, also Ruzzo if you make any attempt to scape either Rafael or I will not hesitate to shoot you, understood?"

"Yes sir, understood".

Ruzzo said laughing.

The following day everything was set up for the sting, a female officer was assign to be Ruzzo's Grandmother, some makeup had to be apply so she can look older, several agents were posted in different locations inside and outside the house, Ruzzo was sitting in a sofa closed to the living room, Rafael and Kurt were hiding in the kitchen, Internal Affairs agents and the agent that took   Ruzzo's grandmother place was also in the living room, every was set.

Alex Corbin arrived around 11am, he seen apprehensive about the hole thing, he entered the house and immediately started talking to Ruzzo.

> "Here Ruzzo, your lousy money, I don't want to see you or Willie's face again next to my wife or me, a promise I will kill you".

> Immediately after Ruzzo received the bribe IA agents apprehended Alex, he was shock and almost fainted, the mold is gone, at least that's what they hoped.

> Alex was transported to the Fulton County lockup pending charges, later that day Cynthia his wife was also taken into

custody, Rafael and Kurt were satisfied the worst thing you can have is a corrupt cop.

That same day Rafael and Kurt took Ruzzo back to Alabama, after arriving at the prison Ruzzo was moved to a special section where ex cops, former gang members and snitch reside.

"Remember Ruzzo, take advantage of the opportunity we are giving you, don't come back to this place".

Kurt said.

Off course wishful thinking on the part of Kurt, most inmates return to prison in about a month.

Rafael and Kurt arrived at GBI headquarters very late, the Director was waiting for them, first thanking them for a great job but also to inform them that Alex was talking and agreed to cooperate with them, both Alex and Cynthia were charged with several felony charges, their kids went their Grandparents, the Director opened up a bottle of Makers Mark, Rafael, Kurt and the Director had a nice toast.

Yolanda was up waiting for Rafael, he was drained mentally and physically, it had been a very complex and busy week, Yolanda gave Rafael a big hug and a lasting kiss, immediately he hit the sack.

The following morning when Rafael and Kurt arrived at their office they directly went to the Internal Affair dept., they asked for permission to interview Alex and his wife in connection to the cold cases of Alicia and Rosanne and also for any information about Jim Donner, Willie and our mystery man Ernie Silas, they said yes but and IA agent had to be present, they agreed.

Around 3pm they arrived at the Fulton County lockup where Alex was being held, permission for an interview was already approved by the jail authorities, when Alex arrived at the interview room he had black eye, some prisoner have taken the honor of hitting a corrupt cop, Alex lawyer was present so did the IA agent.

"Alex, you know who I am with sorrow because I thought that you were my friend, I need to ask you some questions concerning your relationship with Willie Donner and his group, in connection to a couple of cold cases Rafael and I are pursuing".

Kurt asked Alex.

"Well Kurt, first sorry for all the harm I have done to the GBI and specially you, Cynthia my wife introduced Wille Donner and Ruzzo to me about 2 years ago it seems that Cynthia had a relationship with Wille that went back to their HS years, this I did not know until about 2 years ago, at that time a proposition was made by Ruzzo and Willie to help them with certain information concerning the GBI, the pay was nice and Cynthia always insisted that I did not make a lot of money at the bureau and her needs were not fulfill, I did it because of my love for her I was afraid that if refuse to help Ruzzo and Willie I will lose Cynthia".

"What organization did Willie and Ruzzo belong to?"

Rafael asked Alex.

"It is a branch of the Georgia Dixie Mafia".

"What other persons you know that belong to this group". Rafael asked.

"Personally, none but I remember that Willie was always boosting that Judges and Politicians were involved".

"In your conversation with Willie or Ruzzo have you heard the name of Jim Silas?"

"No, but I did hear Peter Smiths mention the name".

"In connection to what?" Rafael asked.

"To an investigation concerning a homicide that happened a long time ago".

Kurt entered the interview again.

"Alex, have you heard the names of Alicia Roque and Roseanne Slinkis?"

"No, I have not".

At that moment Alex lawyer interrupted and advise Alex not to answer any more questions, their time was up.

Rafael and Kurt walked away, not saying thank you, Kurt was really annoyed with Alex, a so call friend who committed treason against its fellow agents, a corrupt law enforcement individual selling delicate information to a group of hoodlums.

Next came Cynthia Alex wife, a woman with no principles according to the information they have gather, her interview will be for tomorrow at the women section of the Fulton Co. Jail, same setup her lawyer will be present no IA agent since she is not attached to the GBI.

Kurt started the conversation.

"Cynthia, we had a meeting with your husband Alex, you guys are in deep trouble, according to the charges you and Alex are facing a minimum of 20 years behind bars awaits both of you".

Cynthia responded.

"Kurt, what do you want from me?"

At that moment her lawyer interrupted and advise Cynthia not to say another word until a deal can be workout.

"Okay, we'll do that, I will talk to the District Attorney and workout a deal, now if we get a deal will you give us the information we need with no reservation?"

Kurt asked Cynthia.

"I will every detail, those jerks play me, including Alex, he knew about me having sex with Ruzzo and Willie from the first moment we started".

Rafael and Kurt left the jail complex quiet, but Rafael hinted to Kurt that there is something that does not match between Alex interview and his wife Cynthia.

"What is it Rafael?"

"According to Alex he knew about the affair between Cynthia and those 2 guys about 2 years ago, right?"

"Right". Kurt answered

"Well, Cynthia just inform us that Alex knew about the affair immediately after they started which was right when they got married, it does not match".

"Yes, Rafael maybe the marriage was done out of convenience and greed, we need to go deeper when we have the next interview".

Upon arriving at their office Rafael and Kurt immediately made it to the Directors office to brief him on both interviews, the Director asked both.

"Rafael and Kurt, any lead to your cold cases obtain in these interviews?"

"Not directly, but Rafael and I think that Alicia and Roseanne where killed by the same person, and we also think that a connection with this group of hoodlums will be stablish".

"How you guys came to that theory, any link or name recognition by Alex or Cynthia?"

The Director asked.

"Director, Jim Donner, Willie Donner, Ruzzo, they are all connected, specially Jim Donner he had a special relationship with both Alicia and Roseanne now, Jim was   killed for whatever reason Kurt and I still don't know but we have a hunch that his death relates to our interview concerning our cold cases, we are working very hard to stablish all the loose ends".

Rafael said.

"I know you guys are working really hard on the cases, please keep me informed of any new development".

By that the Director left, it was almost 7pm.

Kurt turn to Rafael and commented.

"We need that piece missing, we almost have the answer, there are to many avenues that we have to reach before we have a complete picture".

"I know". Rafael answered.

"By the way Rafael in 3 weeks is Thanksgiving, my wife and I are planning for a big dinner, we will like to invite Yolanda and you join us that night".

Rafael immediately said. "I'll talk to Yolanda about it, but I am certain she will say yes".

Rafael arrived at his home around 9pm, Yolanda already made dinner, pork chops, black beans and a nice salad, and off course a bottle of red wine was already opened.

Yolanda commented to Rafael.

"Honey you look tired, here have some dinner and let's talk later about your day, love you".

"Yes, a tough day being face to face with a traitor to the bureau, yes it was difficult, but them I made it here and look at your face, your lips make me a new man again, and yes I do love you too".

They immediately grabbed each other and started a passionate kiss.

After dinner they sat next to each other at the living room sofa, Yolanda started the conversation.

"Well Rafael tell me about your day".

"We interview Alex Corbin first, what a jerk, he did not give us any new information except that he was a paid informant for a group of Georgians that belong to the   Dixie Mafia, now, Cynthia was more descriptive, I think that Alex used her to stablish his contacts with the organization, she has known Willie for a while and then Ruzzo came later, both a couple of scums".

"How was your day Yolanda?"

"I am involved in an investigation of a homicide that occurred last week, it was young black female about 25 years old, shoot 3 times with a 45-caliber gun, not much to go on, some blood samples".

"My Yolandita will get it done, by the way Kurt is having a Thanksgiving dinner at his house and requested that we attend".

"That's 3 weeks from now, I will call his wife to ask what they need for us to bring, that's great".

They both were tired, so they decided to make it to bed and go to sleep, it was almost 11pm.

"Hoy si hay frio" (is cold today), commented Rafael in Spanish.

The morning was cool, temperature in the 40's, a new experience for Rafael he had a jacket on when he arrived at the office, he looked around there were people in tea shirt and short sleeves, how can this be I am freezing, Rafael thought.

Kurt was waiting for him; he had some news.

"Rafael, I think they apprehended Willie Donner in Arizona, he was on his way to Mexico, I am waiting for a call from the Sherriff of Maricopa County, to confirm it".

"Great news, if they confirm the news when can we have him back in Georgia?"

Rafael asked Kurt.

"Rafael, the procedure can take days, weeks or months, he can fight extradition, we will know soon".

At that moment a note was handed to Kurt from Senator Charles Springdale, it said, call my lawyer Frank Pannel if you want to talk to me, I am too busy for any interview. Signed by Senator Charles Springdale.

"Darn politician, what a jerk" Kurt said.

"Kurt, every country has the same bunch of arrogant people".

"I will follow his instruction; I will call his lawyer right now and every week until we get an interview".

Kurt angrily said.

The office of Lawyer Frank Pannel is at the Peachtree Center North, better known as the Gas Light Tower, Kurt made the call, left a message with Mr. Pannel's secretary for him to call Kurt at the GBI in reference for a future interview with Senator Charles Springdale. ***

CHAPTER 12

"Any fool can make history, but it takes a genius to write it"

Oscar Wilde

A week have pass by and no news on either the apprehension of Willie Donner in Arizona or and answer from Frank Pannel, the Lawyer for Senator Springdale, Kurt immediately placed a call to the office of Mr. Pannel, again left a message with his secretary, them next he called the sheriff of Maricopa County to find out about Willie Donner.

"I was about to call you, it has taken longer to identify the person we have detained, first he gave us a name of Willie Taft, after investigating longer we finally stablish the identity, his real name Williams Donner, better known as Willie Donner, so I guest this is your guy".

The Maricopa County Sheriff said to Kurt.

"Yes, how long before we can have him in Georgia?"

"I will begin the paperwork, as soon I can get an order of extradition with a copy of his arrest warrant".

"We do have a warrant for Willie Donner, for attempted murder, I will get everything ready today and forward it to you as soon as possible, by the way thank you for your cooperation".

"Anytime, good luck".

The sheriff said and hang up the phone.

"Rafael, the process just started, Wille will be on his way back to Georgia, more questions will be answered".

Kurt happily said to Rafael.

Before the day was finish Kurt received a phone call from the office of Mr. Pannel, an interview was set for next Tuesday at 9:30am, the secretary said to make it on time, Mr. Pannel will be taking off with his family for a 2-week vacation on Wednesday. "Great week Rafael, first Wille was identify and now Pannel gave us an interview on Tuesday of next week at 9:30am, isn't that great".

"Today is Thursday, we have enough time to prepare, good work Kurt".

Rafael said, them he went back to his office.

On his way to his office Rafael stopped by Yolanda's office, he asked her.

"Baby, did you call Kurt's wife in reference to the Thanksgiving dinner?"

"Yes, and I offered to take a couple of bottles of wine".

Yolanda responded.

"If we can find them, let's make it Spanish wine".

Back in Macon Mary was still getting phone calls, the person at the other end will hang up as soon as Mary answered, probably to intimidate her, her boyfriend was out of the hospital but still bang up from the beating, she called Kurt and reported the situation, the following morning Kurt set up a tracking system on her phone to determined who was the who was the person at the other end, the problem is that the system doesn't work on hang ups, still they were going to try.

Rafael called Mary and asked her.

"Mary, this Rafael when you get the next phone call please associate any sound in the other end, maybe a motorcycle, a train anything that will associate the caller with the location he or she is calling from, can you do that?"

"Off course for you guys anything, by the way I still like your accent".

Mary responded.

"Thank you but my fiancée likes it even more".

Rafael laughing said.

When Rafael was looking for a file in top of his desk, he saw a note that he did not see before, it was from Kurt friend at the APD, address to Kurt, somebody put it there by mistake, it read.

"Kurt according to forensic, the fingerprints found at the homicide scene of Mr. Donner does not match with That Ruzzo character, please call me".

The note was signed by Jerry Sanders APD, the detective assigned to the Jim Donner homicide case.

Rafael immediately called Kurt and convey the information to him.

"I will call Jerry; we need to find out the match of those fingerprints as soon as possible".

Kurt said.

Kurt called Jerry Sanders; he was very shock to find out to whom those fingerprints belong to.

"Kurt it seems the fingerprints belong to one of your agents, Alex Corbin".

Detective Sanders said.

"Jerry, Alex Corbin is in jail now, he was a mold within the bureau supplying information to a local group associated with the Dixie Mafia".

Kurt answered angrily.

"He will be facing more charges in connection to Jim Donner homicide, our department is presenting the evidence with the District Attorney tomorrow".

Jerry said.

Rafael was there also, he asked det. Sanders a couple of questions.

"Has any test on ballistics being performed, also any other material evidence found at the scene linking Alex with the crime?"

Rafael asked Jerry.

"Yes, and it match the type of weapon issue to law enforcement agencies, including the GBI, also we found in an ashtray some residual of a cigarette, Marlboro brand.". Jerry responded.

"Kurt, can we go over to Alex office and look over his personal belongings and see if any pack of cigarettes match a Marlboro brand?"

"Yes, we can do that Rafael".

Det. Sanders was about to leave when Rafael asked him.

"Jerry, can you let us know when Alex's audience to hear his charges will be schedule so Kurt and I can attend, I want to see his reaction".

"Off course Rafael, I will be in touch with Kurt".

When Rafael and Kurt were along in their office Rafael made a comment concerning the homicide investigation.

"You know Kurt I do not think Alex is capable of killing".

Kurt was surprised of the comment.

"Why you say that Rafael?"

"It takes an angry killer to shoot a person three times, it is either vengeance or personal vendetta, not a contract killing".

"What do you suggest we do Rafael?"

"Let's look more into Cynthia Corbin, she had been involved with Ruzzo and Willie for a long time, maybe she also knew Jim Donner".

"You are right Rafael, she is a vicious woman, will do anything for money or vengeance".

It was Friday, Yolanda had plans for the weekend with Rafael.

"Rafael, tomorrow Saturday I made plans to visit the Biltmore House in Asheville, NC about 4 hours away from our place, you'll like it, we'll be staying at the hotel inside the complex, they have a winery and other attractions".

"Great Yolanda, we need to take jackets according to the weather people it will cold this weekend".

"Don't worry Rafael I'll give you all the warm weather you need".

Yolanda answered and look at Rafael with tempting eyes.

Rafael advised Kurt of his planned trip with Yolanda.

"Kurt we'll be staying at the Biltmore Hotel, anything that develop in the weekend please let me know".

"Don't worry Rafael, enjoy, we are going to have a busy week next week, remember Tuesday we meet with Mr. Pannel".

Rafael and Yolanda left their apartment toward Asheville early in the morning, they arrived around 11:00am at the Biltmore complex, they were directed toward the hotel, after settling in they took a shuttle to the Biltmore House.

it was built by the Vanderbilt family in the 1800's, still in the family now it has become a tourist attraction.

Rafael was impressed, not only the house but also the gardens and the winery, they also visited the city of Asheville, a growing community, Rafael and Yolanda were going to have a wonderful weekend.

They arrived at their apartment around 10:00 pm on Sunday, Yolanda asked Rafael. "Did you enjoy it?"   "Yes, I did, you were right the you gave me all the warm weather I need it". Rafael said laughing. ***

CHAPTER 13

"Life is really simple, but men insist on making it complicated".

Confucius

After doing their daily jog, Rafael and Yolanda left for their
office, arriving around 8:30 am, Kurt was already there he immediately rushed to Rafael's office, he had some great news.

"Rafael, the Maricopa Co. Sheriff left a message overnight, Willie
will not fight extradition, he will be back in Georgia this coming Wednesday".

"YES!!!!, he can answer a lot of pending questions, Kurt this call
for a toast, how about some coffee".

"With pleasure Rafael".

With a happy face, Kurt answered.

The following day a schedule meeting with Mr. Pannel, the lawyer for Senator Springdale, will take place.

Rafael and Kurt have been wondering why the Senator needs a
lawyer now, maybe he is to busy or some other reason.

"I have never seeing a person using a lawyer before any question is requested, it's odd, have you Rafael?"

"No Kurt, I was thinking the same thing, do we have any personal information about Mr. Pannel?"

"No, but I can gather any information we have on him".

Kurt said.

"We need to know if he is connected in some way to Ruzzo, Willie or any other person associated with them".

Rafael asked Kurt.

"We can go into the legal files of different cases investigated by the GBI, also we can ask the APD if they have any cases pending or resolved that Mr. Pannel is or was involved".

Kurt took all day gathering information about Mr. Pannel, from the Bureau and the APD, he was amazed.

"Rafael look, Mr. Pannel have been involved in several cases involving the Dixie Mafia, including Wille Donner, as a matter of fact he is the present lawyer handling his legal paperwork".

"I knew it, there had to be a connection between the lawyer, the Senator and those characters, we can now hope to construct a link that will take us back to 1961 and the homicides of Alicia and Roseanne".

Rafael was certain that the link can be stablished, the only mystery is still Ernie Callan.

Rafael and Kurt were at the office of Mr. Pannel as schedule, his assistant, a beautiful blonde maybe 25 years old, great figure and wearing an extra mini skirt took us to his private office, he certainly enjoys this view every single day.

"Mr. Pannel my name is Kurt, and this is Rafael we represent the GBI, as you know we are here because Senator Springdale decided to have you as middle spoke person this a very unusual situation, situation, the Senator is not a suspect in any way".

Mr. Pannel listened and started talking.

"The Senator have been my client for many years, also a personal friend of mine, he is busy doing his elected role in the General Assembly, please agent Kurt proceed with the questions you have".

"Sir, as you know the Senator is the uncle of the late Jim Donner who was killed a couple of month ago, we need to stablish what kind of information in regard to this homicide".

"Agent Kurt, if the Senator had any information about that case don't you think he would have giving it to you?"

"Well, Mr. Pannel maybe he thinks is not important or relevant to the case, that's why we needed to talk to him on a personal basis".

"Agent Kurt, like I said before the Senator is to busy, if you want you can leave all questions with me and   whatever information the senator might have for you I will gladly forward it".

Them Rafael entered the conversation.

"Mr. Pannel how is the case of Willie Donner going, we also need to question him".

Pannel was silent for a couple of minutes and answered.

"He will be available the moment all his legal matters will be resolved, by the way he is not guilty".

"I am pretty certain that Mr. Ruzzo will be very happy to see Willie Donner, don't you think so Mr. Pannel?"

Rafael asked Pannel, like before he took a couple of minutes to answer.

"Sorry that's all the time I have for you guys, anything else please contact my assistant for any future appointment".

Rafael and Kurt left Pannel's office convinced that the Senator was hiding something, they needed to dig more into his personal life going back to 1961.

Next Thursday will be Thanksgiving dinner at Kurt's house, Yolanda bought a great Spanish wine, it's called "Marques del Riscal" good for any type of meat, Rafael have been thinking about Cuba a lot lately, all those people that have not enjoyed a good meal for a while, rationing have being enforced since the early 70's, a good answer that Socialism does not work.

While Rafael was at his office putting together information that they have gather, Kurt showed up.

"Rafael, I received a message from the warden where Ruzzo is, he wants to talk to us ASAP".

"Do you know why?" Rafael asked Kurt.

"No, but we can find out as soon as possible, I will call the prison where he is and set up a phone interview".

"Great Kurt, call me when you have the warden on the phone".

Kurt went back to his office and called the prison in Alabama.

The warden answered the phone.

"Agent Kurt, I was about to call you, inmate Ruzzo was stabbed yesterday by another inmate, he is in ICU at a Birmingham hospital".

"But warden wasn't Ruzzo supposed to be in protective custody?"

"Yes, but we had a breach of security, we are investigating, this might be an inside job".

"Yes, I will say maybe one of your guards let that inmate in so he could stab Ruzzo".

Kurt responded.

"That's what we are investigating, will keep you posted".

The warden said.

Rafael was getting into Kurt's office, when he gave him the bad news.

"Ruzzo was stabbed yesterday he is in ICU; the warden will keep us posted".

"Wasn't he in .... Kurt stopped him and said.

"Yes, he was in protective custody, I am certain that a guard gave access to the prisoner who stabbed Ruzzo ".

"I'll tell what Kurt, we better keep an eye on Willie, he might be next, first Jim Donner had murdered them Mary and her boyfriend were beaten now Ruzzo is stabbed, did they get the guy?".

"They got him, the warden is also investigating if there might be an inside connection, meaning a prison guard".

Kurt said.

It was not until Friday that the warden called Kurt about Ruzzo.

"Agent Kurt, Ruzzo is out of danger, he is being moved to a private room, we have a police officer assign to guard his room 24 hours, will keep you posted".

Kurt asked the warden to let him know when they can question Ruzzo.

"when the doctor attending him gives me the okay, I will call you immediately". The warden said to Kurt.

The weekend went real fast, Rafael and Yolanda enjoyed a car ride thru North Georgia, new foliage, nice temperature, they were preparing for Thanksgiving the first time for Rafael, he have to give a lot of thanks to this country specially the Lynnards family for opening their home to him, he was also blessed to have meet Yolanda an exquisite woman, gentle but at the same time strong, intelligent and a beautiful woman inside and out.

Early Monday morning after doing their usual jogging Rafael and Yolanda headed to their office, it was around 8:00am, arriving Kurt immediately summoned Rafael to his office.

"Good morning Rafael, I just received a phone call from det. Jerry at the APD, there is an informant that have some information about Jim Donner's murder, he wants us to question him".

"Great news, how fast can we do it". Rafael answered.

"We can do it this afternoon, the informant is not going anywhere, he is in the Fulton Co. jail awaiting a hearing for theft".

"I am ready, bet you this guy will tell us about somebody else involved is Donner's murder".

Rafael was certain that his prediction will come true.

Rafael and Kurt arrived at the Fulton Co. jail around 4:00pm, Jerry was already there, they walked to a large reception area where the informant was, his name is Bryan Delany, 25 years old from Cartersville Ga. He had been an informant for 1 year bringing positive results to the APD.

"Bryan, this are agents Rafael and Kurt from the GBI, they would like you to tell them about the information you gave concerning Jim Donner's murder".

Jerry asked Bryant. Bryan immediately said yes. "Bryan, what is the information you have, and please be as detailed as possible". Kurt asked Bryan.

"Well you know, there was this lady, you know, her name is Cynthia Corbin, you know she had an affair with Jim, so she decided to fall in love with him, I don't, know, Jim was a jerk, you know, somebody told me she killed him".

Bryan said.

Everybody in the room remained quiet for a moment.

Them Rafael entered the conversation.

"Bryan are you sure, you trust the person who gave you the information, we have proof that maybe somebody else might have committed the crime".

"Listen man, as Jerry said, you know, I am good on my sources, you know, if you don't want to believe me that's your problem, you know".

Rafael, Kurt and Jerry move away from Bryan, them Kurt asked Jerry.

"Jerry, didn't forensic found Alex fingerprints and not Cynthia's at the crime scene?"

"Yes, but I believe Bryan, he needs my help in the hearing before the judge, certainly he will not lie".

Jerry answer back.

"I also believe Bryan, now we have to determined how Alex prints were found at the scene, I might have a theory".

Rafael commented and proposed his theory.

"I think that Cynthia killed him and them in a moment of desperation she called Alex and asked him to help her out, Alex rushed to the scene to clean the mess and left some prints at the scene".

That's my theory, Rafael said.

Jerry and Kurt looked at each other, them ponder for a moment, Kurt said to Rafael.

"Rafael, it makes sense, Alex is more in love with Cynthia than she is with him, he will do whatever she asked him to do".

Them Jerry asked.

"How are we going to handle this, you guys are investigating a couple of cold cases, I am investigating a recent one, I know there is a link to both situations, so we have to share as much information as possible".

"Rafael and I concur, we can do a joint questioning session with both of them, by that more information can filter to all our cases".

Kurt said.

Rafael, Kurt and Jerry agreed; they will wait until after Thanksgiving to do the interview.

When Rafael and Kurt arrived at the GBI headquarters they immediately went to the director's office and updated him with the latest information.

"You guys are doing an excellent job, please stay with it and you will see positive results".

The Director said. Rafael and Kurt went to their respective office to organize all the information they had gather in the past week, it was going to be a short week.

That afternoon Rafael arrived at the apartment Yolanda was already there, Rafael suggested to have Chinese, Yolanda approved, it had been a while since they had Chinese food.

"Hong Kong" Chinese restaurant is not to far from their apartment, they had a table closed to the door facing a beautiful garden.

Rafael started the conversation.

"Yolanda, we interview an APD informant and he implicated Cynthia Corbin with Jim Donner's murder".

"What, that's amazing, she looked so down to earth every time we met her conversation was centered on her kids".

"It looks like she was having an affair with Jim Donner, maybe she demanded to divorce his wife, he said no and that's when Cynthia took her revenge, we cannot confirm that, but it looks that way".

Rafael responded.

"Well, we'll see what happens, by the way the Lynnard's are also going to the Thanksgiving dinner this Thursday at Kurt's house".

Yolanda reminded Rafael.

"You know Yolanda after this week we should do a "Pernil" (pork shoulder) with the regular black beans, "mariquitas" (fried bananas) and invite the Lynnard's and Kurt and his family, can we do that?"

"Yes Rafael, that's a great idea".

Thursday is here, temperature in the 40's, to cold for Rafael, but what the heck he is living the best years of his life, jogging at 7am, breakfast and getting ready for Kurt's famous Thanksgiving dinner, he was mesmerize with Yolanda, she could run 4 miles every morning, him maybe 2, she looked so fit, ready and sharp.

Around 4pm Rafael and Yolanda left their apartment for Kurt's home, they arrived about 20min later, the Lynnard's were already there so was the Director and his wife, Rafael was surrounded by good friends.

After some drinks before dinner they sat down and immediately Rafael got up and made a beautiful comment.

"To all my friends here specially the lynnard's who I consider my family, thank you for given me a chance to procced with my life, may God bless you all, and to my beautiful Yolandita, te quiero!(I love you)" .Kurt gave thanks for a blessed year, and after that everybody shouted "Cheers!" The conversation at the table was mainly personal, not work related, Rafael made some comments about the turkey, "It needs some garlic", everybody laughed. "Rafael, are you criticizing my dinner? I thought you were my friend".

"No Kurt, just making a comment, you know how Cubans are, we talk to much, I am full, the Turkey was esquisito. Everybody laughed. It was a great dinner. ***

CHAPTER 14

"In truth, men speak to much of danger".

Jose Marti

After a relax week Rafael and Kurt returned to their office facing new challenges, Jerry from the APD called early and left a message for Kurt, he wanted to let him know that they found new evidence linking Cynthia with the murder of Jim Donner.

Kurt immediately placed a call to Jerry.

"Jerry, I understand your forensic group found new evidence, what is it?"

"After I heard the statement from Bryan the informant, we went back and looked at some items we pick up at the Donner's house, there was this jewelry box and after we examined it for finger prints guest what, Cynthia's finger prints appeared, I don't know how we missed that".

"Jerry, it happens, the important thing is that now we have proof of Cynthia's participation in the murder of Jim Donner".

Them Rafael asked Jerry.

"Jerry, were you able to go back to Alex Corbin house and find any connection with the cigarettes butts and any package of Marlboro at his home?"

"No Rafael, we are planning to make a more detail search by the middle of this week".

"Will you keep us posted?" Rafael asked Jerry.

"Off course, I will".

In the meantime, they needed to call Mary in Macon, she needs to give us a follow up on her situation with the phone calls she had received, Kurt placed the call.

"Mary this is Kurt, Rafael and I were wondering if you had received any more of those weird phone calls?"

"No Kurt, it stopped about a week after I spoke to you guys, it is indeed weird".

"By the way how is your boyfriend doing?"

"He is fine, he left the hospital a week ago, still hurting some, those sons of bitches really did get to him, by the way how is my Cuban love?"

"Your Cuban love is fine, making preparation for his weeding".

"Please tell him that I send my love".

"I will Mary, by the way Willie is in jail in Arizona, soon to be extradited to Georgia".

"Great news, when you talk to him tell him to go to Hell".

"I will Mary Goodbye".

"Rafael, I think Mary is in love with you".

"Okay, maybe in my next life I will marry her".

It's the first week of December, a hearing is schedule for the 14'th of December a Wednesday, for Alex and Cynthia Corbin, Alex will be charged with conspiracy to aid and support a criminal enterprise under the RICO act, conspiracy against public officials and for both first degree murder charges, Rafael and Kurt have been invited to attend the hearing.

Rafael and Kurt were preparing several questions that will be given to Mr. Pannel in according with his instructions, them he will forward those questions to Senator Springdale.

"Kurt, can we issue a subpoena to the Senator so he can appear in person and answer the question we are giving to Pannel?"

"Rafael, I have to check with our Director, it is a sticky situation, the Senator is the highest-ranking member in his party, he holds a lot of influence".

"According to the US constitution nobody is above the law".

Rafael reply.

"Right, unless you are Senator Springdale".

After Kurt answer back to Rafael he made it to the Director's office, he was having a meeting, so his assistance suggested to come back in an hour.

Rafael made it back to Yolanda's office.

"Yolanda, are you hungry?"

"Yes, what about Kurt?"

"He'll be back in an hour, took off to some personal stuff, we are having a meeting with the Director in an hour, so let's grab something fast".

Yolanda and Rafael made to a pizza place not to far from their office, at that time Yolanda asked Rafael.

"Rafael, baby have you thought about our wedding day?"

"Off course, we are in December, let's plan on May 30th, that was the wedding day of my parents".

Yolanda was static, then asked Rafael again.

"Have you thought about how many kids we'll have?"

"Yolanda I was the only child, always wished to have a lot of brothers and sisters, how about 10".

Yolanda almost fainted, she suddenly lost her appetite.

"Yolandita, what happened, are you all right, maybe we should have 20 kids, will that make you happier?"

Yolanda them knew that Rafael was pulling her leg, they both laughed and continue eating their pizza.

As soon as Yolanda and Rafael made back Kurt was waiting, he said to Rafael.

"The Director wants to talk to us; we should go his office now".

"Let's go I have all the questions for Pannel here".

"It's not about the Senator, it's something else".

"Kurt you sound to serious".

"It sounds serious Rafael".

They went up the elevator to the 5th floor where the Director's office is located, he was waiting for them.

"Guys, I have a mission for both of you, since Alex Corbin is still an agent of the GBI they want the bureau to assign a couple of agents to escort him and his wife to his hearing, now Rafael I will deputize you so can carry a weapon".

"No problem sir, we are ready, I understand is next week".

Rafael said.

"Yes Rafael, now Kurt you wanted to ask me something, sorry I was in a meeting".

"Yes sir, how can we get Senator Springdale into our office so he can answer some questions?"

"What happened with his lawyer, did he answer any of your

questions?"

"He wants us to give him written questions so he can forward it to the Senator, and them they can determine which one they would answer".

"It does not sound good, we need him to answer the questions directly, I will consult with our legal dept. to find a solution to this matter".

"Great sir, thank you".

Both Kurt and Rafael left with a smile on their face. Rafael

The day to pick up Alex and Cynthia Corbin had arrived, Rafael and Kurt were accompanied by Det. Jerry Sanders from the APD, they took both prisoners into a van that was waiting outside, the wore bullet proof vest in case any problem develop.

The van took 15min to arrive at the courthouse, first Jerry came out them Rafael and last with the Prisoners was Kurt, moments after the Corbin's got out of the van a fast car approach the group suddenly there were shots, BANG,BANG, Rafael that was standing Behind Jerry hit the ground took his revolver out and started firing, Jerry was hit in the leg, Kurt in his abdomen, he was bleeding profusive, a couple of shots hit Alex, Cynthia was not hit, it was done in 2 min, there were some officers in the area, they assisted Kurt and called for assistance immediately.

Rafael check Jerry first, but he told him to check on Kurt first.

"Kurt my brother, hang in their help is on the way, I will put pressure on your wound, you'll be fine".

The ambulance arrived in 3min, Jerry was assisted on the spot by the medics, Kurt was transported to Grady Hospital in Atlanta not to far away from the courthouse, another ambulance took Alex, he was in bad shape with wounds to his abdomen and head.

Cynthia was taken back to the Fulton Co. jail, with 24 hours surveillance, the hearing was postponed.

About 3 miles away the car that was used on the shootout was found, after checking the serial numbers it came back as an stolen car that was taken 2 days ago in Marietta, GA, they found some blood, so it seems one of the perpetrators is wounded, immediately they check the hospitals, an order to report the APD if any wounded person was treated, the hunt was on.

The GBI director was notify of the incident, he advises Yolanda, and both made it to Grady Hospital where Kurt and Jerry were treated, Kurt's wife also arrived sobbing immediately embracing Yolanda.

"Any information on who did this?"

The director asked several agents that were present.

Nobody could give him an answer.

"The only thing we have director is that there were 3 shooters, all white, and young, according to a police officer that was close to the incident".

"let's find those criminals, I want them apprehended ASAP".

At that moment the doctor that was treating Kurt appeared at the waiting room where family and friends of agent Kurt were waiting.

"Any family member of agent Kurt present?"

Hearing the doctor Kurt's wife rushed to see the doctor.

"Doctor, I am Kurt's wife, please give me some good news".

"Agent Kurt was shoot on the left side, missing vital organs, he should be fine, if everything goes as planned, he should be back in action in 2 weeks".

By that time Rafael, Yolanda and the Director hear the good news, they started to hug each other, it was a nightmare, thank God is passing.

Alex was not doing so good, put into induce coma to control inflammation of the brain, the bullet might have hit several nerves in his brain causing some king of paralysis, the doctor attending him will make an assessment in 24 hours.

Jerry was doing fine just a superficial wound, with 5 stiches in his leg he walked out of the hospital on his own.

Now the hunt was on, 3 young white men, some evidence was found in the stolen vehicle, fingerprints, a note containing the details of the transfer from the   Fulton Co. Jail to the Court House in downtown Atlanta, it's was a daring attack.

Rafael stayed at the hospital for a while, Kurt was transferred to a regular room later that day, his wife, and Yolanda were also there, the director left earlier, he wanted to be involved in the plans for the apprehension of the criminals.

For the next two weeks Rafael will have to work alone, maybe even more, after Kurt leave the hospital, he might need some rest, Rafael needs to plan for the next phase of the investigation without Kurt.

Yolanda and Rafael made it to their apartment around 10pm, Kurt's wife stayed longer, an APD officer was assigned to guard the room 24 hours.

"Rafael you are so lucky not to be wounded in the attack, what are your plans now?"

Yolanda asked Rafael.

"At least for the next 2 weeks put everything in order and see what direction we might take concerning a couple of interviews that Kurt and I had planned".

"You mean the Senator, and who else?"

"I want to ask Cynthia if she has any idea who the shooters were, she might know, she might be more involved with this group than Alex was".

Rafael said.

"Do you need any help from me?"

Yolanda asked Rafael.

"Let me figure out where we are in the investigation, but yes I do need your help".

The following day Rafael arrived at his office around 6am, first he checked for his messages there was a note from the director he wanted to see him this morning, Rafael called the director's office he answered the phone and asked Rafael to go up to his office now.

"Good morning Rafael, are you doing okay?"

"Yes sir, thank God, still worry about Kurt".

"Rafael the reason I asked you in is to see if you need me to assign a new partner for the next 4 weeks until Kurt recuperate and start his daily task".

"Director thank you, but I think I can handle the investigation until Kurt get back, now can I use Yolanda to assist me if the need arises?"

"Yes, you can use her to help you in your investigation".

"Thank you, director by the way any luck on the request for the Senator to appear in our office for questioning?"

Rafael asked the director.

"I am supposed to check with our legal dept. today, I will keep you posted".

"Thank you, sir,".

And by that Rafael made back to his office, he needed to call Jerry so he could arrange a meeting with Cynthia Corbin, but he just remember that Jerry had taken the rest of the week off, now he needed to concentrate on   follow up phone calls and put together the questions he will need to ask the Senator when the approval for his interview is made. Rafael's agenda was full, at least for the rest of the week.

At lunch time Rafael and Yolanda made it to Grady Hospital where Kurt is, upon entering the room they saw Kurt's wife reading the latest news to Kurt who was sitting and enjoying a big glass of milk.

"Mi hermano Kurt" (my brother Kurt), how do you feel?"

"I feel fine, should be out of here in a week, how are handling the situation?"

"I am trying to concentrate on the interview with the senator and also looking forward to ask Cynthia if she knows who might be behind the shooting, and off course Willie's extradition".

Rafael said.

"Has the director offered you extra help while I am out?" "Yes, but I said that none is needed, if I need extra help Yolanda can assist me in a couple of areas".

Rafael answer, Yolanda and Rafael sat for a while them departed promising that they will be back tomorrow.

A week has passed since the shooting occurred, Alex is still in ICU, Kurt will be leaving the hospital tomorrow and Jerry was back at his desk in the APD.

Rafael left a message for Jerry a week ago, immediately after Jerry came back to his office, he called Rafael back.

"Rafael, good morning this is Jerry you left a message, what can I do for you?"

"First, how are you doing?"

"Doing great, just a scratch, how is Kurt doing?"

"He is leaving the hospital tomorrow, should be back to work in about 2 weeks".

"Jerry, I wanted to see if it is possible for me to interview Cynthia Corbin and ask her about the shooting, can you arrange that?"

"I 'll try Rafael, first I have to call her attorney and arrange it, I will get on it this morning".

"Thank you, Jerry keep me posted".

Immediately after Rafael hang up with Jerry a message was given to him, it was from the warden in the Alabama prison where Ruzzo is in, he wanted to talk to me about the shooting.

Rafael placed a call to the warden.

"Sir, this Rafael with the GBI, I understand that Ruzzo might have some information about the shooting that occurred here in Atlanta a couple of weeks ago".

"Yes, he wanted me to call you guys about that matter, I will call you back when we get Ruzzo to a safe place where he can talk to you"

"Thank you, sir, I'll be waiting in my office".

Today Rafael might get some information as to who was involved in the shooting.

About 30 min later the warden called Rafael back.

"Rafael, I have Ruzzo here in a safe office let me put him on".

Them the warden handed the phone to Ruzzo.

"Mr. Rafael, I might have some important information about the people that did the shooting in Atlanta".

"Okay, let me hear it".

"Not so fast Rafi, first I need to go someplace else, maybe on a witness protection plan or something similar, if I stay here in prison, they will kill me, they already tried once, and I know they will try again".

"Ruzzo, I do not have the authority to make you that offer, I can ask the director, but it will take a while".

Rafael answer back to Ruzzo.

"I'll wait but tell the warden to put me in a real safe place".

"I'll tell the warden, by this afternoon we'll have the answer".

Rafael was certain that an arrangement can be set up for Ruzzo, but he needed the approval from the director.

Rafael explained the situation to the director, he immediately picked up the phone and called the Governor's office, the director needed a written agreement between Georgia and Alabama for the transfer of Ruzzo, but first they needed a signed agreement from Ruzzo and his lawyer confirming the transfer.

It took more than a day to get the transfer approved, but finally Rafael can call Ruzzo and give him the news.

Rafael called the warden, who passed the phone to Ruzzo.

"Ruzzo, everything is set, tomorrow morning 2 agents from the GBI will be there to pick you up, you should be in our bureau by late afternoon, after you arrive we will tell you the condition of our agreement, don't worry you will be safe, and that I promise you".

Rafael them hang up and started to laugh loudly, he them called Yolanda, she arrived and saw Rafael with a big smile.

"Yolanda, this afternoon Ruzzo will be here, has information about the shooting".

"Rafael that's wonderful, call Kurt right now".

"Already did, he was jumping with joy".

Rafael continued.

"Yolanda are you willing to be present at the interview?"

"Off course Rafael, who else will be present?"

"The director said he will be here, plus Jerry from the APD".

The year was almost over, it was the second week of December,

CELSO FERNANDEZ

soon 1977 will be here. ***

CHAPTER 14

"It's fatal to enter any war without the will to win it"

Gen. Douglas MacArthur

Cynthia Corbin was sitting in her lonely cell wondering what went wrong, her personal life was in shambles, her husband is close to death, she will loose her kids and all the material things she has accumulated thru the years lying and helping a group of law breakers, only saying the true will save some of it.

"Mrs. Corbin your lawyer is here, he will like to speak with you".

The officer at the jail said.

"Yes please, I will be ready in a minute".

Cynthia combed her hair, clean her eyes of constant crying and prepared mentally for her lawyer.

"Cynthia, I received a phone call today from officer Jerry Sanders of the APD and agent Rafael Chaquet from the GBI, they would like to question you about the shootout

that happened 3 weeks ago, you don't have to say yes, so it's up to you".

"Yes, I'll meet with them, I want to come clear, they will pay".

"Them I will arrange it". Cynthia's lawyer said.

In the meantime, Willie's extradition has been delayed, due to some legal hurdle, Rafael spoke with the Sheriff of Maricopa County, everything is set for this week he said, finally Willie will be here.

The director called Rafael and said that the Senator is refusing to appear in person.

"We are trying, Rafael we are going to get him here sooner or later".

The director angrily said.

"Director, the Senator, Willie Donner and the mysterious man named Ernie Callan or Silas are the missing pieces of both Alicia and Roseanne cases, by the way Director will you be present when we interview Ruzzo tomorrow?"

Rafael asked the director.

"If you want me there, yes, who else will be there?"

"It will be you, Jerry from the APD, Yolanda and me".

"Great Rafael, let's get ready"

"I am already ready, as a matter of fact more than ready, I want to get those jerks that harmed my partner".

Willie arrived at the Charlie Brown airport west of Atlanta, that airport is used for delivering prisoners moving thru Georgia, officers from APD, GBI and the Marshall's office were there to greet him.

Wille is in big trouble, first he been charged in federal court for transporting a minor between states lines, secondly, he is wanted in Georgia for arm robbery that occurred in Jasper co., and lastly the GBI.

Wednesday morning second week of December, temperature in the 30's, no jogging this morning for Rafael, instead he put on a jacket that looks like he bought it in Alaska, Yolanda also was ready but she   decided to jog this morning, she takes care of her physical appearance and her health.

Around 9:30am they left for the GBI headquarters, Ruzzo and the director were already there, the director introduce himself.

"Mr. Ruzzo, I am the GBI director, agent Rafael another agent and myself will be questioning you, Rafael will be here any minute now".

Ruzzo sat back and asked for a cigarette, he was ready to talk.

Rafael and Yolanda made it in, they sat next to the director facing Ruzzo.

Immediately made a comment.

"Well at least we won't have ugly people in our room only, a beautiful woman is present, Rafi no offense".

Rafael was fuming, but Yolanda showed a grin in her face.

Rafael started the conversation.

"Ruzzo, you wanted to talk to us about the shooting the other day, as you know my partner Kurt was wounded and that really makes me mad".

"Rafi, I can give you names, addresses and motives of the people involved, but since my parolee hearing was cancel I need assurance that I am put in some kind of protective custody, if I go back to prison my days will be counted, I want to live".

Them the director enters the conversation.

"Ruzzo, that have been taken care off, after you give us the information a team of agents will take you to an undisclosed location, only people that are present plus agent Kurt will know where you will be".

Ruzzo started smiling, he was comfortable with the arrangement, he asked for a writing pad and a pen.

"Okay you guys what I am going to write in this pad are the names and locations of not only the people who participated in the shooting but also people connected with our organization, you will be surprise when you see

the names, now I need to disappear from the world, these people are real bad people".

Ruzzo started writing, Rafael and the director were anxious to read the name, will they recognize any name?

"Here it is, 25 names, their locations and rank within the organization, please do not take any action until I have disappeared".

First the director read the list, a couple of names look familiar, them Rafael saw the list, immediately he saw a name, Ernie Silas, that's the guy we have been looking for.

"Ruzzo, there is a name in the list, Jim Silas, there is no address for him, do you know where we can locate him?"

"No, he is a mysterious man, the only thing that I can tell you is that this guy after serving time in prison disappeared, good luck finding him".

"Okay Ruzzo, you have done a great job, now is our turn outside 2 agents are waiting for you, they will take you to the location we promised you, they will be with you for a while, the Marshall's office is also involved in your relocation, do not try to communicate with any family member or close friend, do not do anything illegal or try to escape, that will void our agreement and back to prison you will go, understand?"

"Yes sir, I understand".

Ruzzo responded to the director, he was in heaven, no more prison walls for him.

After Ruzzo left, the director turned to Rafael and made a comment.

"Rafael, I will set a meeting tomorrow with members of the FBI, APD and the Marshall's office, this list contains names that they might be interested also, we can also set up the parameters to proceed, so get ready for tomorrow".

"I will sir, one name is very important to our cold case investigation, Ernie Silas, we need to find out more about this character".

"Rafael maybe the FBI might have some information on him".

"I will make a comment tomorrow, maybe the FBI can help us out".

Rafael said.

Rafael and Yolanda went back to their offices, he needed to be prepared for the meeting tomorrow, the director asked him to call detective Jerry and inform him about tomorrow.

On the way back to their apartment Yolanda and Rafael stopped by Kurt's house, he was sitting in a recliner watching tv, they sat next to him and started talking about today's meeting.

"Kurt, Ruzzo gave us a list of names, to be precise 25, including the 4 shooters and guest what Jim Silas, he doesn't know where he is, at the meeting tomorrow I will ask the FBI to help us locate him, they might have some information, he disappeared after serving time in prison".

"Rafael, how I wish to be in that meeting".

"Kurt, just relax I will gather all the information from the meeting and give it to you".

Rafael and Yolanda stayed for a little while them left, on the way home they stopped for dinner, Italian.

Rafael arrived at his office around 7am, the director was already there, he mentioned to Rafael that the meeting was set for 10am, plenty of time to prepare, agent Roscoe wills from the FBI, Robert Adams from the Marshall's office, Jerry Sanders from the APD and also Peter moon from the Marshall's fugitive squad.

"Director, I want to find out about Ernie Silas, is he the same as Ernie Callas in Costa Rica, that is one of the main pieces of our puzzle, we need to find out where he is".

Everybody arrived on time, they sat down and started the meeting.

"Gentlemen, we are meeting to here today to disseminate the information that inmate Ruzzo has provided, it contain the names of 25 individuals that belong to a criminal enterprise based in Georgia, of those 25 names, of those names 4 participated in the shooting of one of my agent and another agent that was going to be arraign on several charges, his wife was also present, she was not wounded, agent Rafael Chaquet who is here was not wounded either, he had time to shoot back at the perpetrators maybe wounding one of them".

The director kept talking.

"Between our agencies we can coordinate the capture of the mentioned names, first we have to stablish a plan, maybe agent Moon with the fugitive squad can explain the method used by his agency in capturing fugitive criminals, agent Peter Moon the floor is yours".

"Thank you director Carlisle, the first step is to determined if any of those names have an standing arrest warrant, legally that makes it easier, after capture what agency will take possession of the capture criminal, example APD might have several names in that list that match pending arrest warrants, in the case of the shooters if no arrest warrant is pending the GBI will initiate a criminal file charging them with attempted murder, but we have to find out the status of each one of them first".

Agent Moon finished his presentation.

After almost 2 hours the meeting was over, they took the list to their respective agencies to determine the next step, a plan must be set up nobody beside the participants needed to know the name of the inmate that provided the list.

"Director have you heard from the agents guarding Ruzzo?"

Rafael asked the director.

"Yes, they did call me immediately after arriving at their destination".

"Great, Ruzzo gave us very important information, he needs to be kept safe". Rafael said.

"I agree Rafael, he will be kept safe".

After a week all the participants in the first meeting met again, this time with detailed information about each one of the names on the list, the majority of them had outstanding warrants, except three one Deputy Sheriff in Jasper Co, another Sheriff in McIntosh Co and off course Jim Silas, it seems the Mr. Silas have disappeared from the face of the earth, no state, federal or any other data available.

"Director Carlisle, we have updated the pending arrest warrants on all the individuals on the list, and obtained the necessary warrants for the Sheriffs mentioned in the list, next step is to set up a date and coordinate with the different departments how many officers and agents we might need for this operation, it will be one of the biggest operation that law enforcement will conduct in our state, we might need several groups of officers/agents to articulate a precise and positive capture, they are in different parts of Georgia from Dahlonega to Columbus".

At that time agent Moon put up a chart as to where everyone is located.

"As you all can see we 8 individuals located in Cobb, DeKalb, Fulton and Gwinnett counties, 1 individuals in Jasper county, 1 individual in McIntosh county, 3 in the Columbus area, 4 in Albany, 5 in the Savannah area and 3 more in the Macon area, this requires a massive participation from each department".

The meeting was over, it took 4 hours but the operation was define, each department including local authorities pledge a certain amount of officers, excluding Jasper co and McIntosh co, since both individuals in those counties were law enforcement officers they did not want to have any leak concerning the arrest.

The operation was named" Catching Birds", the date was set also, December 21, 1976.

The GBI selected the four individuals that participated in the shootout the wounded agent Kurt, Rafael oversaw one group, they went to Cobb co., the director

took charge of the group that went to Gwinnett co., the other 2 group of agents were assigned to apprehend the individuals in DeKalb and Fulton Co., they were assisted by officers from the various counties.

At 3:00am on the 21th of December with temperature in the 30'th all group off agents and officers gathered at various assigned positions, before 6:00 am they were inside the individuals houses, with warrants in their hands, the operation was a success no major problems, a couple of scuffle, the deputy Sheriff in Jasper co. fled but was capture 4 hours later near Valdosta Ga.

As soon as the operation was over and the 4 individuals that participated in the wounding of Kurt were apprehended Rafael called Kurt and said.

"Mision Cumplida (mission accomplished) Kurt". ***

CHAPTER 15

"Truth always ends by Victory; it's not unassailable, but invincible"

Ignatius of Loyola

The end of 1976 was almost here, it has been an interesting year, after the operation that nabbed 24 of the 25 persons in the list provided by Ruzzo Rafael was now involved in three persons of interest, Willie Donner, he was already in Georgia being held at the Federal Detention Center in Lovejoy Georgia awaiting for arraignment on several charges, Cynthia Corbin being held at the Fulton County Jail and off course Senator Springdale, no word on when he will appear in our offices for an interview.

Rafael and Yolanda were already making plans to celebrate New Year's Eve, the Lynnard's were hosting a get together, they asked Yolanda if she will bring some Latin music, Yolanda agreed.

"Please don't tell Rafael about me bringing some music, I am planning to get some Cuban music so Rafael can feel at home".

Yolanda said to Charles Lynnard.

"Great, I hope the music don't make him to melancholic".

Charles said.

Roscoe Will with the FBI called the GBI director to congratulate him on the way the operation was carried out and to remind him that Willie will be available for questioning in the next couple of weeks.

"We are anxious to interview Wille, thank you for your cooperation".

Rafael arrived at Kurt's house early in the morning, he needed to brief him on the operation that apprehended the four shooters, also to let him know about Willie, he was already in Georgia.

"Kurt, I understand that you will be back in a couple of weeks".

"Yes Rafael, ready to make those people life miserable".

"I am with you".

Rafael smiling responded.

New Years eve was here, the Lynnard's prepared a delicious dinner, they also invited besides Yolanda and Rafael another 3 couple plus some friends of their kids.

People began to arrive around 8:00pm, the kids already had their music full blast it was going to be fun.

Mrs. Lynnard announce that dinner was ready, and when everyone was sitting she began with a prayer, them everybody began eating, ham with pineapple, mashed potatoes with bacon, asparagus, a Caesar salad and off course a good wine, after dinner around 10:00 pm they began to dance, the celebration was at full force.

Mrs. Lynnard asked Yolanda if she had any Cuban music, she said yes, "go ahead and put it on", Mrs. Lynnard said, Immediately Yolanda grab a Beny More record, a song caught her eye, COME FUE (How it was).

She put the song in the record player, called Rafael and started dancing, you could see Rafael's eyes, tear was coming out, his mind was not in Georgia, but at the same time he looked at Yolanda and began singing;

"Como Fue, no se decirte que paso, no se explicarte que paso pero de ti me enamore"

(How it was, don't know what happened, I don't know how to explain it to you, but I fell in love with you)

Them he gave her a soft kiss, everybody was looking at them and a big applause fill the room, at that time midnight came.

HAPPY NEW YEAR!!!!! HAPPY 1977, a new year for Yolanda and Rafael, a new year that will bring hope and a final solution to the pending cases.

"Alicia and Roseanne, I will promise you that we will find your killer, I will promise".

Lifting his glass and almost crying Rafael said that.

The first 2 weeks of 1977 were a little quiet, Alex Corbin was out of danger but he probably will not be able to walk again, Cynthia his wife will be arraign next week at the Georgia Superior Court of Murder on the First Degree, the Georgia Attorney General will be easy on the charges if she give information about the structure of the Georgia group associated with Dixie Mafia, meanwhile the four shooters have been identified, they hold an extensive criminal record dating back to 1960, still we are looking for Ernie Silas.

It was January 18, 1977, after the morning jogging Rafael made it to his office, a big surprise awaited him.

"Rafael, I am back".

It was the voice of Kurt, 100% ready.

Rafael immediately hug him and welcome him.

"You have taken to many days off, let's get to work".

Rafael laughing said.

"Si senor", (yes sir), Kurt said.

"Where do we begin Kurt, Willie, Cynthia or the Senator?"

"Let's take an easy one first, Cynthia she should be pissed because of what happened to her husband Alex".

"All right let's call Jerry at the APD to arrange a meeting with her".

Said Rafael.

Kurt called Jerry who was emotional elated to hear Kurt's voice.

"Okay Kurt, give a couple of days to arrange it, and welcome back".

"Thank you, Jerry keep us posted".

At that moment Yolanda showed up at Kurt's office welcoming him with a big hug and saying that they missed you and your family at the New Year's Eve gathering.

"I understand it was great, you even had some Cubano music for Rafael, what kind?"

"It was mainly Boleros; Rafael became very melancholic".

Said Yolanda.

"Rafael, think about the positive time in Cuba, you start thinking about the bad time you experience and them you will lose it, you are in the US now and we love you specially Yolanda".

With a smile in his face said Kurt.

"I know Kurt, but I can not forget the atrocities that the government of Cuba have done to its citizens".

Later that day the director summoned Rafael and Kurt, he had some good news, the Senator agreed to be interview at our offices, it will be next week, he is taking a week vacation I think he is going to Panama or Costa Rica. "Costa Rica?"

Rafael immediately thought, Ernie Callas.

"Director, Costa Rica is where this fellow Ernie Callas lives or had a residence there, I find this Senator trip very suspicious". Said Rafael.

"I know Rafael, but we don't have any authority to stop him or question him about his trip, beside the Senator is 70 years old and his movement will be monitored by our embassy and the Costa Rica Government".

Kurt got into the conversation.

"Director, can the US Embassy in Costa Rica advise us when he leaves for the US?"

"Kurt, I'll make sure of that".

Before the day was over Kurt received a phone call from the Marshall's office, the Lovejoy Detention Center where Willie is being held is having a prisoners riot, Willie is not in a segregated area so they are trying to locate him, he might be in trouble, will keep you posted.

Kurt rushed to Rafael's office, he was about to leave, when he received the news of the riot, Rafael and Kurt immediately called the FBI office in Atlanta and spoke to special agent Roscoe Will.

"Mr. Will have you heard about the situation in Lovejoy Detention Center?"

"Yes Kurt, the prisoners have a list of demands, we are trying to find Willie Donner but to no avail, it seems he was taken to another cell by a group of inmates, we will keep on looking, our office will notify your agency of any news".

"Thank you, we'll be waiting, this guy Willie is very important to our investigation".

After hanging the phone Kurt turn to Rafael and said.

"Rafael, we might have a problem with Willie, they can not locate him, ha was taken by a group of inmates".

"Are the authorities going in to stop the riot?"

Said Rafael.

"It's a very delicate situation, they first have to meet with the prisoners committee, then they will decide after that the course of action".

Kurt explained to Rafael.

"Are we staying here and wait for their call, or anything else is needed?"

"No Rafael, there is nothing else we can do, so let's go home, the Marshall's office has my home phone as soon as I have more information, I will call you and let you know".   "I will wait for your call".

By that they both departed to their homes, hoping that they can find Willie.

Rafael and Yolanda settle for a quiet dinner, turn on the tv, the Love Boat was on Yolanda made a comment.

"You know Rafael, we should take a short cruise for our honeymoon, maybe to the Caribbean, what do you think".

Rafael responded.

"Yolanda with you to the end of the world".

Around 11:00pm they went sleep, but 45 min later the phone rang it was Kurt.

"Rafael sorry to bother you so late, they found Wille he is a little bang up but fine, he wants to talk to us as soon as possible".

"Kurt, great news let's set it up as soon as possible".

After that phone call Rafael slept like a log.

Back at their office the following morning Rafael and Kurt began to plan the next step now that Willie was fine, also the interview with Cynthia is going to happen in the next day or so, a busy week is in front of Rafael and Kurt.

Around 11:00 am Jerry called.

"Kurt, Cynthia is ready to be interview, either late today or tomorrow morning".

Kurt answered right away.

"Today, the sooner the better, what time?"

"Any time after 2:00 pm". Said Jerry.

"We'll be there at 3:00 pm, is that okay?" Kurt responded.

"Great Kurt, see you guys them".

Them Kurt turn to Rafael and said.

"Rafael, 3:00 pm interview with Cynthia".

"Perfecto", Rafael said enthusiastically.

"Let's concentrate on Cynthia first them we can call the FBI and ask permission to see Willie".

Said Rafael.

Rafael and Kurt arrived at the Fulton Co. Jail around 2:30pm, Jerry arrived 10 min later, they were guided toward the same room they have being using on the last interview, Cynthia arrived precisely at 3:00pm, she looked nice, she is a beautiful woman, her hair was brushed nicely she even put on some makeup.

"Hi Cynthia, you know us, we are here to ask you about the situation that happens around 4 weeks ago, where your husband was shot, or any other information concerning that particular organization". Kurt said.

"Well, I have a lot of information for you guys, these people try to screw me, I had it no nicer lady, to hell with them".

At that moment Cynthia was crying and shouting obscenities, she was mad.

"Cynthia, please relax, we are here to help you, you give us the right information and I promise you we will talk to the District Attorney about your charges".

Kurt enthusiastically said.

"First I don't know who the shooters were".

Rafael interrupted Cynthia he made the following comment.

"Cynthia, we had an operation and grab 25 people connected to the organization, the 4 shooters were captured in that group, sorry go ahead and finish your conversation".

"Shit yes, that makes me really happy, those jerks are mean, they need to be behind bars for a long time".

"Okay, now what information you had for us?"

"Sorry, I am going to give you 4 names associated to the organization, all of them knew Jim Donner, Willie and Ruzzo since the 1960's and even 2 of them went to the same High School as Jim, Jerome Brooks one of the head guys here in Georgia the guy is loaded own several Strip Clubs all over Georgia, I used to perform in one of those clubs when I was 17 years old, Sam Pelling mean person, he handles all the finances of the group, Saul Reading, Robert Sabb and William 'Billy bob' Samins all enforcers".

"Impressive, we'll check and see if any of these guys was caught in the operation last week, anything else?"

Rafael asked Cynthia, he was certain one or maybe more of this name can be linked to Alicia and Roseanne murders.

"Yes, I am sure these guys have inmates connected to the organization; I need to be in a safer place".

At that moment Jerry made a comment.

"Cynthia, everything has been arranged for you to be moved to an isolated place, it all depended on your   information, you did great, this will happen in about an hour".

"Cynthia, we wish you the best, we'll be in touch".

Kurt said, and by that Rafael and Kurt left the Jail, Jerry stayed behind to finalize all the arrangement for Cynthia's move.

Back in their office Rafael and Kurt started to compare the names that Cynthia gave them with names of the persons apprehended in the operation last week. "Rafael, I only see 2 names here on the list that match the names that Cynthia gave us, Saul Reding and William Samins, the rest are not here".

"Can we find out the names of the Strip clubs owned by Jerome Brooks?"

Rafael asked.

"Yes, we can start here in Atlanta, I am pretty sure he owns one here". Said Kurt.

"Strip Club means prostitution, drugs and women slave trade, we might need the help from one or more of our departments".

Rafael meant the departments in the GBI handling those criminal enterprise.

"I will contact the director and ask for his authorization to use them, I know all the heads of those departments they are very dedicated bunch".

Kurt replied to Rafael.

After gathering all pertinent information Rafael and Kurt presented it to the director, asked for guidance and support from the other department in associating several names to their investigation, they were certain that some of those individuals might be connected to the murders of Alicia and Roseanne.

The next interview was with Willie Donner, he was recuperating from a beating at the Lovejoy facility, the FBI had informed Rafael and Kurt that Willie was ready for an interview next Monday, that's four days from today.

in the meantime, they needed to follow up on several individuals that were interview before.

Alex Corbin was still at the prisoners wing of the hospital, he is confine to a wheel chair one of the bullets hit his spinal cord and will not be able to walk again, Rafael and Kurt arrived around noon time, Alex was having lunch they sat next to him and began asking him some questions.

Kurt began the conversation.

"Hello Alex, we just had a meeting with Cynthia this week, she gave us a lot of information that I think will help us in our case".

"You guys know that she might be in danger, right?"

"Yes, we know Alex, we have made arrangement for her safety".

Rafael entered the conversation.

"Alex, I know that officer Jerry Sanders with the APD is handling your case, but can you give us anything else that can tie any individual in the organization with our pending cases?"

"Are you talking about Alicia Roque?"

"Yes, we are". Rafael said.

"Beside Willie and Ruzzo, what other names did Cynthia gave you?"

"She gave us, Jerome Brooks Sam Pelling, Saul Reading, Robert Sabb and William Simins".

After Rafael gave Alex those names he came back and asked him.

"Alex can you give us any information about these guys?"

"Well Rafael, Jerome Brooks inherit some money when his father pass away, he was also a member of our group in HS, at that time he opened his first strip joint and hired several girls from our school, Alicia was in that group, she had a well shapely body and also beautiful, Sam was also in our HS, a nerd he had a brain for Math, became an associate of Jerome and helped him about any financial dealing".

"Alex, we understand that Cynthia was also a dancer at Jerome's Strip Club".

"That was after I graduated from HS, she is 7 years younger than me, but yes she did dance at that Club, I think it was called "Young Desire".

Them Kurt asked Alex.

"Alex, did you know a girl by the name of Roseanne Slinkis?"

"Yes, she was also beautiful, she was Jim Donner's girlfriend, he really did love her, but something happened that they broke up, and yes she was also a dancer at the same club as Alicia".

Kurt looked at Rafael, are we getting conspiracy, are they getting closer to solving the case?

"Hey, you guys, tell my wife I love her a lot". Alex was taking to an isolation cell; his future was done. ****

CHAPTER 16

"Accept the challenges, so that you may feel the exhilaration of victory"

General George S. Patton

Habersham Rd extend from West Paces Ferry to Wesley Rd and beyond, in the middle of Buckhead an area north of the City of Atlanta, costly homes and well groom yards, not your typical neighborhood.

On 223 Habersham Rd sit the home of Jerome Brooks Strip Club entrepreneur, millionaire and head of the Georgia criminal organization called the Dixie Mafia, Mr. Brooks have never been convicted of any crime, even thou he have appeared several times in court to face charges, he is married have 2 small children and very active in the arts community philanthropist, he is also represented by the law firm headed by Frank Pannel, the same lawyer representing Senator Springdale.

All the sudden Jerome Brooks was on the list that Rafael and Kurt have of persons they were trying to interview, to many coincidences, the Senator, Jim Donner, Willie, Ruzzo and off course Ernie Silas or is it Callan, all connected in some way to Alicia and Roseanne.

Monday, the day that they were going to interview Willie Donner is here, he is been held at the Lovejoy Facility a private company owns the place but it's main client is the US Marshall Service, the facility is about 50 minutes away from the GBI offices, Rafael and Kurt arrived there by 10:00 am, Willie was already there also there was an FBI agent and Willie's lawyer John Andersenn, by the way his lawyer also belong to the Frank Pannel law firm.

Kurt started the conversation.

"Willie, my name is Kurt and this is Rafael we represent the GBI, we are investigating a couple of cold cases from 1960, their names, Alicia Roque and Roseanne Slinkis, we need to know your relationship to them and any information you might have that can help us solve the case".

Willie asked for a cigarette and began talking.

"Yes I knew them both Alicia and Roseanne use to hang out with our group, even thou we left school 4 years before they did not mind to be with us, we were older and had cars, it was nice they both were very beautiful and easy".

"What do you mean by easy?"

"You know, easy, kissing, touching, you know easy".

Rafael intervened.

"Since they were easy your group took advantage of them, right?"

"Hell no, we were just having a good time, they liked it, never complained, we had fun".

Rafael was fuming, here a group of men taking advantage of HS girls.

Kurt got involved again.

"Willie, tell me more about your group relationship with Alicia and Roseanne, please be as descriptive as possible".

Them the lawyer said something to Wille's ear, after that moment Wille said.

"by the advised from my lawyer until I get assurance that not a word, I say here will be used against me I will keep quiet".

Rafael and Kurt looked at each other thinking, what will be the next move.

"Willie, you know that we don't have that authority, we need to consult with higher up's, it might take a couple of days".

Willie came back.

"Take all time you want, I am not going anywhere, ha, ha".

Willie was taken back to his cell, Rafael, Kurt, the FBI agent and Willie's stayed for a brief meeting.

Addressing Willie's lawyer Kurt said.

"Mr. Andersenn, we are not here to incriminate your client, we just want to get some information about our case".

"Okay agent Kurt, Willie is facing several Federal charges, if he says something that might look incriminating, he will be in a position to be charged by the State of Georgia of a crime he didn't commit".

"So, what is it you want us to do?" Kurt replied.

"Willie will cooperate with the GBI after a written statement from the State Attorney General giving Willie

Any immunity to provide information on those cases".

Them Kurt turned to the FBI agent and asked him.

"Will the FBI be okay with these?"

"Yes, as long it does not interfere with our case against Willie".

After the brief meeting Rafael and Kurt left, thinking how they are going to approach their Director concerning Willie's testimony.

After arriving at their office, they immediately headed to the Director's office, he was having a meeting, so they waited, this needs to be resolved as soon as possible they thought.

After 20 minutes the Director's meeting was over, Rafael and Kurt step into his office, them the director asked them.

"Agents, what can I do for you guys?"

Kurt them brief him about the meeting with Willie.

"Sir, we have a complicated situation, in order for Willie to provide us with any information concerning our case his lawyer needs a written statement from the AG saying that Willie will have immunity from prosecution connected to our case".

"I don't have a problem with that, I will call the AG today and explain the situation, I am sure we can come up with an agreement".

Them Rafael and Kurt left confident that an agreement can be reach.

On his way back to his office Rafael was meet by Yolanda, she asked Rafael if he wanted to go to the moves, "there is a great movie that I want to see it's called Jaws". Rafael responded affirmative, they just needed to check the time the movie start, it was showing not to far away from their office.

"The movie begins at 5:00pm, them after we can have some dinner, is that okay?"

Yolanda commented.

"Yes, let me finish some pending paperwork, we still have close to an hour for the movie to start".

Said Rafael.

BANG!!, an explosion just happened outside of the GBI headquarters, agents were running with their guns drawn, "is on the parking lot", an agent shouted, Rafael ran to Yolanda's office to check on her, she was fine, next to Kurt's office he was also fine at that moment they both ran outside to check the blast, they were   astonished, it was Kurt's car somebody tried to install a pipe bomb under the hood but it exploded in his hands causing the perpetrator to died instantly he was burned beyond recognition, in a matter of moments the place was swamped with FBI, Decatur Police dept. bomb squad and GBI agents including the director.

The director commented to Rafael and Kurt.

"From now on you guys will take extra precautions, it looks like you are closing on the case and somebody wants to stop your investigation".

"How the hell they knew it was my car?"

"Kurt remember we have gone to all interview in your car, somebody was trailing you, mucho cuidado mi amigo-be very careful my friend".

"I will Rafael, let's get those jerks as soon as possible".

Yolanda was inside the GBI complex, Rafael approach her and recommended to cancel going to the movie until next week, Yolanda agreed.

"Let's go home we'll cook some dinner and relax, what just happened is making me sick".

"But first let's take Kurt to his home, his wife is also worry and they need all our support".

At the time Rafael and Yolanda dropped Kurt at his home Rafael said.

"Kurt remember, anything you hear, or see any suspicious situation call me, at any time remember you are mi hermano".

"Yes, Rafael don't worry I will surely call you".

On the way home Rafael was thinking who might have ordered to place the bomb on Kurt's car, maybe it's this guy Brooks, he has all the connections and is connected in some way with all the detained suspects.

Rafael and Yolanda arrived at their apartment, cooked dinner and relax, before Rafael went to bed he checked on Kurt, everything is quiet.

The following morning Rafael pick up Kurt at his home, when they arrived at the GBI parking lot Kurt burning car was not there, but a visible burn stain was there, they made to their office as soon as they arrived a note from the director was delivered to them, he wanted to see them ASAP.

Rafael and Kurt made it to the director's office not knowing what was all about, they sat and the director's started talking.

"Gentlemen, I yesterday before the blast I spoke to the AG about the situation with Willie, this morning I received his confirmation that he will provide the written agreement giving Willie immunity to any information he gives you concerning your case, and only your case, the FBI have been notify of this action they are okay with that".

"Sir, that's great news, we know that Willie can provide some vital information about the case". Rafael said.

"I'll call Willie's lawyer and set up the next meeting, also   the FBI will be informed, thank you sir, this is great news".

After arriving at his office Kurt called Willie's lawyer, he will get in touch with Willie today to set up the meeting, also the FBI was informed.

Yolanda called Rafael, she will meet him at the entrance of the GBI complex, "I have a surprise for you", Yolanda said to Rafael.

Yolanda was waiting for him at the main door.

"Look Rafael, look outside".

"Snow, the first snow I have seen in my life, this is beautiful".

Rafael laughing said.

Before the day was over Willie's lawyer called Kurt and confirm the meeting, it was set for this coming Monday at 10:00am, the FBI was also notified.

"Rafael everything is set for Monday's meeting with Willie, we have several days to prepare". ***

CHAPTER 17

"Faith, Joy, Optimism. But not the folly of closing your eyes to reality".

Jose Maria Escriva

Early Thursday morning the GBI director received a phone call from the Miami Customs office, Senator Springdale have arrived in the US, he is in a wheelchair according to one of his family member he suffered a stroke in Costa Rica, his communicating skills have deteriorated, is this going to make it more difficult to interrogate him?

Rafael and Kurt were summoned to the director's office.

"Guys, we might have a problem, Senator Springdale had a stroke in Costa Rica, his ability to speak might be limited".

"Can we get any proof that it really happened?" Said Kurt.

"According to immigration in Miami, the lady that was accompanied him did have some kind of medical documents verifying the stoke, now they also said that she looked young to be his wife, but she had all the legal papers confirming her identity and she was able to enter the US".

The director also suggested that they should be in contact immediately with Mr. Pannel, Springdale's lawyer.

"we'll do that". Rafael said.

Kurt rushed to his office and placed a call to Pannel hoping a quick meeting will be schedule with the Senator.

"Law offices, can I help?"

Kurt heard the voice of Pannel assistant, he immediately pictures her shapely body and her convincing walk in his mind. "Yes mam, this is Kurt with the GBI, I need to talk to Mr. Pannel, is he available?"

"No Mr. Kurt, he will be back to the office tomorrow morning, can I help you?"

"Please, ask him if we can set schedule a meeting with Senator Springdale as soon as possible in my office?"

"I will pass the information to him Mr. Kurt".

Rafael and Kurt need to concentrate on the next person, Willie Donner, they were certain that he will untangle several knots in their investigation.

Yolanda kept in touch with her mother constantly, in one of those calls Yolanda found out that her mom was engage to her neighbor, a nice man he served with Yolanda's father in the Army.

"So, mom when is the weeding?"

"I'll let you know mi Niña, by the way how is Rafael?"

"He is good, we also have plans, the weeding is planned for May".

"When are you coming to visit me again?"

"Soon mom, Rafael is involved in a very delicate case, his time is limited".

"Okay baby, talk late, love you".

"Me too mom".

It was around 4:00pm that Rafael received an anonymous call.

"Hey man, we don't like foreigners in our state, you better get the hell out or pay the consequences".

Them Rafael replied.

"If you are such a man why don't you come by my office and kick me out yourself?"

"Just get out man, just get out". Them he immediately hung up.

Rafael went to Yolanda's office, he asked her.

"Yolanda, are you allowed to carry a weapon?"

"Yes, Rafael why?"

"Some jerk just calls me and threating me, your safety is more important to me than anything else".

"Rafael, don't worry, we'll be fine".

Them Yolanda hug Rafael and gave him a long kiss.

Rafael informed Kurt and the director of the phone call, Kurt reassured Rafael that they were prepared to face any inconvenience, the director asked Rafael if he needed any extra resources to assist Yolanda and him.

"Thank you, director Yolanda is well trained to face this and me, well I can handle these, I have face worse situations and always came out on the winning side".

Yolanda and Rafael made it to their apartment, and they noticed an unmarked car parked outside, it was one of them, they had a quiet dinner and after watching 'The Love Boat' on TV they went to bed.

It was a tense, but quiet weekend, Rafael and Kurt kept in touch constantly, they were planning for the meeting with Willie on Monday, confident that the information that will be provided by him can give them more answers concerning the Alicia and Roseanne murder investigation.

Monday was here, after grabbing a quick breakfast Rafael and

Kurt headed to Lovejoy to meet with Willie, they arrived around 9:30 am, the FBI agent and Willie's lawyer were already there, they had a quick meeting, Kurt gave a copy of the letter from the AG to the lawyer and set up the parameters for the interview.

Willie was taken to the room where they had the last meeting, he was still showing the scars from the beating he received 2 weeks ago but upbeat.

"Good morning Willie, I have provided a copy of the letter from the AG as you requested, your lawyer have approved it, are you ready to answer some question that Rafael and I will provide?"

"Yes, off course, but first I need a cup of coffee and a cigarette, is that okay? "A cup of coffee and a cigarette was provided to Willie, them Kurt preceded to ask him   about the information he might have concerning Alicia and Roseanne.

"on our last meeting you mentioned that you knew Alicia and Roseanne, right?"

"Yes, they use to hang around with our group, they were manageable, I mean they participated in all our activities, if you know what I mean".

Them Rafael entered the conversation.

"I know that they use to dance in a strip club, but what other activity are you referring?"

"Well, agent Rafael engage in dating with other men, specially connected and well to do, they acted as let's say spies, mainly with politicians that provided information we needed to do our thing".

"Was any of those politicians named Charles Springdale?"

"Oh, you mean 'chuky', yes he was one of them, he was a constant client, very mean and dirty fellow, he was I think a Judge now a Senator".

Rafael and Kurt looked at each other with amazement, here they have the first clue that maybe the Senator might be involved in the murders of Alicia and Roseanne.

Kurt proceeded with the questioning, his next question involved that illusive man name Ernie Silas or Callan.

"Willie, did you have a relationship with a guy named Ernie Silas or Callan?"

Willie was silent for a while thinking what he was going to answer, this question put him in a very delicate position, he approached his lawyer and asked him something, Rafael and Kurt were very anxious to hear his answer.

Willie began to talk.

"I don't know how to answer that question, yes I knew him, he was in prison for a while, a mean SOB, didn't trust anybody had a complex personality, and yes a jerk".

"Did he belong to your organization?" Kurt said.

Them Willie's lawyer intervene.

"Agent Kurt that question is not within the parameters we stablish, my client is collaborating with the FBI on certain situations and I am afraid that question can put my client in personal jeopardy".

Rafael them tried to be more specific into why they need for Willie to answer the question.

"Okay Wille, let me put it this way, did Jim participated in any way in the disappearances of Alicia and Roseanne?"

Willie hesitated for a moment, light up another cigarette and began to talk.

"Yes, he was the facilitator of the group, he moved girls from the strip joint to the motels where the paying clients were waiting, them stayed outside to make sure the girls didn't have any problems".

"Willie, what we are trying to stablish, did Jim in any way participated in the murder of Alicia and Roseanne?"

"In a way maybe he did, like I said he move the girls around, maybe he did, I don't know".

Rafael and Kurt were getting annoyed with Willie's answer, when all the sudden Willie said.

"You know what, Jim had a special relation with 'chuky', the Judge, he uses to drive him around all over Atlanta looking for young girls, maybe he did introduce Alicia and Roseanne to the Judge, will that help you?"

"Great, Willie now what about Jerome Brooks, did he have any relationship with any of the women in the group?"

"Off course, he is a charmer, money, culture and connections, lots of connections, his father was wealthy left Jerome a huge amount of money, he put it to work by creating the strip joints, liked Alicia a lot, when she disappeared you could see the sadness in his face".

Kurt asked Willie.

"Willie, going back to the Judge now Senator Springdale the one you call 'chuky', you mentioned that he used to drive around Atlanta with Jim looking for young girls, was that before or after Alicia and Roseanne disappeared?"

"That was before and after they were killed, that guy is mean, even thou he was married he used to get young girls all the time".

"To do what with the girls, Willie?" Rafael asked that question, even thou he had an idea what he will do with the girls, he needed Willie to be more specific.

"Man, what kind of stupid question is that, I guest to rape them, to do sick stuff, who knows, maybe you can ask Jim Silas".

Rafael and Kurt looked at each other, did he say ask Jim Silas, is he alive.

Calmly, Rafael asked Willie where Jim Silas is now.

"I think he lives in Georgia, he changed his name, he lived outside of the US for a while and them came back, ask the Senator he might know".

That is our next person, Rafael thought.

After questioning Willie for another hour Rafael and Kurt left, they were quiet most of the trip back, trying to put together all the information they acquire from Willie, they will concentrate in mainly in three persons, Senator Springdale, Jerome Brooks and Jim Silas, first they have to find Silas.

Back at their office Rafael and Kurt received a phone call from Mr. Pannel, he informed them that Senator Springdale health was fragile and it will take a while before he can talk to them, Rafael and Kurt were very disappointed, they thought that the Senator could clarify the information that Willie gave them concerning the Alicia and Roseanne murders.

"Well, Rafael let's concentrate on Jerome Brooks, I will make arrangement for him to come to our office for an interview". Rafael agreed.

At the Decatur city morgue, a body was wheel in, a John Doe, no wallet, no ID of any kind, according to the

examiner it looks like homicide, before autopsy was perform 3 bullets holes were noticed, 1 to the head 2 to the lower abdomen, a white male maybe on his 50's there was a noticeable tattoo's 'an eagle' on his chest no birth marks, it looks like he have been dead for almost a week, the information about the body will be disseminated all over Georgia, the GBI will be also notify.

When Rafael and Kurt received the information about John Doe they immediately began to inquire about the body, they needed to stablish the origin and the design of the tattoo, maybe it will have some variance on their case, they were interested to see if the body was that of Jim Silas.

Later that day the body was identify, it belonged to William 'Billy Bob' Samins, one of the people that was detain in the raid last month, he was shoot execution style.

Yolanda didn't make it to the office today, she stayed at the apartment trying to get everything for her wedding in May, even thou are only January Yolanda likes to plan ahead, while she was preparing some coffee somebody threw a rock thru the Living Room window with a note attached, it read:

"Hey, foreigner stop snooping into our business if not face some consequences you have 48 hours to leave Georgia".

Yolanda ran to the bedroom grab a 38 Smith & Wesson and looked thru the window, nobody was there, what a coincidence the officer that was assigned to be their lookout was taken yesterday.

Yolanda was calm, she grabbed the phone and called Rafael, he informed Kurt about the note and left for the apartment, at the same time Kurt called the DeKalb co. police, when Rafael arrived he looked at Yolanda, she was still grabbing her 38, pale but calm.

"What happened baby?"

"Somebody threw a rock with a note, look at it".

"Yolanda, don't worry, I will find out who the jerk that is".

"Rafael, we just need to be more careful in every activity we do".

At that moment Kurt called Rafael.

"Rafael is everything okay with Yolanda?"

"Yes, she is fine, a little shaken but fine".

After a couple of days Kurt informed Rafael about a call he just received from the Lovejoy facility.

Rafael, Willie might have some information about the incident in your apartment, he thinks who did this".

"Is he still at the Lovejoy detention center?"

"Yes Rafael, and we can call him back or see him in person, what do you want to?"

"Yes, the fastest the better, let's get in touch with him".

Rafael drove back to the GBI headquarters, there Kurt and the director were waiting for him, he rushed to   Kurt's office and called the Lovejoy facility, they immediately brought Willie to one of the office, the call was set up with an speaker phone so members of the facility could monitor it.

"Willie, this is Rafael we understand you might have some information about the incident at my apartment this morning".

"I might, according to sources inside here, the incident was carrying it out by members of the organization".

"Okay Willie, but gave the order to carry it out?'

"Agent Rafael, these are mean people, it could be any one higher up".

Rafael was getting up tied, he needed Willie to give him more precise information, who was it, from where the order came.

"Willie, I need names, places, who the hell is involved, I need it now".

"Okay, okay, it could be Jerome Brooks or 'chuky' thesenator, maybe somebody from Alabama, that's all I can give you, please don't inform my lawyer about this call, my life will be on the line, you see he belong to the same firm as Pannel, 'chuky's' lawyer".

Rafael knew it, Jerome, the Senator, he turned back to Kurt and the director and said.

"We need to get those guys here, we need to start getting answers, I am certain Kurt that they are deeply involved in our cases".

"Willie, thank you, do you need anything from us?"

"No Rafael, they are moving me today to a safe house, I have agreed to be government witness, you know, 'a rat', good luck, I hope you get those bastards".

Kurt and the director agreed, so they devised a plan to get them here at the GBI headquarters for questioning.

"Rafael, the first thing we need to do is call Mr. Pennel and pressure him to bring those guys in, I don't know who is Mr. Brooks lawyer but if is not Mr. Pennel we need to get the name of that lawyer and get him on board"?

The director angrily said.

To no surprise Pannel is also Jerome brooks lawyer, he runs a law firm of 10 criminal lawyers, they will probably find that the majority of their clients are associates or connected in certain ways with the Dixie Mafia, they cover Georgia, Alabama, South Carolina and North Carolina it's an extensive territory.

Rafael and Kurt spend 3 days looking into all information available about the organization, names, places, contacts and any connected politician with the group, the main target is the person or persons involved in the murder of Alicia and Roseanne but if they find some other information about their criminal activities, that will be a plus. "Kurt, have you called Mr. Pannel yet?"   "Yes, left a message for him to call me, I do hope it will be soon".

Later that afternoon Pannel called, he informed Kurt of the situation with Senator Springdale and gave more information about Jerome brooks.

"Agent Kurt, as you are aware Senator Springdale suffered a stroke in Costa Rica, his ability to speak is very limited, about Jerome Brooks, he is a very busy businessman and his time is limited". Kurt interrupted Pannel.

"Mr. Pannel, we understand that, but we need him here as soon as possible, unless you want us to get a warrant to force him here, is up to you".

Mr. Pannel was quiet for a moment, he calmly said.

"Well if you guys insist, I will have Mr. Brooks in your office to-morrow, I will call later to give you a firm time".

"That's all we want, Mr. Pannel".

Rafael responded, them turn to Kurt with a smile on his face.

Later that afternoon Pannel called, he and Jerome Brooks will be at the GBI headquarters the following day at 2:00

pm, Senator Springdale is under medical treatment and will not be able to make it now, Rafael and Kurt will be anxiously waiting.

In the morning of the interview Rafael arrived around 8:00am, ready to face Jerome Brooks, Kurt arrived 20 minute later, after gathering all the pertinent information for the interview they went to the director's office, Rafael and Kurt needed to define certain parameters since their main concern was the cold cases of Alicia and Roseanne, the director commented that they should concentrate on those areas, if anything else comes up another department within the GBI will take over.

The director was right, but everything tied together the Alicia and Roseanna dancing at the club, Jerome relationship with them, all this information comes together into one big case. ***

CHAPTER 18

"The truth wakes once and never dies"

Jose Marti

Jerome Brooks looks younger than his age, well groomed and with a diverse vocabulary, calm, and by the initial introduction of his lawyer, Mr. Pannel willing to cooperate with Rafael and Kurt, the director also asked Charles Lynnard to be present in the interview in case additional inquiring is required.

Kurt opened the conversation.

"Mr. Brooks, I am agent Kurt, this agent Rafael and Asst. Director Charles Lynnard, we would like to ask you some questions in reference to a couple of cold cases, one is of Alicia Roque and the other is Roseanne Slinkis, we understand that you knew both of them".

"Agent Kurt before we proceed, I will like to clarify that my client came on his own free will, no investigation is even conducted on him and only will answer questions on those two cold cases".

Mr. Pannel firmly said.

"Mr. Brooks, this is Rafael gives a detailed picture of your relationship with both women?"

"Rafael, is that Spanish?"

"Yes, actually Cuban".

"I did not know that the GBI had foreigners working for them".

Rafael looked at Kurt, did he say 'foreigners', did that sound familiar?

"I did know them both they worked in my first club for a brief period, both beautiful and full of live it was a shame they were killed, they were in the same HS, even thou I graduated first".

Rafael kept the questioning, he wanted for Jerome to be more open about their relationship, but also the remark he made about 'foreigners'.

"Jerome, you don't mind if I call you Jerome?"

"No go ahead, Rafael you can call me Jerome".

"Jerome, I need for you to be more precise, tell me more about the time they worked at your club, I understand they were doing other things beside dancing, we just need to know, we also have information about an attempt to injured one of our agent by throwing a rock at his home".

At that moment Pennel interrupted the questioning.

"Agent Rafael, my client only can answer any question regarding their work at his club, or any personal contact regarding their friendship not any activity the women engage outside their place of employment".

"I understand, but we have some information that they also engage in activities inside his club, and we need to know".

At that moment Jerome got up and exploded in rage. "I came here as a good will gesture, to answer questions regarding the murders that occur in the 60's, and them you are trying to link my business as an illegal dump, also to tied me to that rock incident, to hell with it, I am leaving".

Mr. Pannel was shock, he immediately intervened and try to calm Jerome, but to no avail.

"Mr. Brooks, the only reason we are asking you those questions is that we have several witnesses that can verify our information".

"What, people that are professional liars, ex-convicts, come on man, I am leaving, are you going Pannel?"

Both Jerome and Pannel got up and left, the room was quiet for a couple of minutes, them Mr. lynnard made a comment.

"Guys, we have something here, the fact is that Jerome is hiding something not only about your case but also about the activities that lead to the murders, keep up the pressure, if you need my help let me know".

After sharing information, the group went to their respective offices.

"Rafael, you know we should ask the FBI and the Alabama AG to let us share Willie and Ruzzo so they can testify against Jerome and the Senator in case more information comes our way".

"That will be perfect, we have to keep the pressure on Jerome, and off course the Senator too".

At that moment the phone rang in Kurt's office, it was the director.

"Kurt, I have asked our legal department to solicit from the court a search warrant for Jerome's strip club here in Atlanta, that will keep him guessing if we have anything else".

"Great, I will tell Rafael he is here with me".

Rafael and Kurt were overjoyed, they knew that Willie and Ruzzo could facilitate more information that will put Jerome in a bind, now they needed the Senator to answer some questions, they knew it will be almost impossible to get him to do that, but also, we need to find Ernie Silas or Callas this person can add to our inquire.

The following morning the director call Rafael and Kurt, he wants to see them at his office now, Rafael and Kurt made it upstairs to the director's office, he received them with a smile.

"Gentlemen, we have the search warrant, one of our undercover agents just made a cocaine buy at Jerome's strip club".

"Director we can do this tomorrow, the time, well not in the morning not many people show up at a strip club in the morning, maybe after 7:00pm, we also need the cooperation of the APD".

"Kurt are you in agreement?"

"Yes, let's get the ball rolling", The ball rolling, are we going to a baseball game? Rafael laughing asked.

Everybody in the room started laughing, by that time Charles Lynnard showed up, he provided the following information.

"I assumed that the director informed you guys that a search warrant was approved, according to reliable sources there are a number of armed guards in the premises, we have to be very careful when be begin the search".

Rafael and Kurt were ready, they were going to be joined by several agents from the GBI plus several officers from the APD, they gather at 5:00 pm in a shopping center about 4 miles from the club, they assigned each group an area and duty, the APD will be covering the perimeter, the GBI including Rafael and Kurt will proceed with the search warrant.

The agents arrived at the strip club at 7:10pm, they were received by a muscular black man, after showing the warrant they proceeded to enter the club there they found the manager a guy by the name of Ralph at thebeginning he showed some resistance but after a couple of minutes he got out of the way, there were 2 floors in the club, Rafael with another 3 agents took the top floor, Kurt took the first floor with the same number of agents.

All of the sudden, Bang, Bang...... several shoots were fired on the second floor, one of the agents shoot a guy when he tried to use his pistol, Rafael was fine, they found several bundles of marihuana and some cocaine, on the first floor on the side of the dancing floor Kurt and the agents found about 3 rooms dedicated to service prostitution, they apprehended 2 clients, one being a prominent lawyer in Atlanta, another guy tried to get away thru the back door but was stopped by an APD officer, they also found several documents concerning funds the were deposited in Grand Cayman and Costa Rica, do we hear Jim Silas?

Rafael and Kurt made the final report to the director;

2 bundle of Marihuana, 25 ounce of cocaine, 2 arrest on prostitution charges, 1 wounded guard he will charge with resisting arrest and carrying a weapon without a permit, another person was apprehended by the APD trying to escape.

In addition to the raid in the Atlanta club, the other 3 clubs in the rest of Georgia was put under surveillance by the GBI and the local authorities.

The following day an arrest warrant was issue for Jerome Brooks, the charges will be under the RICO act, he is facing several years behind bars, unless he can provide useful information to the GBI.

After his arrest, Jerome Brooks was transported to the Fulton County jail, he immediately called for his lawyer Mr. Pannel in about an hour both were meeting with Charles Lynnard, Rafael and Kurt, they informed Pannel of his client charges.

Charles Lynnard began reading the charges to Jerome.

"Mr. Brooks, you have been charged with several counts of possession and distribute of a control substance, 3 counts of promoting prostitution, plus evidence of money laundry by your organization".

At that time Pannel requested a private meeting with his client.

After a meeting that lasted for about 40 min Jerome and Pannel again were joined by Rafael, Kurt and Charles.

Charles asked Pannel.

"well, do you have anything to say about those charges?"

"No, but my client asked me to propose some kind of a deal that can help him overcome those charges".

Rafael immediately thought 'this guy is going to sing like a bird'.

With a grim on his face Charles ask Pannel to be more specific.

"My client had decided to cooperate with the authorities in solving not only the cold cases you are trying to resolve but also several other situations concerning the working of his organization".

Rafael looked at Kurt, 'this is getting interesting', they thought.

Rafael asked, "What other situations?"

"Let's get some kind of a deal on the table, then we'll talk".

It is amazing how fast a person can fall, Jerome Brooks just hours ago was a prominent member of his community, after the raid of his club, a parasite looking for a hole to hide.

Jerome's wife was contacted, her husband was facing a lot of years behind bars, unless he can come up with something that will appeal to the authorities, her world was falling apart in front of her, what would happened to her, to her kids, if Jerome get a deal they would have to be moved by the government under the witness protection plan, she will have to hide her new address from her immediate family, and her friends.

"Mr. Pannel, I will advise the AG of our conversation, we should have an answer for you by tomorrow, is that okay?"

"Yes, tell the AG that Mr. Brooks have a lot of valuable information, also he needs to be on separate cell, a lot of inmates know who he is and might take some kind of retaliation against my client".

"I will advise the jail superintend of the situation".

Jerome was taken away, them Pannel left, Rafael, Kurt and Charles stay behind, they commented on the meeting.

"Rafael, Kurt this is amazing, we might have the answer for your cases plus important information to put a lot of crooks behind bars".

"Yes Charles, what's the situation with the rest of his clubs here in Georgia?" Rafael asked.

"They are been raided as we speak, with luck we might find more evidence to put this guy away for a long time".

Arriving at the GBI headquarters Rafael stop by Yolanda's office, gave a hug and a big kiss, he was planning to have a very quiet evening, it has been a hectic week.

"Yolanda, how about a dinner and a movie?"

"Yes, any movie on your mind?"

"You know I like the James Bond movies, the new one is 'The Spy Who Loves Me', let's go and see it".

Rafael and Yolanda enjoyed a quiet evening together, dinner at an Italian restaurant and them the movies, Yolanda was not too impressed with the movie, but Rafael did like it, "a lot of action" Rafael commented, "those Russians they are evil".

Arriving at their apartment they noticed a message in the answering machine, it was from Kurt.

"Rafael, I received a message from the FBI giving us permission to use Willie and Ruzzo as witnesses in our investigation, see you tomorrow".

Rafael turn to Yolanda pick her up and kiss her, he could not contain how happy he was listening to Kurt's message.

"Yolanda, why don't we open a bottle of wine to celebrate not only the news from Kurt but also our future together, I hope you know what you are getting into".

Yolanda with a smiling face said.

"Claro que si mi amor, I have love you from the first moment I saw you".

Rafael pour the wine and both holding their glasses promise eternal love.

The week will very challenging for Rafael and Kurt, the final steps in closing the Alicia and Roseanne case was near, with the deal that the AG will present to Jerome Brooks, and the testimony from Willie and Ruzzo will be enough to seal the case. ***

CHAPTER 19

"Aspire to have no more than one right; that of fulfilling your duty"

Jose Maria Escriva

"Good Morning Rafael, we have several meetings this week, first Willie's and Ruzzo's lawyers, we need to set up the parameters for their deal, also it looks like Jerome is going to provide a lot of information not only for us but to different law enforcement agencies".

"Good morning Kurt, great we need to set up an agenda and have the right questions for these guys, I am confident that the closing of our cold cases is near".

Challenging week? heck yeah, later that afternoon the law firm that represents both Willie and Ruzzo decided to withdraw their services, yes, it's Pannel law firm, we wonder why.

"Rafael change of plans, the court have appointed new lawyers for Willie and Ruzzo, we have to go over with

them the complete deal structure, hoping they will approve"

"Kurt, Since Willie and Ruzzo are willing to testify against Jerome I don't think we will have any problem".

"let's hope and pray Rafael".

In the meantime, Jerome was asking for a better secure place for him and his family, he heard thru his associates that there was contract hit on him, there was a couple of criminal organizations tied to his case, the Bonnano Mafia family that control the drug trade and the Dixie Mafia that handled the prostitution side of the operation, his future was complicated, the GBI and conjunction with the Marshall's office decided to move him and his family to a government safe house, they will end up in the witness protection plan his life as he knew it was over.

There is a couple of loose ends, the questioning of Senator Springdale and finding Ernie Silas, both essential to their case.

"Kurt have we tried to get the Senator to talk to us again?"

"Rafael, according to the doctor that is treating the Senator his ability to respond is very limited, we might never be able to speak with him".

"What about his wife?"

"we have some information on her, her name is Dalila Diaz, born in San Jose, they have been married for 3 years, she is 25 years old, and guest what, she used to dance at the strip club in Costa Rica owned by Jerome Brooks".

"can we interview her?"

"I will call Pannel today and arrange a meeting at his office with her".

"Kurt, I am certain that we can get some information about the activities of the Senator in Costa Rica from the past years to now".

"I will get on its Rafael".

It was around 11:00 am when Kurt placed a call to Mr. Pannel.

"Law Offices".

"Mr. Pannel please, this is agent Kurt with the GBI".

"Hold sir, I will transfer you to his assistant".

She passes the call to Pannel assistant, I call her 'Betty Boop', she has the same shape as that comic characterBetty Bop.

"Agent Kurt, Mr. Pannel is with a client, can I help you?"

"Yes, please tell him that since we can not speak with Senator Springdale we need to interview his wife, either at his office or in the GBI headquarters, also advise him that if we have to get a warrant, we'll do it, thank you".

About 20 minutes later Pannel called, he agreed to meet with Rafael and Kurt the next day at 10:00 am, the Senator's wife will be there also.

"we'll see what kind of information we can get out of her". Said Rafael.

Willie, Ruzzo, Jerome and his family were moved to different parts of the country and placed under the witness protection plan, they will be sent back to Georgia when their court hearings are schedule, in the meantime Rafael and Kurt were busy putting together all the information they gather from them and different sources now they need to interview Mrs. Springdale, she can furnish valuable information on the operations of Jerome in Costa Rica and shed some light on the whereabout of Ernie Silas.

The morning of the meeting Rafael and Kurt arrived at Pannel's office sharp at 10:00 am, Pannel assistant 'Betty Boop', directed them to his office, there was Pannel and Dalila Diaz, a beautiful woman too young for the Senator, she introduced herself with perfect English, we later found out that she studied in the US.

Kurt started the conversation by introducing himself and Rafael.

"Mrs. Springdale, my name is Kurt, and this is Rafael we are agents from the GBI, we want to ask you some questions regarding Senator Springdale activities in Costa Rica".

Pannel intervene and made the following comment.

"Mrs. Springdale will provide as much information as possible within the parameters of the law, is that clear?"

"Yes, off course". Kurt replied.

"Dalila, how many years have you known Senator Springdale?"

"Now, let me see, I was about 19 years old when I meet him, I was working as a waiter at a men's club in San Jose, he was real sweet and offer me the world, at first I took lightly, a lot of men offered me the world but never delivered, if you know what I mean".

Rafael entered the conversation.

"Dalila, 'que nombre mas lindo', what a beautiful name".

"Oh, hablas espanol', you speak Spanish". Said Dalila.   "Yes, originally, I was born in Cuba, anyway, when you   said you worked as a waiter in the club, did you have any other activity there beside been a waiter?"

"Senor Rafael, what kind of question is that, can you be more specific".

"well, what I meant is that were you involved in any management activity of the club?"

"After working there for 5 years I was promoted to manage the exotic dancers, that's when the Senator proposed to me".

"Usted bailo alguna ves? 'did you at any time danced at the club?'

Pannel interrupted.

"Agent Rafael, I don't think that question is relevant to your case".

"Mr. Pannel, it is relevant we want to stablish what other men stablish a relationship with her, specially a man by the name of Ernie Silas".

Pannel approach Dalila, he spoke to her ear, them she came back to Rafael.

"Yes, I did have a relationship with several gentlemen before I married the Senator, and yes, I did meet Ernie Silas, we never associated with each other, he was a crazy man, very explosive not good manners".

Rafael turn to Kurt; Rafael knew he was thinking the same thing.

"Dalila, did he have any connection with the club at all?"

"He was there almost every night; he got his drinks free and mingle with the club personnel, whenever Mr. brooks came to check the club, he was his constant companion".

"So, he did have a connection to Mr. Brooks".

Pannel stopped the questioning of Dalila by Rafael.

"Agent Rafael, as you are aware, I represent Mr. Brooks, any information concerning him will be not be available until a formal deal can be arrange".

"I understand Mr. Pannel, but I just want to stablish the identity of Mr. Silas and his whereabout".

"Rafael, when we get a formal deal you, Kurt and the GBI will have that information, in the meantime if you don't have any more questions for Mrs. Springdale the meeting is over".

At that moment Kurt asked Pannel the following.

"Mr. Pannel, I understand your firm will not represent Willie or Ruzzo anymore, can I ask why?"

"Our firm choice, anything else?" "No, thank you Dalila for your time, can we contact you in the future if we need any more information about the operation in Costa Rica?"

"But first call Mr. Pannel, whatever he advises me I'll do".

Rafael and Kurt got up and walk away out of the office.

When they got into their car they started to talk about the meeting.

"Rafael, I think she knows where the heck Jim Silas is".

"I know Kurt, after the deal is done between the federal authorities and Jerome Brooks we need to talk to her again".

Arriving at the office there was a message from officer Jerry Sanders of the APD, Alex Corbin committed suicide at the Fulton CO. jail this morning, even thou he could not walk due to injuries he managed to strap a bed sheet to his neck and hung himself.

The Atlanta connection of the Dixie Mafia was falling apart, all the major players were willing to testify in court about their activities and connections with that organization, Rafael and Kurt were very happy that they have helped in that endeavor, at the same time working toward solving the cold cases of Alicia and Roseanne. Willie and Ruzzo will provide important and crucial information about the criminal enterprise, the Federal Government will tied it to the RICO act. ***

CHAPTER 20

"El deber de un hombre es estar alli, donde es mas util".

Jose Marti

It is in the middle of March already, temperatures raging in the low 40's, Rafael wears a sweater plus a coat and yes a wool scarf, it is colder than Cuba, 'voy a cojer una pulmonia', I am getting a pneumonia!

It has been 3 weeks since a deal was approved by all the parties involved, but before they can forward any information to Rafael and Kurt concerning their case the FBI, DEA and any other government agency needs to get theirs first.

"Rafael, according with the director we can start with our interview of Willie, Ruzzo and Jerome as soon as tomorrow, all of them have been taken back to the Lovejoy facility from their witness Protection area outside of Georgia".

"Are we going to be able to interview Dalila again?"

"If we need to yes, we only have to call Pannel and arrange it".

Rafael and Kurt are trying to tied some loose ends, Cynthia Corbin is awaiting trail accused of first degree murder in the homicide of Jim Donner his lover, she have declared that after the death of her husband Alex her life doesn't means much, Mary Lunquin is fine, still with her young boyfriend and still living in Macon, other members of Jerome brooks organization have either been apprehended or killed in confrontation with law enforcement officers.

Early Friday morning Rafael and Kurt are on their way to the Lovejoy facility, they are almost certain that the meeting bring some definite answer to their cases, they will interview first Willie, Ruzzo and Jerome will also be interview separately, the information that they will provide will be crucial to solving their cases.

Kurt and Rafael arrived early, around 8:30am, they were directed to the same room that the first interview with Willie was done, agents from the FBI, DEA and Wille's new lawyer was there.

"High you guys, ready for some gossip, it's going to be interesting".

Willie made that comment with a big smiling face.

"Well Willie, we don't consider that gossip, the information you have provided will result in the cleaning of the streets of Georgia, they are your companion in crime, but at the same time you will be doing a good deed".

Rafael was very agitated when he responded to Willie.

"Okay, yeah, now hit me with the questions".

"You have answer questions from different government agencies, now is our turn, we need to know about the murder of Alicia Roque and Roseanne Slinkis, how was it done where, and by whom".

Willie sat back, light up a cigarette and with a grin on his face began talking.

"Yeah, it's complicated, you have several people involved, not actually in the killing, but involved, you have Jerome Brooks that supplied the girls you have the clients, Senator 'chuky' Springdale that performed the rape and them the final step the hired killer".

Kurt beaming with anger, but calm asked again.

"Them who was the killer?"

"That sick and weird guy, Jim Silas".

"Okay, where is Silas now".

"I don't know, ask the Senator, he was very close to him, also you might want to ask his present wife, Dalila she was very intimate with him".

Them Dalila was lying, she mentioned that she was never closed to Silas, Rafael thought.

After a couple of more question Rafael and Kurt were finished with Willie.

"Willie, we hope you can find your way to redemption, life have giving you opportunity, grab it, don't let it go".

"I won't you guys, if you need me again, I will be in the same place for a while".

Rafael and Kurt waited about an hour to interview Ruzzo, he also had information about our case.

They brought Ruzzo to the meeting room, before anybody could talk Ruzzo said something to Rafael.

"Rafael, 'como esta usted' how are you Rafael, did you liked that Rafi, I learn that here in this hell hole, how do you like it?".

Rafael want it to go and hit Ruzzo but was restrain by Kurt.

"Well Ruzzo, not bad, here is another word for you, 'te voy a meter un piñaso'".

"What does that mean Rafael?"

"It only means you are a nice guy". Them Kurt feeling the animosity between them started the conversation.

"Ruzzo, you have provided valuable information to various Federal Agencies, now we need to ask you for your help in solving the murder of Alicia and Roseanne, can we get your cooperation?"

"Off course agent Kurt, what do you need to know?" "We need to know the activities they were involved before they were murdered, boyfriends, friends or any relevant information you can give us".

"They were good dancers, made a lot of tips, had a lot of admirers, but the main guy Jerome, demanded that they do extra activities with his best clients, you know, doctors, lawyers, politicians, that's where Senator Springdale came into the picture, he wanted to be with them all the time, Jerome permitted it as long as the Senator 'chuky' took care of some legal matters".

"What about their disappearing and them murder, who was involved?"

"After Springdale used them, he will instruct Silas the weird one to get rid of them, you know kill them, he did not want any of the girls to interfere with his political future".

"Did Jerome have any part in their murders?"

"Well, he facilitated the girls and the place, after they were murder Silas move them to different places".

"So, they were killed at Jerome's strip club, right?"

"Yes, like I said he facilitated the place".

Rafael and Kurt had enough evidence to put the Senator and Jerome behind bars for a while, they only thing they need now is finding Silas, maybe Dalila can provide that information, while they were waiting for Jerome Kurt asked Rafael if he had any idea after all the information they have gather if Silas was still alive.

"Oh, yes he is, alive and well, we might have to go back to the names of people we have in our list, he probably will be there".

After 10 minutes of waiting Jerome was brought into the meeting room, he didn't look that good, his hair was all

mess up, his face looked like a locomotive pass thru it and his demeanor was not there, them Rafael started the conversation

"Hi Jerome, we meet again, off course on different circumstances, I am hoping your family is doing fine, their security is important to us".

"Yes, they are doing fine, now according to my lawyer the deal I made with you guys allows me to describe certain information about your case, so what's that you need to ask me?"

Them Rafael went up with the interview.

"Jerome, according with several sources Alicia and Roseanne were killed at your club, is that accurate?"

"Yes, that maniac Silas killed and disposed of their bodies, he used to work for me in Costa Rica, Alicia was killed first them he went after Roseanne, the poor girl she was hiding somewhere in Atlanta, but he found her and killed her". "Any reason or did anybody order to kill her?"

"No, she just witnesses the murder of Alicia".

"Did Senator had anything to do with this?"

"Yes, he used them, rape them and ordered Silas to kill them, he is another monster".

Them Rafael paused the interview turn to Kurt and whispered, "Did Jerome just declared himself a saint?" Kurt began to smile, Jerome didn't kill them, but he corrupted and abuse them, it's like what Silas did to them.

Jerome have given Rafael and Kurt plenty of information about the murder of Alicia and Roseanne, but there is a missing chapter, Ernie Silas, their next step is finding him, is he is still alive, they don't know but they will find out soon.

Rafael and Kurt arrived at the GBI headquarter by 5:00 pm, the director was waiting for them, he needed a report of the interviews, "can I have it in the morning?" the director asked them.

"Yes sir, we will have one ready by mid-morning".

Said Rafael.

"Did you guys get solid leads?"

"Not only solid leads, we have the whole picture, persons, dates, and places, you will read everything in our report".

"Rafael, we need to bring charges against the Senator first, then interview Dalila later, we don't want her to tell the Senator about our findings".

"Tomorrow when the director reads the report, I assume that charges will be immediately presented, I think the AG is already working on that, now concerning the Senator, yes charges first them Dalila interview later, the only piece of the puzzle missing is Jim Silas and she will have to resolve her comment about any relationship with him".

Later that night a fire was destroying Jerome's Strip Club in Atlanta, there was still some documents that were left

behind for later examination, all probably gone the APD suspect arson, some criminal associates of Jerome didn't want those papers to be made public. Rafael and Kurt were advice that Senator Springdale was taken to the Fulton Co. Jail for processing, later release due to his medical situation, later assigned to house arrest.

Kurt was making the necessary preparation for Dalila to have the second interview at their office, he received some resistance from Pannel, but later agreed to the location of the interview, it was set for the following morning at 10:00 am.

The Georgia State Senate schedule a session for next week to deal with the indictment of Senator Springdale, the Democratic majority will impose a suspension until all the facts are known.

In the meantime, the local authorities were trying to gather all the documents that were salvage in the strip club fire, including bank records that can tied some mafia families with Jerome, also salvage was some photos that included Ernie Silas, it was difficult to distinguish his face, the fire has destroyed a lot of important information but the authorities managed to remove the majority of the files before the fire.

That morning Dalila and Pannel arrived at the GBI headquarters on time, Rafael and Kurt were waiting, they walked to an interrogation room close to Kurt's office, Rafael started the conversation.

"Good morning Dalila, thank you for let us expand the information you provided before, I am certain you know that the Senator was indicted on conspiracy charges, and as a matter of fact Mr. Pannel will be defending him".

"Yes, I know, now what is it that you need to expand on my information".

Dalila responded; her tone of voice was not to amicable.

"Well, Dalila in your first interview you mentioned that your relationship with Jim Silas was minimal, right".

"Yes, so what is the problem?"

"Dalila, we have credible information that you engage with Silas in a more complex relationship". Rafael said.

Dalila was quiet for a moment, then she approaches Pannel, ask him something, he responded, them Dalila turn back to Rafael and said.

"De acuerdo a mi abogado debo decir la verdad", in English please, Rafael reminded Dalila that Kurt didn't spoke Spanish.

"I am sorry Mr. Kurt, what I was saying is that my lawyer reminded me not to lied".

She proceeded.

"Yes, Silas and I had a closer relationship, before the Senator asked me to marry him Jim did, we were together for a couple of years, he was very abusive, not physically but verbally, for a while he was Jerome's enforcer in Costa Rica, a weird fellow".

"So, Jerome knows him?" Rafael asked.

"Yes, I think he lives here in Georgia now".

Rafael knew that Jerome and Silas were at one-point associates and close friends, he was just testing the trustfulness of Dalila testimony.

"Dalila can you describe him?" Kurt asked her.

"Well, he is 5' 10", on the chubby side, dark hair, maybe now he has change it, when he is okay, he sounds like a preacher, that's all I have".

"So, we have the mysterious Ernie Silas in our midst".

Rafael said to Kurt.

Pannel instructed Dalila not to answer any more questions, so they departed immediately the GBI headquarters.

Rafael and Kurt had the whole cases of Alicia and Roseanne in front of them, they needed to find the main perpetrator, Ernie Silas.

A week has passed, and Rafael and Kurt were concentrating all their detective work on finding Jim Silas, in the meantime one of the criminal organizations

involved with Jerome in Georgia and beyond were doing some more cleaning themselves, two bodies were found in South Georgia, riddle with bullets, they were later identify as Sam Pelling Jerome's bookkeeper and Saul Reading one of Jerome's enforcer, they were found in the trunk of a Mercedes Benz, belonging to Sam Pelling, the Bonanno family out of NYC it is suspected of been the perpetrator.

It was the middle of March, Yolanda and Rafael were making all the necessary plans for their weeding in May, Rafael was notified that his swearing in as a US citizen will be next week, Yolanda was making arrangement for a surprise party at the Lynnnard's house, Yolanda knows that it will be a very emotional moment for Rafael, he loves Cuba, but at the same time becoming a citizen of the country that open their arms for him is without any doubt a proud moment, he will surely remember at that moment all the gratitude that the people in the US have given him, he rebuilt his life, found his true love and gain a family, the Lynnards. ****

CHAPTER 21

"I am a slow walker, but I never walk back"

Abraham Lincoln

Rafael was ready, he already had passed the citizenship test, the constitution, the presidents and the bill of rights, the United States have the most detailed and practical constitution of the world, we have the right to be free, to dissent, to question and most important to select our leaders, even thou they might not be 100% perfect, but we have the right to get rid of them by a orderly and respected right , the right to vote.

The swearing in ceremony was perform at the Civic Center, located in downtown Atlanta, there were 100 future citizens presents, their wives, husband, parents and friends, Yolanda was there, so was Kurt, Lynnards and his wife and the Director and his wife.

After the ceremony they all departed to the Lynnards house where more people were waiting, his friend during his political prison years Capt. Carlos Urquiza was there so was his wife and a group of Cubans representing their community.

Rafael was static, very emotional and melancholic all at the same time, Yolanda approach Rafael gave him a kiss and began to address the group.

"Friends, well should I say family members, we are here to celebrate a new chapter for Rafael, the man that I love and respect, the man that have gone thru hell and back, the person that have embrace our great country with pride and respect".

Everybody applauded and demanded that Rafael say a few words.

Rafael looking very emotional began to talk.

"My dear friends, or like Yolanda said family members, today my heart is divided, one side belongs to Cuba the other to my new nation the United States, my thoughts are with Jose Marti and George Washington, my old family in Cuba and my new family here in Georgia, thank you for giving me this great opportunity to develop my free mind and soul, love you all".

And by that, sobbing he embrace Yolanda.

Jerome, Willie and Ruzzo are under the witness protection plan and were sent to different places inside the United States, somehow where Jerome was sent was discovered by the Bonnano family, since Jerome's head had a $100,000.00 price it was obvious that somebody inside the system provided the information, so on a Friday morning Jerome was attending the garden in front of the house they were assigned when a black van pulled over and shot Jerome several times, his wife that was inside heard the shots and immediately called the assigned FBI agents, they went ahead and called 911 and an ambulance was rushed to the site, but it was to late, Jerome was declared dead on site, after the shooting the FBI started an internal investigation and discovered the source that provided the information to the Bonanno family, it was 20 year veteran of the force with less than a month to retire.

Rafael and Kurt got the news about Jerome that same day, Jerome was the main source that would provide the identity of

Jim Silas, now he will be harder to identify, they still have Senator Springdale and his wife Dalila, the Senator is disable, so Dalila will the only one to provide any valid description of Jim Silas.

After the debacle with Jerome Willie and Ruzzo were immediately moved to a different location, they still need to testify in upcoming trials of New York Mafia and several of the Mississippi and Alabama Dixie Mafia members.

Rafael arrived at his office that Monday morning not expecting a surprising call from Pannel, he immediately summoned Kurt to his office, "it must be very important when Pannel is calling us", Rafael said to Kurt.

"Pannel, this is Rafael I have Kurt here with us, what can we do for you?"

"I have some very bad news for you guys, Dalila have

disappeared, she closed her bank account and just disappeared".

"So, you have no idea where she might be?"

"No, no idea at all, I called you since it is my duty as her attorney". Pannel responded to Rafael.

"We have a problem Pannel, we wanted to ask Dalila to be more descriptive concerning Jim Silas, since Jerome is no longer with us and the Senator is mainly a vegetable".

"Wait, what do you mean Jerome is no longer with us?"

Pannel asked Rafael.

"You didn't know that Jerome was gun down over the weekend?"

"No, how did it happened, he was supposed to be protected at all time".

"We think it might be an inside job, since his location was kept secret, only known by his wife and you as his lawyer, we are investigating, we should have an answer real soon".

Pannel kept quiet for a moment, then began to talk.

"I am shock, why I was not informed sooner?"

"You have to take that with the FBI, Pannel".

Rafael and Kurt knew Pannel was notify, there was something wrong in the way he answered that statement, why did he lie? Pannel knew 1 hour after Jerome was gun down, maybe there is a connection between Jerome's shooting and Dalila disappearance, the truth will come out sooner or later.

Concerning Willie and Ruzzo, they were already moved to any another safe house, Rafael and Kurt were given all the necessary information in case they wanted to interrogate them again.

It was late on a Wednesday afternoon while Yolanda was working in one of her cases a GBI agent show up at her office asking for Rafael, Yolanda smartly ask the agent for some ID since she did not recognize him, he showed the official GBI badge, but still Yolanda was suspicious, why a GBI agent from another dept. was asking for Rafael?

"Rafael is on the field; can I ask I what you want from him?"

"Just routine, when do you expect him back?"

The agent asked Yolanda, but she will not give him any more information.

"Let me check with Captain Lynnard, he might know".

But the agent left abruptly, without saying goodbye, that's when Yolanda determined that person was not a true agent, she immediately called Captain Lynnard.

"Captain, an agent just showed here in my office asking for Rafael, he had all the necessary ID, but I was suspicious and told him that I was going to call you he left abruptly, what do you recommend I do".

Then Lynnard responded. "Yolanda I will be down, stay calm, we might have an impostor in our headquarters".

But Yolanda was calmed, she just needed to get in touch with Rafael, but how, he and Kurt were out on the field, she was hoping that the impostor will be caught before Rafael and Kurt arrive at the GBI headquarters.

Lynnard called the Sergeant in charge of security for the headquarters, advise him of a potential impostor in the premises, be on the lookout he told the Sergeant.

When lynnard arrived at Yolanda's office he could see a Ruger .380 that Yolanda has placed next to her desk, she was ready for any situation, she was calm a true professional, lynnard mentioned that all the security options have been put in high alert, the director also was notify and extra security guards were placed at various exit doors.

20 minutes have passed since Lynnard gave the alert that an impostor might be inside the complex a guard at section 3 on the Southside of the building have noticed a suspicious character and after the guard gave him the order to stop he ran away from the guard, the Sergeant

head of security gave the order to concentrate in that section, for a while they thought that they have lost the individual but after further inspection of the area the person was located, he began shooting at the guards, they responded by shooting back, after several minutes of engagement they noticed that he was not responding, after an inspection of the area they found him laying in a pool of blood, he was hit by one of the guards.

Now they needed to identify the body, how did get a hold of an GBI ID, in the meantime Rafael and Kurt made back to headquarters not knowing what was happening they were summoned to the Director's office, there they will know the reason for all the commotion.

"Rafael, Kurt, we had a situation here but everything is under control, early today an individual approached Yolanda asking for Rafael, after he left her office Yolanda called Captain Lynnard, he immediately applied the security protocol and after an encounter with our guards the subject was terminated". "Is Yolanda okay?" Rafael asked the director.

"Yes Rafael, now I need for you guys to lay low for a while, we need to determine who this guy was and if anybody else is involved".

After the briefing with director, Rafael ran to Yolanda's office, arriving he embrace her and asked how she was doing.

"I am doing fine Rafael, I have my baby next to me her name is Ruger.380, what did the director said?"

"Kurt and I have to lay low for a while until they can determine what happened".

"Them Rafael, let's live early and enjoy a quiet evening together, we'll figure out tomorrow the next step to take".

"Let me talk to Kurt first to set up plan of action".

Rafael said to Yolanda, he steps out of her office and walk to Kurt's office.

"Kurt, I am taking the rest of the day off, going home let's be in constant touch, tomorrow we can set up a plan of action, we don't know who else is involved, go home to your wife talk later".

Kurt signaled positively and left for his home.

After Yolanda and Rafael arrived at their apartment, they noticed an official car parked outside, it was one of them, the director has ordered a detail to guard Rafael and Kurt homes.

After a quiet dinner Rafael and Yolanda watched tv for a while, Gilligan's Island was on, around 11:00 pm they went to sleep, next to their bed their babies, a Ruger.380 next to Yolanda and next to Rafael a 45 caliber Smith and Wesson, they were hoping for a quiet week, maybe not.

Rafael arrived at his office around 8:00 am, Kurt was already there, he gave Rafael some new information about Dalila, where she might be and with whom.

"Rafael, it looks that Dalila left for Central America, no country specifically yet waiting for immigration to give us more detail".

"Well Kurt, knowing that Dalila was born in Costa Rica, we might look there first".

"Right, and also remember those bank account statements found in Bonner's home, they were from The Bank of Nova Scotia in San Jose, they were under the name of Ernie Callan".

"Yes, a name fabricated by somebody to hide an identity, maybe Silas".

"Let's wait for the additional information from the immigration department".

10 minutes after the director showed up at Rafael office.

"Rafael, we have some information about the person that was shoot here yesterday, matching his fingerprints gave us a name of Leo "Leone" Talazia, a well-known hit man from the Bonnano family out of Chicago, we still don't know why he was asking for you so please be very careful on your daily activity, that also goes to Yolanda". "We will sir, please keep me posted on any new development".

"I will Rafael, by the way any news on Dalila, where she might be?"

"Kurt and I are waiting for more information from the Immigration office concerning her where about".

"Great, keep me posted, we need to grab her as soon as possible".

After the director left Rafael's office Kurt and Rafael began to work on a plan of action, not only to protect themselves but also to detain Dalila and whoever was with her.

Later that afternoon they received more information about Leo Talazia, it seems that he flew from Chicago to Omaha Nebraska where Jerome was settle stayed there for 2 days and them flew to Atlanta, the local authorities could match the days that he arrived in Omaha with the shooting of Jerome, still not clear why he came to Atlanta looking for Rafael.

Yolanda and Rafael left the office around 6:00 pm, they stopped at a restaurant close to their apartment, they wanted to make sure nobody was following so they drove around the block for a couple of times, the restaurant name was the Beef Cellar, not to fancy but great stakes, they sat in a table facing the door, them Rafael began to talk.

"Yolanda, who the heck wants to kill me?"

"Baby, I don't know, you just have to be a little careful".

"I have tried to put all the different situations on my mind, nothing clicks".

Don't worry Rafael, let's concentrate in our dinner and try to be alert, That's all".

Dalila was already at least 2 weeks ahead of the authorities, she arrived with a man in San Jose, Costa Rica, where some people were waiting for them at the airport, one of them was Carlos Gerras, a known head of a criminal organization in Costa Rica affiliated with the American Mafia, Mr. Gerras took over the Strip Club in Costa Rica previously owned by Jerome.

The moment Dalila got into the limousine with a grin on her face she started talking.

"estupidos, all of you are bunch of idiots, we created a good organization and look what happens, Willie, Ruzzo and specially Jerome, they all became RATS!!, them you send a no-good hit man that could not finish the job, we gave Jerome everything and he screw it up, we told him to only handle prostitution and get the human traffic of young girls going, but no, he decided to get involved with drugs, estupido".

Currently Dalila was getting explosive.

"I WANT THAT RAFAEL GUY FINISH, FINISH, MUERTO".

Everybody was quiet, thinking how to respond to the insults that Dalila have made.

"Miss. Dalila, the hit man was recommended by our associates in Chicago, they are aware of situation and have sent another person to Atlanta, they promise they will get rid of Rafael Chaquet as you have ordered". Carlos Gerras said.

"the hit on Rafael is a favor to an associate from Cuba, he has help us to move some girls thru Cuba into Europe, he knows Rafael well, he is the reason his father and brother are both dead". Dalila said.

Dalila was talking about the younger son of Commandante Sosa, and the brother of Captain Sosa, his name was Rogelio Sosa now a Coronel with the Cuban Intelligence service.

After Dalila have calmed, she turns to the man that arrived with her from Atlanta.

"Jim, you knew how to take care of things many years ago, I wish you could the same now".

Jim is Jim Silas, he finally appeared, and it looks like Dalila have a closer relationship to him than previously known.

"Rafael, we just got word that Dalila left for Honduras with a man, according to his passport, are you sitting down, Ernie Callas, we found him Rafael, we found Jim Silas".

"Yes, but you know what Kurt, even thou they flew to Honduras, I bet you their final destination is a country they feel comfortable, and that is Costa Rica".

Even thou they were happy to find Silas, Rafael needed to find out why they want it to get rid of him.

About 8:00 pm a flight from Chicago to Atlanta brought an individual, he had an assignment, get rid of Rafael Chaquet, it will easier said than done, the Illinois State Police already have notify the GBI that a Goivanno Assanse was on his way to Atlanta, 'Goyi' as he was known in Chicago checked into the Hyatt Regency hotel, already an uncover unit from the GBI was on his tracks, Rafael and Kurt were also notify of the situation and were ready to prepare for the unexpected.

The moment that Giovanno left the hotel was grabbed by the GBI agents, they found a Colt revolver on him and some notes concerning Rafael, he was charged with possession of a firearm without a permit, he was taken to the Fulton County jail for processing.

Rafael was notified of the apprehension of Giovanno, he immediately wanted to interview him he was anxious seeking the reason why anybody wanted to kill him, he approached the director and asked for permission the director gave the okay, but he needed to take Kurt with him, so Rafael and Kurt made plans to interview Giovanno that afternoon.

The processing of Giovanno took longer, he have a massive criminal record dating back to the late 50's, in one instance he was charged with a felony and served 7 years at the Joliet prison, he was also charged of several other acts but never convicted, Rafael and Kurt arrived at the Fulton County jail around 4:00 pm, a jail guard took them to the same room where they interview Cynthia Corbin, after 20 minute waiting Giovanno was brought in, he didn't look that menacing, a short guy maybe 5'8", a little bit on the heavy size and a chain smoker.

Rafael started the conversation, very calm but precise.

"Mr. Assanse......." Giovanno interrupted Rafael.

"I know who you are, I have been studying you for 2 weeks, Mr. Rafael Chaquet".

"Well, since you know me that well, can you tell me why you

wanted to kill me?" Rafael asked very angrily.

"I don't know, and don't care, as long as they pay".

Giovanno answered Rafael with a smile.

"But who gave you the order?" Rafael asked again.

"Gentlemen, I need a lawyer, I already had said enough".

And by saying those words the interview was over, Rafael needed to expand his investigation, his personal case is getting complicated and not only his life was in danger but also that of Yolanda, no way he was going to permit anybody to harm his Yolanda, especially now that in only 30 days their wedding was going to happen.***

CHAPTER 23

"The ideal man bears the accidents of life with dignity and grace, making the best of circumstances"

Aristotle

The Escalante neighborhood is an exclusive area in San Jose Costa Rica, Dalila Diaz runs her enterprise from there she lives in an spacious condominium with 5 bedrooms, the day after arriving in San Jose an officer with the Ministry of Public Security who is on the Dalila payroll arrived at her place with some news, it seems that the Americans law enforcement agencies are looking for Dalila, they still don' know where she is but when they find out they will demand from the government of Costa Rica her extradition.

"It doesn't scare me, I have very good connections in the government, some of them owe me some favors and also I have hidden information that might damage their reputation, I am not worry at all". Dalila said.

Back at the GBI headquarters Rafael and Kurt had two important tasks ahead of them, how to get Jim Silas apprehended and find out the reason why there was a contract on Rafael, "it doesn't make any sense", Rafael commented.

"We'll get to the bottom of this Rafael; I promise you that".

"Thank you, Kurt any word on the whereabout of Silas and Dalila?"

"Nothing yet, we should hear something any day now".

Due to the government red tape in many Latin American countries the whereabout of Dalila and Silas have not been stablish yet, they flew on a private jet from Tegucigalpa Honduras to San Jose Costa Rica, by bribing the local authorities in Honduras no exit documents were archive.

Dalila received a phone call 2 days after she arrived in Costa Rica from the Chicago Mob advising her that no more individuals will be sent to Atlanta, the 2 that they

sent were apprehended and there is a possibility one of them might flip and start helping the authorities, in which case the reason for the hit on Rafael Chaquet might be uncovered and hers and the Chicago Mob activities might be in danger of being exposed.

Dalila was mad, she needed to terminate Rafael or her trafficking operation to Europe from Cuba might be in jeopardy, Coronel Sosa will be in San Jose next week, he will be very annoyed if nothing has been done about Rafael Chaquet.

Dalila decided to finish the work herself, with the help of Silas they could sneak into the US get rid of Rafael and sneak out again, she still have some contacts that can help her accomplish her plan, it will be a big risk but she needed Sosa to rely on her so the Cuba connection will stay intact, she got in touch with a Costa Rica government official that provided her and Silas new identity, new passports, new driving license and a couple of falsify credit cards issued in Costa Rica, later she contacted an associate of the Dixie Mafia, she needed   their help by transporting her and Silas thru Georgia and later making a getaway.

Everything was set, next week they will depart from San Jose to Montreal Canada, there they will flight to Charlotte, NC and them finally drive to Atlanta, GA, that final portion with the help from the local Dixie Mafia associate.

Back at the GBI headquarters Rafael and Kurt were frustrated at the authorities in Costa Rica, they have not provided any information about the whereabout of Dalila and Silas, it appears that they never arrived in that country even the US State dept. could not provide any information about them.

"It's only Monday Rafael, maybe before the week is out, we should have some information about their whereabout".

"Let's hope so, those are the only 2 persons left to close our case".

Rafael commented to Kurt.

About 2:00 pm on Monday, an FBI agent arrived at the GBI headquarters, he needed to talk to Rafael and Kurt, he was directed to Kurt office, Rafael was there them the agent gave them the following information.

"Hey guys, just to let you know Mr. Pannel is in custody, he is been charge with money laundry and several other situations in conjunction with the Dixie Mafia, it looks like he was their money man".

Rafael and Kurt were not surprise, they always knew that Pannel had a close connection with those criminal elements, first by representing them and later to clear their illegal gains, they were hoping to flip Pannel and start to cooperate with the Federal authorities.

Rafael asked the FBI agent.

"Can we interview Pannel, maybe he can shed some light into the whereabout of Dalila and Silas".

"I will ask permission from my superior for your interview with Pannel".

"I hope it will today so we can interview him tomorrow".

Rafael said.

Dalila and Silas were making the final preparations for their flight to Montreal, they already had their fake passport, her new name Dolores Trellos and Silas will be William Serrach, they also have changed their exterior appearance she has become an stunning blonde with some facial modifications, his look will be older and more passive for a change.

The Pannel interview was approved by the FBI, they scheduled it for tomorrow morning at 10:00 am, it will be conducted at the Federal Facility at Lovejoy, Rafael and Kurt knew the drill, be there early and be precise in the questions as possible.

Rafael and Kurt left their office early, stopped at a Cracker Barrel on the way to Lovejoy, they were ready, they needed to get the right answers from Pannel concerning the whereabout of Dalila and Silas it was the main point of the interview, Rafael and Kurt were directed to an office, an FBI agent was present and also Mr. Pannel attorney, at first Pannel was reluctant to meet with them but he was reminded that any collaboration will weight on his eventual conviction and sentencing, Pannel was ready he entered the room wearing the customary orange jumpsuit, he looked older than his regular age of 61, Rafael started the interview.

"Mr. Pannel, we meet in different circumstances, we hope that you can give us information concerning the whereabout of Dalila, is she in Costa Rica?"

"Agent Rafael, I have instructed my attorney to get some documents that will take into consideration my collaboration with the pertinent authorities, meaning the GBI".

"Well, Pannel you are in luck before we came in the GBI attorney issue a letter of recommendation to the Federal District Attorney and to the presiding judge in your case to take into consideration your testimony concerning Dalila Diaz and Jim Silas".

Rafael enthusiastic said.

"Okay, but the part concerning Silas, I don't know where he is, I know about Dalila, she flew to Honduras them took a private flight to Costa Rica".

"Concerning Silas, it was determined according to Federal authorities that Jim Silas left with Dalila".

"Okay if you say so". Pannel answered back.

"Concerning Silas, did you at any time knew that Silas was living in the US?" Rafael asked Pannel.

"Off course, he was living under an assumed name, he was here under your noses".

"What was his assumed name?" Rafael asked.

"It was 'Reverend' Henry Wall, a thru Christian, ha, ha, ha".

Panel could not stop laughing, a true Christian he sent people to Heaven and Hell.

At that moment Kurt looked at Rafael and made a comment.

"Rafael, we interview Henry Wall before, he didn't look that menacing, he also had an affair with Joann, and we cleared him".

"I know Kurt, we were fooled". Rafael said.

"Pannel, thank you we might need you later with more questions".

Kurt said and him and Rafael left the room.

"Just imagine Rafael, that innocent looking guy we had in front of us is a cruel Serial Killer".

Rafael was as surprise as Kurt, he looked very astonish.

The following morning Dalila now Dolores Trellos and Silas now William Serrach boarded the Air Canada flight from San Jose to Montreal, they should be arriving 9 hours and 40 minutes later, connecting in Montreal for another flight that will take them to Charlotte in 3hrs and 20 min.

Under the witness protection plan Willie was sent to Laramie Wyoming, a quiet city, to quiet for Willie, after been there for 6 months he was apprehended trying to break into a house, he was sent to the Laramie county jail where he meet a dubious local fellow named Isle Preston that was also in jail for armed robbery what Willie didn't know was that Isle already knew about the price on Willie's head from the Bonnano family and he was going to get it.

"Hey Willie, do you want to get the heck out of here?"

Isle asked Willie.

"Yes, the sooner the better".

"I got a friend of mine who works here, he can let us out tonight for the right price".

"How much is the right price?" Willie asked.

"He wants 10 Grants, and we will out tonight".

"How the hell I am going to get 10 Grants tonight?"

"Don't worry I will give him the 10 Grants and you pay me later, okay?" Isle said.

"Great let's do it". Said Willie smiling.

Around 10:00 pm Isle friend took over his shift, the County Jail in Laramie is not big, so only 5 guards were on duty at that time, one of them was Isle friend who was were together on this, the amount was $50,000.00.

Isle friend took them to a back door where a car was parked, Willie entered first, Isle stay behind not getting into the car to Willie's surprise there were 2 other men waiting for him, the immediately hit Willie on the head knocking him down them drove away to a farm nearby.

The car stopped, Willie was push from the car the 2 other men walked out of the car and kept hitting Willie, he was bleeding profoundly, them one of the men started talking.

"Willie today is your lucky day; you are meeting the creator or maybe not".

Them the other man began hitting Willie with a baseball bat until Willie dropped dead, they dig a hole big enough to place the body of Willie, them after they left to meet Isle and compensate him for his information, Isle was going to be very surprised.

They meet Isle about a block from the jail, shoved him into the car and shot him 3 times with a .22 caliber pistol in the head, they went back to same place where Willie was and dropped Isle in the same hole, covered it and left, no witnesses.

The Federal authorities were slow in react to the situation and the lead agent taken care of Willie was demoted and sent to another post, it was very demoralizing they needed Willie to testify in the coming trails, now he is gone, they immediately surrounded the locale where Ruzzo was sent in Burlington Vermont, Ruzzo was always complaining about the cold weather "a guy from Mississippi should not be here".

Ruzzo was transported to a safer place somewhere in the South with 24 surveillance and zero free time, no visitors, no shopping and no mingling with the locals.

The following day Rafael and Kurt were notified about the killing of Willie, they knew that the Mafia was very effective in carrying out their task, now the Federal authorities need to keep Ruzzo as safe as possible, right now he is indispensable in their quest to bring certain members of the NY Mafia and the Dixie Mafia to trial.

Back in Lovejoy Pannel heard the news that Willie was killed; he thought that because he is behind bars the same group that killed Willie can assumed that he can also flip and start providing information to the Federal authorities, difficult times for Pannel he already helped Rafael and Kurt identify Jim Silas, he was quiet for a moment them all of the sudden started to shout, GUARDS!, GUARDS!, when the guards arrived at Pannel cell he told them that he needed to meet an FBI agent as soon as possible, he had important information about certain criminal elements, the FBI knew which criminal elements he was talking about.

Pannel was taken from the Lovejoy facility to a safe house in Atlanta for further questioning, present were   several FBI agents from the Organize Crime Task Force, a lawyer from the FBI and the special agent for the Atlanta section, them the FBI started to go point by point the information they needed to know and would happen next to Pannel.

"Mr. Pannel, we brought you here because you have notified the authorities in Lovejoy a desire to cooperate with us concerning the structure and dealings of the Bonanno family in the South with the help of the Dixie Mafia, is that correct?"

The FBI agent in charge of the questioning asked Pannel.

"Yes, I am willing to provide you guys with any information I have, and I do have a lot of information, but with one condition".

"What is that condition". The agent asks Pannel.

"That I go to a real safe place, look what happened to Willie".

"Yes, we will provide you with a safe place, what

happened to Willie was a breach of security and we have corrected the protocol for future safe locations".

Then Pannel grabbed a cup of coffee relax and began to describe the history and the mechanism of both the Italian Mafia and the Dixie Mafia connection in the South.

"It all began in 1969, the then Vice President of Citizen and South bank William Burtinsaas now retired but still alive in the Buckhead branch ask to meet with me, I have done some legal work for him before I remember it was a Wednesday, when I arrived at the Buckhead Branch in Peachtree Rd there were 2 more men, they introduced themselves as Mr. Guissepe Vallonera from NYC, and Jeff Sprondile from Biloxi Mississippi, at first it was a conversation regarding my legal help for them concerning a Strip Club they wanted to open in Atlanta, at that moment I thought of Jerome he owns a small Club in Atlanta why not connect this 2 business men with him".

"was anything discussed about money laundry or drugs, prostitution or any illegal activity they plan to conduct in Atlanta?"

The FBI agent ask Pannel.

"Not at that time, but a week later another meeting was called, at this time Jerome was there so was the guy from NYC and Jeff from Biloxi, and off course William and me, at that meeting they start to talk about drugs and prostitution and other illegal activities, they created an structure to where the NYC Mafia will handle the drug trade and the people from Biloxi will handle the prostitution and other illegal activities".

"How did Jerome got involved at this time?"

The agent asked Pannel.

"Jerome was given the opportunity to be involved in more clubs in the Atlanta area and later expand to other areas of the South, off course Jerome will manage the clubs with a percentage of the profits while the other group will enjoy a bigger cut".

"What about the rest of the people involved in the first meeting?" the agent again asks Pannel.

"You mean William the bank VP, well he was involved in the laundry of the profits from all the illegal activity perform by the organization, he received a hefty percentage of all the money he received from the group, he retired from the bank about 2 years ago and still lives in the same house in Buckhead, he should be around 60 years old ".

"Beside the Atlanta bank, anymore banks were involved with the operation?" the agent asked Pannel.

"You see, the money was laundered thru the Atlanta bank and later transferred to a branch of the Bank of Nova Scotia in San Jose Costa Rica, by the way Jerome opened another Strip Club, or should I say the group opened the Club and named Dalila Diaz as the head of the Club".

"Was Dalila involved in other illegal activities in Costa Rica?" another agent asked Pannel.

"Well her family did, her Father ran a numbers racquet and a prostitution ring since the 1940's, later Dalila married a member of her father group, he later was killed by the security forces in San Jose after a botched robbery of a jewelry store, later Dalila took over after her father became ill, she is a ruthless woman".

"now, what about you, what was your place in the organization?"

"I was their legal counsel, I defended or my firm did many members from both organizations, including Jim Silas and now ex-Senator Charles Springdale, a sex maniac, I told agents Rafael and Kurt from the GBI, he was involved in the cold cases they are trying to solve, I also handled some cash transactions for them".

All the FBI agents were pleased with testimony that Pannel have provided, they arranged that same day his transfer to an FBI safe house, they also requested the Marshall Office to handle his security arrangement.

"Well Mr. Pannel, we are satisfied, we can assure you that your safety is our most important task right now, we will advise you what the next step will be, thank you".

Now the federal authorities have 2 witnesses to testify against those criminal organizations described by Pannel, Charles Springdale is under house arrest due to his disability, an arrest

warrant was issued against William Burtinsaas the ex-bank official.

The location of Dalila and Silas have become number 1.
***

CHAPTER 24

"Every new beginning comes from some other beginning's end".

Seneca

By weeks end must of the people involved in the organization were either apprehended or were already in prison.

Guissepe Vallonera was apprehended in NYC after a confrontation with the FBI agents, he was wounded and transported to a nearby hospital where he remained chained to his bed for 2 days, Jeff Sprundille the head of the Dixie Mafia was already in an Alabama prison serving a life sentence after been convicted of first degree murder in connection to the killing of an ex-member of the Dixie Mafia, William Burtinsaas was already in the Fulton County jail awaiting charges of money laundry and other charges in connection with the organization.

Dalila and Silas were already in Charlotte, NC, waiting for a member of the Dixie Mafia to transport them to

Atlanta, after 2 hours waiting the guy show up, he had tattoos all over his body except his face his name was Mike "but everybody calls me mickey" maybe 6'2" and very muscular.

The drive will take about 3 hours, on the way to Atlanta they stopped in Greenville, SC to grab something to eat, while they were having dinner Dalila made a phone call to Pannel's office, the assistant answer the phone informing her of the latest development concerning Pannel.

"Silas, Pannel have been taking into custody and there is possibility that he might flip, what a jerk".

She didn't know that Pannel already was providing information to the Federal Authorities.

"Should we proceed to Atlanta or turn back?"

Silas asked Dalila.

"Hell yeah, we are going to finish our job, Rafael will be terminated, or our operation will be ruined".

Dalila's eyes were full of rage, her remark was final.

The director asks Rafael to come over to his office, there is some information he needed to relay too Rafael.

"Rafael sit down, we just have received reliable information that there is an individual or individuals, we don't know who they are, that want to kill you we have contacted all various law enforcement agencies and asked for their help in trying to locate those individuals".

Rafael was a bit shock but recovered fast.

"Thank you, director please keep me updated about any more information concerning my situation".

Rafael ran over to Yolanda's office, he immediately told her about the conversation he had with the director, he didn't want her to be scare but he needed for her to be inform and prepared, he also talk to Kurt about the danger they might face, no detailed description of the subjects was known.

"Yolanda, from now on we have to be very vigilant and alert, I will never allow anybody to harm you because of me".

Yolanda responded immediately.

"Nobody is going to harm us Rafael, we are going to be prepared, we will get over these".

In a matter of seconds Kurt arrived at Yolanda's office Rafael was still there, Kurt began to talk.

"Rafael, I just spoke with the director he will assigning us 2 more agents, we should be armed at all time and prepared to engage whoever those individuals are".

"Kurt, Yolanda and I are armed, we hope we don't have to use it, but if we do, we won't miss".

It was already the beginning of May, the first set of hearings against a group of members of the NYC Mafia and the Dixie Mafia was taking place, Ruzzo was brought back to Atlanta as the main witness, the group was been charged with murders, racketeering, prostitution and more all under the RICO act, Cynthia Corbin was found guilty of first degree murder in the homicide of Jim Donner, she received a sentence of life without parole a week ago, Cynthia offered herself to be a government witness in the hope that her sentence will be reduced, Dalila and Silas have been in Atlanta for a week already, they have been recording with the help of 'mickey' all Rafael movements it will be difficult task to carry out their plan, Rafael is under constant guard, also several federal agencies are also looking for them, but that did not deter Dalila she needed to finish her plan as soon as possible.

From the information they gather on Rafael, Dalila knew that almost every Wednesday Rafael and Yolanda had dinner at a Chinese restaurant not far from their apartment, and after dinner they usually visited a neighborhood bar close by, that will be the right moment to go ahead with the hit, but they encounter a problem, 'mickey' was arrested on DUI charges the night before making it almost impossible to move around Atlanta, also they were afraid that he will divulge the plans to kill Rafael they needed to find a solution, the only option was to rent a car but that would make them vulnerable since every law enforcement agency was looking for them, Dalila and Silas decided to stay low for a while until the situation with mickey can be solved, their stay at the Sheraton will be somewhat prolonged.

The following day they were informed that mickey will not be out for a while, he broke his parole and will be returned to prison to serve the remaining of his sentence which is 7 years.

"We are dealing with a bunch of idiots, for a stinking drink he will be out for 7 years, what a bunch of idiots!!!!"

Dalila was furious, her plan to eliminate Rafael was looking more distant now, she needed to find a solution to her dilemma.

Them Silas gave her a suggestion.

"Dalila, do you remember the name of that fellow that helped me dispose of some of my victims?"

"Yes, that was Henry Dollsis, isn't he in prison?"

"No, he got out about a year ago, and I think he lives in Macon, he did a job for me about 6 months ago".

"Really, why don't you give him a call, maybe he can help us out".

Dalila was very excited, Silas found a new source to help them out in their quest to finish Rafael Chaquet, maybe their Cuba-Europe operation can be saved.

Kurt was still at his office so decided to call Dr. Slinkis the brother of Roseanne, he wanted to inform him of the latest developments.

" Good Afternoon Dr. Slinkis office can I help you?"

"Yes, this is agent Kurt Janus with the Georgia Bureau of Investigation is Dr. Slinkis in?"

"Yes, agent Kurt, I'll get him for you".

In about 2 minutes Dr. Slinkis grab the phone and started a conversation with Kurt.

"Agent Kurt what a pleasant surprise, I hope you have some news about the murder of my sister".

"As a matter of fact, yes it seems that Jim Silas murdered your sister, she was having an affair with Judge now ex-Senator Springdale, the day of the murder she refused Springdale that day and he ordered Jim Silas to kill her".

Kurt could hear Slinkis sobbing at the other end of the line, even thou she was murdered more than 10 years ago he still remember that day.

"Agent Kurt, has Silas been apprehended yet?"

"No Doctor not yet, we know where he is but is a foreign country, we have activated an arrest warrant thru INTERPOL, he will be apprehended soon, I will keep you posted".

"Thank you, agent Kurt please do".

When Kurt finished the conversation, he went back to work, Rafael already has left on his way to Aiken, SC to visit Yolanda's mom, she was also planning to marry a friend of her husband, she has been a widow for 4 years now and on her 70's, she needed a companion.

While he was at his office Kurt received a strange phone call, the person at the other end identify himself as a member of the Atlanta Police Dept., they were asking for Rafael.

"He is not here now; can I help you".

"Do you know when he'll be back?"

Kurt immediately became suspicious and asked the caller for his badge number, when Kurt ask him that information, he remained quiet for a moment and hang up his phone. Rafael left Yolanda's mom phone number in Aiken, so Kurt called Rafael and inform him of that suspicious phone call.

"Rafael, be very careful, keep your and Yolanda's eyes wide open, I did not like that phone call".

"Thank you, Kurt, we'll do, please keep me updated, we'll be fine".

After Rafael hang up the phone, he relays the information to Yolanda, she wasn't to happy but been a strong woman she was ready for any situation.

"Silas did you call Henry Dollsis?"

"Yes, I did, left a message with his girlfriend".

"How about the call to Rafael's office?"

"Yes, he wasn't there, I hang up the phone fast the guy at the other end became suspicious and ask me for my badge number".

"That's probably Kurt, his partner, I hope he did not trace your call".

"He didn't have time".

10 minutes have passed when the phone rang at their hotel room, it was Henry Dollsis.

"Hey Silas, how are you man, I thought you were out of town, how are you doing?"

"Doing fine Henry, listen is you available to do a job for me?"

"What kind of job Silas?"

"I need somebody to drive me and my partner around Atlanta to do a specific job".

"You mean killing somebody?"

"Something like that".

Henry was quiet for a minute them responded to Silas.

"Man, I don't do that stuff anymore".

"Henry what about $10,000.00, will that convince you start

again?"

"Well, that surely sounds tempting let me think it over, call you later, okay".

Finishing the conversation with Henry Silas turn to Dalila and said.

"I think he will be on board, he sounded enthusiastic when I mentioned the 10 thousand dollars".

"Silas, we have to be careful, look at those people we trusted, they have turn against us". Dalila said to Silas. What Silas and Dalila didn't know was that Henry was a Police Informant with the Macon Police Dept. the week before he was caught with DUI violation, Henry was on parole, that violation surely will send him back to jail after posting the bond he contacted the officer handling his case, "If you help me with my pending trail , I will help you with some important information you might need", this is the perfect time to betray Silas and Dalila.

Back in Aiken, SC, Yolanda and Rafael were a little apprehensive but try show calmness in front of Yolanda's mother, they were enjoying a good Puerto Rican Dinner that Yolanda's mother prepared when the phone rang.

Rafael pick up the phone it was Kurt, he had some information about Silas and Dalila.

"Rafael, we might have a lead as to the whereabout of Silas and Dalila, they might be back in the US we don't know the reason or where they are, but they are here".

"that's great news Kurt, we should be back in Atlanta tomorrow".

"Also, Rafael we are still looking into that weird phone call asking for you, just be careful".

"Thank you, Kurt we'll do". Rafael finished the conversation and went back to the dinning room to enjoy his meal, when he sits down at the table Yolanda ask him "who was it?"

"It was Kurt, giving me some news as to the whereabout of Silas and Dalila, nothing to worry baby".

They didn't know that they were here to terminate Rafael, now they needed to be lucky and hoped that Henry in Macon gives the information to his contact inside the MPD.

But it was not going to happen, the following day Henry called Silas and accepted the offer, 10 big ones will be very handy now, specially since he was broke.

"Silas, good morning, I will take your offer, but give me a week I need to tie some loose ends here in Macon". "Okay Henry, but only a week I need to finish this situation as soon as possible".

"Yeah, yeah, only a week I promise you".

Silas turned to Dalila and said, "we got it, he agreed".

"Let's hope he doesn't screw this up".

Dalila reluctantly agreed on the arrangement; it was their only option.

Tuesday evening Rafael and Yolanda were back in their apartment, an assigned agent was posted outside, he will be there until Rafael and Yolanda leave for their office the following morning.

"Yes, I loved my husband and those jerks killed him!!"

Cynthia Corbin was at a Federal court, she was there as a government witness, she exposed all that she knew about the dealings of the criminal organization she used to be associated with, in front of her several members of the Dixie Mafia they were facing several charges, murder, engaging in a prostitution racquet and many others, all charges were tried under the RICO act.

Back in Macon the officer assigned to Henry needed some information so he gave him a call, something was brewing, Henry needed to talk maybe a little pressure can convince him.

"Hey Henry, how are you doing today, man I need some information and I hope you can give it to me".

The officer could hear Henry breathing heavily, he was nervous.

"Hey, how are you, what kind of information you want?"

"Well, henry any information, you know the street people are saying you might know something important and if you want my help, tell me now or I will not be able to help, okay".

Off course the officer didn't know of any situation going on, he was just proving to see if Henry can talk.

"Man, I do want your help, but the street is wrong nothing important is going on if I hear anything be certain I will let you know". The officer was not convinced, he could sense the nervousness of Henry.

"Okay Henry, is your call but if anything happens and I find out you knew, don't count on me helping you".

Henry is in a quagmire, should he spill the beans on Silas and Dalila or just keep the promise to Silas, 10 Grants sounds pretty good, but at the same time going back to prison is even worse, he has a week to follow his instincts. Rafael and Kurt were busy trying to find any clue as to the whereabout of Silas and Dalila, already the DA has place in the system warrants for their arrest, if they are in the US they will be caught, if only they knew that they were not that far away, it will be almost a suicide mission but Silas and Dalila were ready to carry out the plan, of course Silas was not to convince it will succeed but he already was involve 100 %. ****

CHAPTER 24

"Charm is a product of the unexpected"

Jose Marti

Ruzzo was feeling secure, his witness protection address was almost impossible to detect, well not true the criminal elements have a way to find anything they want thru extorsion and payout they will find you unless they consider that your testimony is not worthwhile.

Right now he was secure, he was taking back to Atlanta to be the main government witness against several criminal elements, he will stay there for a couple of days them back to his hideout in the middle of nowhere, the only problem is that the people wanting to terminate Ruzzo found and agent with the Marshall service in deep financial trouble, he was staying with his mistress at a hotel in Las Vegas owned by the Chicago Mafia the agent has a couple of addictions, gambling and women, he owes a lot of money to a gambling joint owned by the NYC Mafia, they knock at his hotel room and very politely

ask to be let inside, the agent was surprise and immediately identify himself as a federal agent they knew who he was, they sat down and gave him a proposition he could not refuse.

"we can forgive your gambling debt of $100,00.00 and don't

mention anything to your wife about the woman you are keeping if you give us information about that rat Ruzzo, and by the way we can forgo the breaking of both of your legs, do you understand agent Richard Simtson?"

The agent became pale and started to vomit, he doesn't have an option, beside Ruzzo is con man and an ex-convict, one less in this world will not matter and by doing that all my main problems will be gone, well Mr. Agent no so fast man, you are dealing with people that will not hesitate to terminate your life.

"What do you want to know?"

The agent shaking asked the member of the NYC Mafia.

Great, we knew you would come to your senses, we need to know where Ruzzo lives now, and how many agents are guarding him".

Them the agent responded.

"you have to give me at least 3days, I need to ask around, I not assigned to that detail, I need to ask around".

"Okay, no problem we can handle 3 days, but don't disappoint us".

The agent was still shaking when the individuals representing the NYC Mafia left.

After testifying Ruzzo was taken back to Denver where he will reside from now on, it is cold like his last residence, but he doesn't have a choice is either Denver of be taken out of the witness protection plan, it's up to Ruzzo.

"Rafael, May 30 is almost here are you excited?"

Yolanda is talking to Rafael, but he was not there, he could not get his mind concentrated in anything else except finding out why people want it to get rid of him.

"Sorry honey, yes I am excited and looking forward to my promise of us having 20 kids".

"Rafael, I love with all my heart but if you want 20 kids you are marrying the wrong woman".

"Baby I was only kidding; I do love you with all my heart also".

They both hug and kissed, Rafael and Yolanda were surely in love.

Agent Simtson already had the information they wanted, he calls them but before he divulges the whereabout of Ruzzo he needed an assurance that the elimination of his debt and the information of his mistress will be carry out.

"Off course agent Simtson, we take care of people that helps us, you can be sure that all be forgotten".

"Denver Colorado".

Now, one thing is given him assurance and another to comply with it, agent Simtson will be very surprise in the next 2 weeks.

Ruzzo was settling in his new residence, assured that nothing will happen to him, but he made a grave error, like Willie he broke the law, he was involved in a fight at a local bar, he was apprehended and taken to the local jail, After posting the customary bond he was free, on his way to his residence a black SUV was tracking him they will not do anything now, to many people around but they already knew where he lives, maybe next time he will not be so lucky.

Henry was meditating, he was trying to set up a plan where he can collect the 10 grants from Silas and at the same time give the information to the Macon police, a daring plan for a man with an IQ of a cat, sorry a cat is more intelligent, he put his plan to work, first he needed to call Silas the week was up and he might become suspicious, he will demand his money upfront after he gets his money them, he will call his contact at the MPD, what a great plan he thought, how stupid can he be.

Henry grabbed his phone and call Silas.

"Good morning Silas, this Henry when do we start?"

"We are ready, are you?" Silas said.

"I am, the only thing is you have to pay me upfront, I need the money now".

"Henry my man, let's do this I'll give you half now, and half later, will that cut it?"

Henry was trying to con a con man; how stupid can he be.

"Okay Silas let's do that".

Henry was ready to betray Silas; he needed to find a way to get the money and at the same time call his police contact it was not a smart move.

Ruzzo was trying to lay low for a while, he doesn't' need anymore headaches, his trial on the bar fight was coming up next week, the Marshall office was aware of was going on and they were trying to get Ruzzo off the hook the head of the Regional office was meeting with DA and the Judge today to see if they can drop the charges if they succeed them they will move Ruzzo to another state, maybe Alaska.

The individuals assigned to eliminate Ruzzo were waiting in a motel nearby ready to strike, they already had a plan Ruzzo always walked in the direction of the motel everyday accompanied with an agent to get a pack of cigarettes and grab a something to eat, they waited until they were close hit them hard to make them unconscious, they grabbed the agent and put him in a garbage bin, the agent was not their target, they moved Ruzzo inside their room and kill him by using a bat as their weapon, later disposing of the body in a nearby ditch, mission accomplish one of them said.

It took the Marshall's office 1 day to find the agent he was fine only a big bump in the head and a lousy headache, but the body of Ruzzo was not found until 3 days later, no clue was left behind.

The Marshall Regional Director was fuming, 2 witnesses that

were supposed to be guarded 24 hours a day killed, who the hell knew about their safe house except the detail assigned to them, only an inside source was the culprit.

Agent Richard Simtson was enjoying his new found luck, no more debt and he can keep his beautiful mistress he was at the top of the world, but for how long the persons he made a deal with don't like to leave a clue behind specially a crooked agent, Richard and his mistress were invited to a party at the hotel he usually gamble, the party was on the 15th floor room 1504, they knock at the door but they were surprise only 4 individuals were present "where is the party?" Richard asked.

In a fast move two of them grabbed Richard given him little time to grab his pistol, the other 2 grabbed his mistress, took their clothes off and tied them to a couple of chairs immediately they forced Richard to swallow a large amount of alcohol making him dizzy, they untied both and walking toward the balcony they made the following comment.

"You two love birds are really going to fly".

They pushed them to jump from the balcony making it look like a couple of suicide.

Henry drove from Macon to Atlanta to meet Silas, he parked his car about a block away from the hotel where Silas and Dalila were staying.

The moment Silas opened the door Henry asked for his money.

"Henry don't worry, I have your money here, let me tell what I want". Silas explained to Henry what the plan was.

But Henry insisted to see the money first, before he left Macon, he placed a call to his contact at the MPD telling him that he will give him some important information in a while, his plan was get the money, find an excuse to leave the room them call his contact, easier said than done.

After a brief conversation Silas, Henry and Dalila left their hotel room ready to carry out their plan, Henry had his money but Silas insisted to leave as soon as possible so Henry didn't have time to call his contact, the second phase of his plan could not be carried out.

The 3 of them drove to Decatur where the headquarter for the GBI is located, parked the car about a block away, nearby a public phone Silas was the first to get off he was carrying an Springfield M1903-A4 Sharpshooter rifle, his plan was to call Rafael's office and tell him that he had a message from a friend from Cuba, when Rafael was in sight he will shoot him from a distance.

"This is Rafael can I help you". Rafael answered the phone; it was Silas calling.

Silas tied to talk with an accent, "Rafael my name is Carlos, I have a message from one of your friends from Cuba, can you come outside I am in the parking lot".

Rafael was a little suspicious, but he took the bait, having news from Cuba was very important to him since a lot of his friends are still there.

"Okay Carlos, I will see you outside".

But before he made it out he called Kurt and told him about the phone conversation, Kurt also was suspicious and advised Rafael to wait he wanted to check the area first, Kurt made it to the parking lot, nobody was there except the regular guard, Kurt asked him if anybody not associated with the Bureau have check in, he answered no, right away he put his previous call and the one that Rafael just received and knew it was a setup, there was somebody outside wanting to get rid of Rafael he went inside and advised Rafael to stay put, them Kurt, Rafael and a couple of more agents went thru the back door and started to comb the area, Kurt also called his friend Jerry Sanders at the APD, Kurt wanted to get his assistance in closing a mile wide radius and check any suspicious character.

About a block form the GBI headquarters one of the agents directed Rafael to look at a roof nearby, there was something moving, he could not determined what it was, an animal or a person, Rafael grabbed a pair of binoculars that another agent had, right away he saw it was an individual and he was armed, he signaled Kurt about the person on the rooftop, when Silas noted that they made him he started shooting, one of the agents with Rafael was hit in the leg, at that moment elements of the APD show up, Rafael and Kurt began shooting back, Silas was cornered, on one side the APD on the other Rafael, Kurt and another agent, Silas was not be taken alive he made a promise "I will never see the prison walls again", Silas was running of ammunition he still had a .45 pistol and 2 clips, when Rafael tried to move in the direction of the building where Silas is a shot disable him, he was hit in his left arm, this time it was not Silas it was Dalila that after hearing the shootout came to help Silas she was hiding on the side of the building where no clear shot from the authorities was possible.

Dalila was overjoyed, she shot Rafael her main target now she needed to run, she went back to Henry's car and with her pistol pointing at him push him out of the way "Henry you are on your own enjoy your money" and left, Henry was on the side of the road scared with no way of getting back to Macon he surrender to the authorities and created a false story about been kidnapped, Rafael was on the side of the building bleeding and badly hurt, paramedics arrived patch in up and took him to the hospital.

Silas was hit by an officer from the APD, Kurt approach him, Silas identify himself he was hit several times and looked in real bad shape before the paramedics arrived to take him to the hospital Kurt wanted to verify his identity and ask him.

"Are you Jim Silas?"

"Yes, and like I promised, I will never go back to prison, is Dalila still alive?"

"No, she got away, do you know where she might be heading?" Kurt asked Silas.

"No, she probably would like to get back to Costa Rica, she is travelling under the name of Dolores Trellos, good luck, she is very astute".

At that moment Silas died from his wounds, Rafael was on his way to Grady hospital seriously wounded, there was 2 shots, one to the arm and one to the abdomen.

Yolanda the director and Lynnard, were on the way to the hospital, Kurt was already there with the other agent who also received a superficial wound, Yolanda rushed to the nurse station asking for any information about Rafael, she was informed that Rafael was on surgery and as soon as the doctor finish with the procedure he will talk to her.

Silas was dead, now they needed to get Dalila, the director asked the Federal Authorities for help, they advised all airports, rail stations and bus terminals to be for the lookout for a Dolores Trellos, bur Dalila was very smart, without Silas knowledge she also obtain another false identity, she was not Dalila or Dolores anymore her new identity is Carmen Diez, Dalila knew that already had the full information about Henry's car, so dumped it next to a bus station and as Carmen Diez took the bus to Charlotte, NC where she will take her flight to Madrid Spain via New York La Guardia airport.

At the bus station in Atlanta where she dumped Henry's car she went to a restroom and put on a red wig, from dark hair, to blonde to red, she was on her way to freedom, she arrived in Charlotte around 4:00 pm in time to catch a Piedmont Airline flight to La Guardia as soon as boarded the flight she was relax, she alluded the authorities in Atlanta and Charlotte, but her luck will run out in La Guardia due to a tip from an airline employee in Charlotte that found her credentials suspicious and informed the FBI , hey notified their office in NYC and a couple of agents were waiting for her, the moment she disembark they apprehended her.

"Dalila Diaz there is warrant for your arrest, please place your hands behind your back, you have the right……"

The FBI agent cuff her, and the saga of Dalila Diaz Costa Rican citizen and the head of a criminal enterprise was over, the US authorities charged her with conspiracy to commit murder, racketeering and running a criminal enterprise, she could face 25 years in prison.

Back at Grady hospital in Atlanta Rafael was in surgery for 3 hours, they removed a bullet from his abdomen, no vital organs were damaged, Yolanda was given a full report on his condition he will have to remain in the hospital for at least a week.

"Thank God is out of danger, but in very delicate condition, but he will be fine".

Yolanda gave all the details to Kurt, the director and Lynnard.

After a couple of hours Yolanda made it to Rafael's room, he was weak but fine, Yolanda gave him a kiss and reminded him that their weeding was in about 2 weeks, they probably would have to postponed it.

"Hell no, Rafael said, even if I have to marry you in a wheelchair, I will walk down the aisle in a wheelchair, I love you too much to postpone the weeding".

Kurt walked into the room the moment Rafael and Yolanda were engage in a kiss.

"Sorry you guys, Rafael you scared the heck out of me, by the way Silas is dead and Dalila was apprehended at La Guardia airport trying to catch a flight to Madrid, Spain".

Jerome, Ruzzo and Willie were gone, Silas was killed attempting to kill Rafael, Dalila in custody "Well, Kurt that means case closed, right?", yes case closed.

****

ACKNOWLEDGMENTS

To Yakaly my beautiful wife, my son, daughter and daughter in law Leonardo, Annaleah and Allison that kept telling me you can do it and but must important my belief in God has been a guiding light in my life.

Writing the first novel has not been an easy task, after spending more than 30 years as a business owner I had to bring to life a brief history of Cuba from the 1950's thru 1970's, the main character represent the accomplishment of an individual in both repressive period of Fulgencio Batista and Fidel Castro.

After an experience of torture and incarceration he made it to the US where he was received with open arms.

Thanks to all my friends and family for all the magnificent support thru the writing of my novel.

"VIVA CUBA LIBRE"

THE NEXT CASE OF DETECTIVE RAFAEL CHAQUET WILL INVOLVE THE GOVERNMENT

OF CUBA AND THE US IN
A SPY THRILLER.

THE FOLLOWING PAGES WILL GIVE YOU AN IDEA OF THE PLOT. I HOPE YOU WILL ENJOY IT.

CHAPTER 1

After spending a couple of week in Miami Yolanda and Rafael returned to their apartment in Sandy Springs, Rafael was recuperating fast, their weeding was perform without any problems, and no, Rafael walked with Yolanda thru the church aisle without any difficulty, at the moment they were unpacking, the phone rang, Yolanda was surprise as nobody knew they were back from Miami, she grabbed the phone and answer it.

"This is Yolanda can I help you?"

"Yolanda, I am sorry you don't know me but a friend of Rafael a gentleman named Gerardo refer me to him, my name is Felipe Andrades and I urgently need to talk to him, is he available?"

"Yes, Mr. Andrades I will get him for you".

Yolanda walked to Rafael and told him who the person on the phone was and who referred to him.

"This is Rafael, can I help you"

"Rafael a mutual friend in Miami named Gerardo recommended I call you, I had a daughter attending Georgia Tech, when I say had a daughter is because she died last month at the university, according to them she committed suicide, I don't buy it, she was an Honor Roll student, high GPA and a bright future and happy".

"So, Mr. Andrades what do you want me to do?"

"I will be in Atlanta next week, if you don't mind, I will like to meet with you, is that okay?"

"Off course let me know when you arrive in Atlanta".

Rafael what was that all about, Yolanda asked.

"This Person lost his daughter last month, she was enrolled at GT, according to the university it was a suicide, he is not convinced and want me to help him find the truth".

The following morning Yolanda and Rafael made back to the GBI headquarters; Rafael was expecting a thank you

and goodbye from the Bureau, he was surprised, when cases dating back to the 1950's, them a big figure was standing at his door, it was Kurt.

"Hola Amigo, we got a lot of work in front of us, are you feeling up to it?"

"Claro hermano, let's do it, then they hugged each other confirming their alliance.

Rafael and Kurt had 3 cold cases in front of them, they needed to select one, opening up the files the case that attracted them the most was the killing of a 52 years old black man, he was beating and them shot in the head, this happened in 1957 in the city of Lawrenceville about 45 minutes away from Atlanta.

"Kurt let's wait, I am waiting to meet a Mr. Andrades, he wants us to look into the apparent suicide of his daughter". Rafael commented to Kurt.

Mr. Andrades arrived the following week in Atlanta, he immediately contacted Rafael and made arrangement for a meeting, they decided to meet at 10:00 am on a Tuesday, when Andrades show up at the GBI headquarters, he was escorted to Rafael's office there they greeted each other after a brief introduction Rafael asked Kurt to join them.

"Mr. Andrades, this is Kurt, my partner and friend we work together trying to solve complicated cold cases, now tell me why you are here".

"Like I mentioned to you over the phone my daughter attended Georgia Tech, last month she was found dead in her dormitory, the university pronounce the case as a suicide, Rafael, she was a 4.0 gpa student, Honor Roll and with a lot of plans for the future, I need to find out the truth".

"Mr. Andrades we are limited to investigate, since the case was probably handled by the APD, we might have to solicit their help also".

"Thank you, Rafael, that's all I ask". Andrades said to Rafael.

"Anything else?" Rafael asked Andrades.

"She went to Cuba 2 weeks before her death, with the CHE Brigade, that's one of the reasons I doubt her suicide, that brigade recruit young university students primarily young Cuban Americans to 'help in the building of true socialist utopia', off course they use them for some sinister activities inside the US".

"The first thing we must do is get as much information from the APD as possible, we'll be in touch please leave all your contact information with us".

Andrades left, them Kurt and Rafael sat down and commented on the meeting.

"What do you think Kurt?" Rafael asked Kurt.

"Well Rafael let's get as much information as possible them we can come to a logical conclusion".

"Okay, let's do that". Rafael said.

****